The Lies We Tell

Copyright © 2022 Torrie Jones

The Lies We Tell #1 - TORRIE JONES
All rights reserved

The characters and events portrayed in this book are fictitious. Any similarity to real persons, living or dead, is coincidental and not intended by the author.

No part of this book may be reproduced, or stored in a retrieval system, or transmitted in any form or by any means, electronic, mechanical, photocopying, recording, or otherwise, without express written permission of the publisher.

Cover design & Illustrations by: Amie Hughes @_artbyames
Editing: DT Editing & Formatting.

To Grandad Norman,

This ones for you old man.

I hope I've made you proud.

AUTHOR'S NOTE:

Please note this book does include mentions of drugs, adoption and a teenage girls murder. If that is something that you can't read right now, I completely understand. Please take care of yourself, your mental health is more important.

TJ x

PROLOGUE

Robert Quinten – June, 2000.

I hold her in my arms gently. She's so frail and so innocent. I watch her as she sleeps in my arms so peacefully. I rub my thumb lightly across her forehead through her pale white hair.

My daughter. Her last name is Quinten, a name she will probably never use, although it is her birth name. I only have a short time with her before the adoption agency take her. I could never be a father to something so little. There would be a hit on her if anyone was to ever find out that she exists.

In my line of work, you only have a small circle of people you can trust, my brothers and sisters, are the extent of it. I'm frightened that anyone will ever find out about her, let alone her mother. A one-night stand that should never have happened. I, a 19-year-old working in London taking over my father's business after he passed away, met almost 17-year-old Arielle Henderson... although that's what she told me.

The lies started when I met her in a bar, first her name was Sophie, then Abigail, lastly, she slipped up and said her name was Arielle. Her long red hair came down to her waist. She was beautiful, every man in the bar wanted her that night. I was the only man she made some sort of effort with that night. Her age was also something she lied about; she had a fake ID saying she was 20. But I knew she wasn't 20. She was looking at the world differently. She was... different.

Not long after she was born, Arielle was left in her hospital room alone to sleep, the pain of 24-hour labor exhausted her, or so I thought I would grab a coffee while they took our baby to get some tests. When I returned Arielle was gone, as was her bag with a note saying I'm sorry. That was 24 hours ago. I haven't left her side since. I feel like such a failure as a father, I'm letting her down and she's only 36 hours old. My daughter will only see me as someone who disappointed her, who didn't do enough to keep her. When I am doing this for her. For her safety.

I hear the door open, and I turn my eyes to look in that direction. My brothers and sisters standing there looking at me like I am not the man who grew up with them, the man who vowed to never bring life into this earth as we wouldn't want to burden them with the last name Quinten as it only brought death and destruction.

"She's small." my brother Oliver says breaking the silence in the room.

A light chuckle leaves my lips. He hates children and wasn't particularly pleased when he found out I was having one of my own. He's the youngest, and the thought of a family or even a wife has always put him off and made him cringe. He sees himself as nothing more than a member of a pack, a leader maybe in the future.

"She's perfect." I correct him as I look at him with a slight smile. He shakes his head before walking towards the window, disgusted with what I have just said.

"She will be the death of us all and you know it." He continues. I look at him with sad eyes, he doesn't understand how hard this is, handing her over to some strangers. I know he is right, he's always right.

"Oliver stop it." Serena begs. "This is hard enough as it is. She's our family too, remember that." She reminds him.

Oliver scoffs before shaking his head. "She's not mine." He says bluntly. My eyes turn to him my blood boiling. Before I can get a word in, my elder sister Felicity stops me.

"Don't even bother giving him the time-of-day Robert, he's being a pathetic little child." She says which only infuriates Oliver.

"What did you just call me?" He storms towards her, his nostrils flaring; anger written all over his face.

"That is enough." My eldest brother Peter announces as he places his hand firmly on Oliver's chest. "She is your family. You may not like it but she is. She has no say in any of this." He reminds him once more. Oliver's eyes still burn into Felicity's. She stands tall glaring at our younger brother.

"Oliver," Peter warns once more. Oliver turns his eyes to look at Peter.

"She will kill us all, just you wait and see." He says before storming out of the room. This outburst isn't unusual for Oliver, he's hated the fact that there was going to be another one of us. I shake my head before looking back at my daughter.

"Ignore him, Robert, he is being dramatic as always," Peter reassures me as I feel him walk towards me. He stands in front of me as I look at him, you can tell he is older. His dark brown hair and bushy brows frown as he looks at me with pleading eyes. He knows I don't want to let her go. That I want to raise her, hand the family business to him, but he would never take it. He refused it once, he wouldn't do it so I could go and raise a child. He knows that by bringing her into the world, I will have put a target on her back if she was to stay with us. And we already have a target on our back.

"Robert, she will have a better life with this

couple." He reminds me, he always seems to be able to read my mind.

"I know that Peter. But I can't help but feel like I'm letting her down." I say quietly, my voice on the verge of breaking. I don't want to hand her to strangers. "What if this couple don't love her like she's supposed to be loved? What if they break her heart?" I question. He looks at me as he places his hand on my shoulder to comfort me.

"Brother, I cannot make promises, the family that you have chosen seem like the perfect people to raise her. She will have a good life; she will be happy." He reassures me.

"And I doubt for a second you would let anyone break her heart. I know you will watch over her. Just remember where your duties lie." He reminds me once more.

I nod lightly as I look down at my beautiful and frail girl. I rub my thumb across her cheek as I bring her closer to me. Tiny sounds escape her mouth as she moves into me. I hold her close, so she can hear my heartbeat. Many of whom think doesn't exist.

I turn away from my brother and sisters who I feel watch me as I walk to the window. I look out into the city. London, of all places for her to be born, it had to be London. A different country to me, a totally different country to her mother, who is long gone.

"Robert?" I hear my sister Serena say behind me. I turn to look at her, tears filling up my eyes as I know I only have a matter of minutes before the adoption agency take her.

"Did you give her name?" She asks softly her brown eyes filling me with hope. I realise after a few seconds that I never told them the name I gave her. Arielle wasn't here to decide on the name, so this is all me.

"Her name is Julianna Eleanor Quinten."

CHAPTER ONE

Juliette Sanders, 14 years later

I slam my face down on my chemistry book. I hate chemistry, always have. It's one of those subjects that unless you're going to be going into a field where your job requires it, you won't ever use it. I unfortunately take it as it will help me get an understanding of what I will see out in the field when I eventually get into the profession I want to go into. What is that profession you may ask? I want to bring down the criminals. I want to study and bring down killers. I want to be a detective.

Now my mother, Amy, doesn't understand why I want to go down this route. None of my family in the past have ever gone into the justice field. But I guess I'm different. Growing up on the likes of Law and

Order and NCIS has given me an understanding that I don't want to just sit around when I know there are criminals out there to be taken down.

My mother finds me peculiar; she says all the time that I'm different, but she always reassures me it's in a good way, a great way even. After my dad, Paul, died it's been hard on my mum. Now being a single parent to me and my sister, Ava, she struggles to do everything but I'm so grateful for what she does for us. I know Ava is also. She still doesn't understand, and if I'm honest we don't know how to explain it to her. She was only 7 when he died and after that happened, we never really spoke about it as a family. We just moved on.

I hear a slight knock on the door as I leave my long stare, remembering all the good times I had with my dad before it got bad and turn my attention to the door. My mum opens it, her short brown hair and chocolate brown eyes meet mine and she gives me a warm smile that's eases my thoughts.

"Hey cherub, you going to make an appearance? Everyone's downstairs." She asks sweetly before looking at the piles of notes and revision books on my bed. I watch the excited smile drop from her face as she walks into my room, closing the door behind her.

"Jules, you know you can enjoy your birthday. You're fourteen today. That's something worth celebrating." She says softly before moving some of my notes and joining me on my bed. I smile back at her, reassuring her I'm fine but I know that she knows that I don't enjoy my birthday for multiple reasons.

"I know, but I do think that birthdays are silly sometimes." I tell her before moving some of my books out of the way.

"I know darling, but today is a special day, your friends are downstairs as is Grandma and Grandad." She tells me. I know she's trying to get me excited, but I haven't enjoyed my birthday since my dad died.

"Yeah, I know mum, I'm coming down. Let me just clean up my notes and I'll come say hi." I say with a smile, convincing enough so that she will leave and I can have a minute to calm my nerves before facing my family and friends. She nods in agreement and makes her way to the door.

"Mum?" I ask her which stops her in her tracks. She turns back to look at me, those chocolate brown eyes meet mine once more, and I suddenly feel guilty for hiding.

"Did they send something again?" I question. The small smile that was planted on her face only a moment ago disappears completely as she looks at me with concerned eyes.

"Of course, they did." She says to me before opening the door and leaving.

I take a deep breath before picking up my books and placing them on my desk. I look in the mirror, my caramel hair falls to just above my shoulders with my hair in a half up half down style. I look exhausted but that's because I spend every single waking moment studying, wanting to build a better life for my family. In the corner of my eye, I notice the box that haunts me every year. I just end up adding new things to it, but only on my birthday.

I turn to look at it. I'll probably have to buy a bigger box soon. It's always the same, a gift for my birthday and then money for Christmas. But it's always expensive items, from someone I don't know.

No note, nothing. Even when we moved to a new house after my dad died, they sent them there too. It doesn't bother me anymore. I used to be very curious, but I know it bothers my mother. We aren't materialistic, and them sending teddy bears from *Harrods*, first addition books, they've even sent me a new wardrobe for my 13th birthday filled with *Prada*, *Dior*, and *Chanel* items.

I know it makes my mum feel bad. She's been to the police several times, but the leads end there. She installed a security camera at the front door, and it still didn't catch them on either occasion. I know it bothers her, because she always feels like she is doing less as a mother when in fact, she is doing more than she should as a single parent. I am proud of her, and how far she's come since my dad died.

I move my gaze from the box and look at my wardrobe. A diamond from a *Chanel* cardigan catches my eye and I decide that since these people, half of whom I don't know, have decided to come to celebrate my birthday, I should try and make an effort. After all, I'm only fourteen once.

CHAPTER TWO

As I begin to walk around the crooked staircase, I see my cousin Tyler and his girlfriend Taylor, a weird combination I know, in a heated conversation. I watch my Aunt Nikki walk over to try and defuse any situation which is on the verge to erupt.

What I know so far is, that Taylor kissed Tyler's best friend Michael at a party a few weeks ago, my cousin Emma told me when she looked after us last Friday. Emma knows everything only because she listens in on everyone's conversations. Like how she already knows Aunt Nikki and Uncle Ric are getting divorced because she caught him in bed with his assistant. All things I, a fourteen-year-old shouldn't know but does because of her sneaky cousin.

As my eyes wander the room, I notice my younger sister Ava, annoying Barnaby, our youngest cousin. He is the son of my Auntie Alison who is incredibly posh considering she grew up on the outskirts of London in the rough areas. She's a CEO now of some big makeup company and sometimes when I look at her; I feel as though I could pop her like a balloon, she's had so much Botox.

"Juliette dear!" I hear a high-pitched posh squeak behind me, oh lord, she's found me.

"Hi, Auntie Alison," I say with a fake smile. I turn to see she has her party face on, her brown hair lightly curled and her freshly whitened teeth glistened as they blind me while she came in for a hug.

"Oh, my dear how are you doing!" She exclaims enthusiastically in my ear while holding me against my will.

"Yeah... fine." I manage to squeeze out. I realise that I'm going to die this way because we've been in this position for a good minute, and she's still not let go. Just as I feel myself slip into a coma, she let's me go and I take a long deep breath. That was a close one.

"Oh, you break my heart. I swear you could do with some therapy after everything you've been through." She says jokingly.

I just stare at her. Yes, I'm a quiet kid, but it doesn't mean I need to talk to some stranger about my problems.

"I think she's just fine." I hear a booming voice come from behind me. I watch as Auntie Alison's face drops from a smile into a scowl. I would recognise that voice if he was 100 miles away.

My Grandad Norman. My best friend and the man I aspire to be like. I turn and run into his arms for a bear hug which he gladly accepts with his walking stick.

"I was only saying she may need to speak to a therapist dad, I wasn't trying to upset her." Auntie Alison says trying to save herself when the truth is, she doesn't get on with her father.

"No, you're sticking your nose into something that doesn't concern you." He brutally reminds her causing me to quickly drop the smile from my face and get away from this situation. I watch as my Auntie Alison rolls her eyes at Grandad and leaves us both standing there. I ignore her pettiness as if anything, Auntie Alison has always wanted the gossip when there wasn't anything.

"Ignore her sweetheart, if she comes over and bothers you again and I'll smack her with my stick." He jokes. I laugh, as always Grandad made sure I wasn't uncomfortable.

"It's okay, she just asks a lot of questions." I remind him, he smiles at me, he knows I'm right. Auntie Alison does ask a lot of questions and she tries to get me into therapy.

"You know what she'll say to you Romeo, 'I

studied psychology, I know how the mind works, I have a degree.'" He says to imitate my Auntie which only makes me laugh. 9 times out of 10 when we see her, she has to mention she has a degree in psychology, more so since my dad died.

"I know Grandad, but we have to love her." I remind him. He exhales harshly while looking back at his daughter who, when I turn around, is deep in conversation with one of my mum's friends.

"I know Romeo." He jokes to me. I laugh at the use of my nickname. Romeo. Grandad tortures me with it because my name is Juliette. "I'm going to find your grandmother, see if she can make me a dicky ticker." He jokes to me as he chubs my cheek. A dicky ticker is a red wine, vodka, and lemonade concoction he invented. It smells horrific.

"Not too many though Grandad?" I question him, which causes him to chuckle as he walks towards the kitchen.

"I'll try, I can't promise anything." He jokes before walking away to annoy my Grandma. I begin to look around the party for any sight of my friends who i notice are standing in a corner giggling while gawking at my older, more attractive cousin. I roll my eyes and march towards them, anytime they see Tyler, they gawk and giggle totally forgetting that he has a girlfriend and that he is a lot older than them.

"Come on, stop looking. He doesn't know you exist." I say as I grab my friend's arms. They whine and object which only makes me grab them tighter.

"Jules come on! For the first time we are in the same room as him and you're pulling us away?" My friend Katy whispers loudly. I laugh as I drag them through the kitchen and into the back garden where there is some sort of privacy so I can remind them of two things:

1. He is too old for them.
2. He has a girlfriend (which they always forget.)

"You two don't know when to quit do you? He has a girlfriend! Since I have to remind you for the millionth time this week." I tell them as they roll their eyes in disgust.

"Jules, a man like that is rare, surely you of all people could appreciate a man like that, smart, strong and seriously irresistible." Mikki gushes. I chuckle under my breath at how open she is about her crush. "He needs to catch the love train." She flirts.

"Since you two also seem to be forgetting he is also 17, he is in sixth form. If he was to catch anything it would be a case because you two are underage." I remind them again, honestly, I hate to burst their bubble but, their fascination with Tyler is simply a high school crush and nothing more.

"I see what this is." Katy explains as she looks at Mikki. I look between them both, who then look to me suspiciously. The looks are making me nervous, and I'm the one who hasn't done anything. "You want to keep him to yourself." Katy continues.

I burst out into laughter, at first the audacity of her and second the blatant disregard at the fact my 17-year-old cousin would in fact not find my 14-year-old best friend attractive.

"He's, my cousin!" I shout, not loud but loud enough for them to know that extremely wrong.

"But it's not illegal." Mikki states. I scoff at her before turning away and walking back into the house.

"Unbelievable and disgusting." I mutter underneath my breath as the door slams behind me, leaving Katy and Mikki baffled.

I begin to walk through the house on the look-out for anyone I do not want to speak to, Auntie Alison being the top of that list. As I investigate the dining room, I notice a present on the table, beautifully wrapped with a gold silk ribbon. That must be it. The present. The parcel I get every year from someone I don't know.

I slowly begin to walk towards it. I should be grateful, a gift from someone else on both holidays, my birthday and Christmas. But every year I get more nervous, nervous that it could be something like a head, or a body part because I have no idea who is sending these packages.

"It was at the front door this morning." A voice behind me breaks the silence and I jump out of my skin. My mother Amy, standing there with a sad look on her face. I meet her sad eyes with my own as she walks towards me.

"You know, I don't think we will ever find out who sends those presents. I did everything the police told me to, I got cameras and they even managed to disable those. I had a hours sleep and in that hour, that was when they dropped it off." She goes on before stopping herself. She looks exhausted, something I didn't realise because my head was too stuck in a book to notice.

"Mum, we will find out, don't give up hope." I say with warm smile, to reassure her. She smiles back before pulling me closer and kissing my head.

"I love you nugget." She says sweetly against my head before pulling away, causing me to look at her. "Now open it. I want to know what it is." She encourages with a smile. I nod before looking back at the present. Every year, every year I'm a bundle of nerves. Surely if they had sent me something horrific it would have smelled by now.

I pull the gold silk ribbon on one side, and I watch as the perfect bow falls apart and to each side of the box. I take a deep breath as I place my shaky hands on either side on the box. I feel a hand on my shoulder to comfort me. Suddenly I feel the whole world stop as I lift the sides of the box slowly. Once the lid of the box is off, I place it to the side and notice a card on top of the gold silk.

Honestly whoever is sending me these gifts has some serious money. Silk wrapping, really? I look at the note which has my name 'Juliette' in the most beautiful writing I've ever seen. I begin to take the card out of the envelope, turning to my mother who gives me an encouraging nod. I lift the card and it reads:

'Juliette,
Happy Birthday. May your day be filled with laughter and love.
All our love.
Q.'

I stare at my mother surprised. "Mum, they signed it. This is the first time they've signed it." I exclaim. Then it hits me like a truck. "Mum, they sent a card." She is just as shocked as me as she takes the card from me, not saying a word as I watch her re-read the card repeatedly.

"Q? Do you know a Q?" She asks me. I shake my head at her as she closes the card to look at my surprised expression.

"Do you?" I ask her in the silence. She shakes her head at me, shock still filling her face. "Mum, they said, 'all our love.' It means its more than just one person." I say to her. She doesn't say anything as she turns her head from looking at me to look at the gift still wrapped in silk.

I follow her gaze and decide enough is enough, it won't be a head, I'm being stupid. I lift the gift and place it on it's side before pulling down the silk bag it's placed in. My mouth drops as I look at the icon on the front.

A MacBook. I turn to my mother who at this point is whiter than Casper the friendly ghost. She looks as stunned as me as we stare in awe.

"Mum, didn't I tell you last week that I was wanting a new laptop for school?" I say to her. She nods to me, still not being able to say a word. She makes ends meet as a widowed parent, and a new laptop would be something I would have to save for, I would never of expected my mother to buy me a laptop not with her job.

"Well, it looks like they've been listening." She says as she looks around the room, the same room we had the conversation in a week earlier. When she says that my heart falls and I begin to feel sick.

"Mum, do you reckon they have bugged the house?" I ask her, my voice breaking. I can't help it, that would panic me even more. But I also feel a sense of relief because if they have, my mum would be able to take it to the police and they would be able to track it.

"I don't know nugget." She says as a whisper. We both begin to look around the room, looking for anything that might be able to hold a bug, more so me than her. She gets distracted as she watches my grandma remove something from the oven.

"Mother! Still have 5 more minutes!" She shouts before she looks at me, noticing my worried face she kisses my forehead before smiling comfortingly.

"Don't worry we will sort this out. But right now,

you must celebrate your birthday. Go find Mikki and Katy, you know they are in some corner drooling over Tyler. I'm going to go in the kitchen before your grandma kills us all." She says softly before placing the card down and walking into the kitchen.

I turn my attention back to the MacBook. My first laptop, and the stranger was the one who bought it? Why? I wasn't desperate for one, I do all my homework in the library at school anyway. I begin the lift the box lid to look at the laptop.

As I remove the box, I notice another letter addressed to me on top of the MacBook. The last thing I want to do is make my mother worry more, so I put the letter in my pocket of my cardigan, place the lid back on the box not even looking at the laptop properly and placing it back in the box. They have never sent me two cards before, and I don't want to make my mother panic any more than she already is. I leave the dining room and walk towards the stairs to head up to my bedroom.

"Jules where are you going?" my mother calls after me.

"Toilet! Be back in a second!" I call back to her before quickly running up the stairs. I do exactly as I said I would, I go into the bathroom and shut the door before locking it and standing against the door. I pull the card which again has my name on and open the card. My heart starts to beat as I read the note.

21

"Juliette,

Someone told me you like solving mysteries.
Let's see if you have the skills to be a detective once you're old enough.
Maybe you'll be able to find me.
You up for a case Juliette?"

I feel a sense of determination pulse through my veins. If this is the way I'll be able to meet this person in the flesh, I'm willing to dance with the devil.

Bring it on.

CHAPTER THREE

Kissing my mother goodnight, I head up to my room. After finding the card from the stranger, it was all I could think about for the rest of my party. Why would they suddenly send another card with a taunt? It doesn't make sense. Even though I don't understand why now, I decided to use that do my advantage. If anything, I can start digging. I open the laptop and wait for it to start up. I can't be bothered to do anymore revising for the test I have tomorrow, I know all the points it's going to include so I'm not worried.

As the laptop slowly starts up, I change into some comfortable clothes. Just a t-shirt and pair of jogging pants before grabbing my dressing gown as I can feel a slight chill in my room.

The laptop takes a while as I'm assuming it has an update to do since after all it is a new laptop. Then the thought suddenly dawns on me – they might have bugged the house. With the party and everyone around I'm assuming my mother had forgot about the potential bug since she headed to her room not long after me. I leap out of my bed and grab the torch I have in my desk. It's only 9pm, but just in case if I'm looking under any ornaments, I need to be able to see clearly and I don't want my mum to be alarmed if she wakes up for the toilet to see a light on in the dining room.

I slowly open the door and begin to make my way downstairs. I can hear my sister Ava watching *Disney Channel*, something she watches almost every day. As I get down the stairs, I turn on the torch and the bright light blinds me for a second. I turn right down the crooked staircase and walk into the dining room. I shine the light into the dining room. The rest of the presents from my party are still on the table waiting to be taken up to my room. I begin to lift ornaments on the coffee table that's next to the wall.

Nothing. Damn it. I look underneath the coffee table hoping that it's in one of the corners. Nothing. I walk around the room looking at all the walls and the floors. I look underneath the dining table and all the chairs only to be left with nothing. No ornaments, no chairs, nothing has any sort of bug. I begin to become frustrated and every now and again check towards the stairs to see that I haven't woken up my mum. Thankfully, I haven't.

I begin again, I refuse to believe that there isn't anything in here that would be a bug. I had only mentioned it to my mother, not Katy or Mikki, not my cousins. Just her. I doubt she had told anyone.

I open some of the cupboards next to the side table under the window, just papers and rubbish. The same with the drawers, filled with documents, old school pieces and little bits and bobs. I exhale loudly. I'm probably being paranoid, surely mum has just told someone and whoever the stranger is, just happens to be listening to the conversation. I decide to call it a night and go back upstairs. Maybe the laptop has finished doing whatever update it needs to do. As I turn around and admit defeat and I turn around to find my sister Ava standing there.

"Jesus!" I whisper loudly. I feel my soul jump out of my skin, she's so light on her feet I didn't even hear her.

"What are you doing?!" She whispers back annoyed that I shined the light in her face.

"None of your business. What are you doing up?" I question her. She ignores me and walks towards the kitchen and grabs a glass of water.

"Getting a drink. That okay with you?" She whispers sarcastically. I take a deep breath and roll my eyes. "You look like you're doing something you shouldn't be." She says inquisitively as she takes another sip of her water. I stare blankly at her.

"Well, you look just as suspicious. Come on." I

usher her upstairs quietly.

"You never answered my question, what were you doing?" She asks once more. As we reach the top of the staircase, I look at her, her soft mousy brown hair is behind her ears and her pale blue eyes stare into me like they are staring into my soul.

"I was looking for something I'd dropped. That alright with you?" I ask her while raising one eyebrow. A light smirk creeps across her face as she takes another sip of her water.

"Guess so." She says before walking into her room and shutting the door. She's sneaky, and I can't put anything past her. I turn around and walk into my bedroom before shutting the door. Clearly, I was just being paranoid. As I reach the bed, I notice that the laptop is up and running. Surely, I needed to set it up? I shake my head; I really am being paranoid. This whole situation is so strange and it's making me lose my marbles.

As I look around the icons trying to work out which one is the internet, I notice a message on the MacBook. I move the cursor over it and click. As the section loads, I feel my heart sink. I knew something wasn't right. I re read the message making sure that my eyes aren't deceiving me.

So, Juliette,

You up for a case?

Q.

I feel sick. I knew the laptop would have needed to be set up. They set it up for me. I pause for a second rethinking my decision. Do I really want to play a game with a stranger I don't know? I'm fourteen, if anything I should be showing this to the police. But although I want to have my trust in the police, they seem to be doing nothing so far.

For all I know they could be a pedophile with a creepy obsession with me? I have no idea who this person is. But if I want answers especially for my mother, I think I'm going to have to play the game.

Only if you answer some questions.

Surely if they want me to work a 'case' I should be able to ask some questions. They owe me that much at least. I watch the screen hoping for some sort of message to pop through. And it does.

I'll allow one question, then every time you solve a piece of the puzzle, you can ask another question. How does that sound?

I think about it for a moment. I mean that does seem fair. I work for the questions I want answered. My heart is beating out of my chest. I am having a conversation with the person who has tormented my family for years and made us question our sanity. I think hard for a moment. What kind of question do I want answered first? I doubt they would tell me who they are, if that's the endgame, then they aren't going to make this easy.

Alright that seems fair. My question is why me?

When I click send, I feel as though sick is going to come out of my mouth. Whatever answer that comes on the screen. I'm going to have to solve this. I need to know who this person is.

Because you are something special.

CHAPTER FOUR

As I sit and eat my cereal the next morning, I can't help but feel guilty towards my mum. I decide it's probably best to not tell her about the messages, and I'm starting to question whether it is a good idea for me to be messaging the stranger at all. I'm only enabling the behavior. I barely slept and that last message is replaying in my head.

'Because you are something special.'

Gives me the creeps just thinking about it. I've seen enough of any crime shows to know that if I kept messaging the person, I'd end up on the news. *'Teenager enabled stalker and turns up dead.'* Or something along those lines. I'm going to turn the laptop off and pop it in that never-ending box. I'll save up for my own laptop, one I can control that isn't going to send me creepy messages.

"Jules, can you get the letters please?" My mother Amy asks as I take pause mid bite of my now very soggy cereal. I stan up, bowl in hand while pushing my chair out making sure to get no milk on my uniform. I head towards the door and collect the letters. There are only a few, *Mum, Mum, Mum... me.*

My heart stops for a second. It's the same writing as the one from the birthday cards. They've sent me a letter.

"Anything exciting?" My mum questions. I look at her for a second and give her a reassuring smile.

"Oh no, looks like another birthday card." I tell her before placing the card in my bag.

"Ava let's go! You're going to be late, and Jules has a science test." My mum screams up the stairs.

"Coming." A mousy sound comes from upstairs. She's more than likely in her pajamas, hair unbrushed and her mouth smelling like a rotten corpse because she is yet to brush her teeth. And if I'm honest, I wasn't far off.

She is wearing her pajama bottoms a long-sleeved t-shirt and a pair of slippers and she yawns down the stairs. It's currently 7:50am and we leave at 8.

"Ava! Come on lazy. Upstairs get ready, put your uniform on." My mum shouts ushering my still very sleepy sister up the staircase. When I see that they are out of sight I turn back to my bag and pick up the card. I open it quickly, every now and again checking up the stairs to see if anyone is coming.

"Juliette,

I want to apologise if my message last night made you feel uncomfortable. You asked a question and I told you the truth. Looking back, I realised it came across as creepy.

I completely understand if you would like to stop this, my actions last night were uncalled for, and I apologise. My plan is just to see how smart you are, although I know you are already. And to answer the question buzzing around in your head, a little birdy told me you were going to save for a laptop. Therefore, I decided to buy you one of your own. You are old enough after all.

Juliette, good luck in your test. Not that you need it.

Q.

P.S – You may tell your mother about this at any time, I don't want you to lie to her."

I read the letter repeatedly, my heart beating out of my chest. I can tell my mum. Surely, it's a test. Funnily enough, in all the years of getting gifts and now letters I have never felt frightened or scared of this person. They haven't given me any reason to be scared, although I feel a little pulsing through my veins right now.

"Jules you good to go?" My mum calls from upstairs. I quickly put the letter back in my bag and grab my coat.

"Ready!" I call back up. As I put my bag on my shoulder, I see my sister run down the stairs, looking like a functioning human being rather than a zombie.

"Pleased to see you decided to join the land of the living." I tease. She sticks her tongue out as she furiously takes a bite of her now cold toast.

"Come on you two, out the door." My mum instructs us as she grabs her bag. As me and Ava reach the car, I look up the street and notice a black car on the corner. My heart begins to race, surely, they aren't watching me? But that thought is quickly out of my mind as my mother shouts once again for me to get in the car.

◆ ◆ ◆

"Jules!" I hear my friend Mikki, scream behind me as I walk towards my locker that is next to the science room. Her black hair and ebony skin glowing as she runs towards me with a smile, brighter than the sun.

"What are you smiling for?" I laugh as I put in the combination for my locker. She does a squeak before looking away and reaching out to someone and pulling them into me.

"Did you hear?" She asks Katy with a smile as she looks around the hall, I'm so confused by this point, what could I have possibly missed in P.E and English to warrant my best friend about to explode with excitement.

"How could I not? It's all everyone is talking about!" Katy squeals as she grabs a hold of Mikki's arm and squeezes.

"Mikki! Spit it out before you die, please." I lightly shout at her. As I place my P.E kit back in my locker and take out my science book before closing my locker once again.

"Have you heard about the new boy?" They squeal in unison. I'm taken back by how in sync they are when it comes to someone new, or a potential new fascination.

"Clearly, I haven't; what makes this one so special?" I ask with a smirk on my face. Their smiles are infectious and it's no wonder we are classed as the weird friendship group, they carry the weird with them. "Oh my gosh! Is he age appropriate?" I ask with a grin. Katy smacks me quite hard on the arm before looking to Mikki and rolling her eyes.

"He's 16 and he's American." Katy says quietly, I nod as I watch her mouth drop as does Mikki's. I turn to see what has them so shocked. As I turn, I lock eyes with possibly the most beautiful boy I have ever seen. He doesn't take his eyes away from me, and I don't take mine off him. His mousy brown hair is in a boyband style haircut.

His blue and black flannel sways as I watch him in slow motion. Our eyes never unlock. Like we are looking into each other's souls. As he turns away, I feel myself take a breath. I didn't even realise I had stopped breathing, never in my fourteen years on this earth have I seen someone so beautiful in the flesh. The sound of the hallway becomes busy again as kids rush to get to class. I feel like I just watched a model walk down a runway.

"What in the world was that?" Mikki asks stopping her mouth from falling open once more. I stare at her bluntly and I can feel my cheeks becoming slightly red, am I blushing? I never blush.

"No idea." I say before walking towards the science room. If I manage so much to pass this science test, now that would be a miracle.

CHAPTER FIVE

As I find a seat in the hall, I take a bite of my apple while I wait for thing 1 and thing 2 to arrive. My science test didn't go too bad. I managed to complete it without thinking of the handsome stranger who is too old for me and way too good looking. I've never had a crush. Like a real like crush, never had a boyfriend or a first kiss. I've never thought of those sorts of things.

I reach into my bag and grab my book for the next class, a light skim over my notes before history won't do me any harm until I wait for the troublemakers to arrive. With my apple still in my mouth, I turn to see that beautiful American standing in the corner of the hall, staring.

Okay, so I may have an apple hanging out my mouth surely that doesn't mean he needs to stare. I suddenly realise I'm staring back at him, and I look away blinking repeatedly. I'm being paranoid why is he staring?

"So, you going to tell us why the new boy is staring at you?" Mikki asks as she takes a seat next to me while taking a bite of her brownie.

"No idea. I think I was staring at him, so it was only fair." I say as I open my book. It's quickly slammed shut by Katy who looks me dead in the eye.

"Jules he clearly thinks you're cute or he wouldn't stare." She says flirtatiously. I roll my eyes, these two think that if you don't find a man that loves you when you're young; you're going to end up alone.

I just don't have that mindset. I don't even want to think about boyfriends or romance. I want to focus on my future. The rest will fall into place.

"Will you two stop! I was staring because he was staring there is nothing more to it." I say as I open my book while giving Katy a warning that if she so much as touches this book, I will take her hands off.

"Okay but do you think he's cute?" Mikki asks leaning in. The smell of brownie fills my nose and I look at her.

"He's a boy, another species, am I meant to find every single one of them cute?" I question. She scoffs before taking my book out of my hand and putting it in my bag. I groan in annoyance. I would do this to them if it was the other way round.

"Okay yes, I find him cute. Happy?" I say as I stare at them both. They nod before taking some of their lunch out of their bags and eat it in silence.

◆ ◆ ◆

As I head to my locker before my last class, I realise that I haven't thought of the stranger or their little game they are playing with me. I smile at myself, thanking God that because of school, they will probably stay clear. Not wanting to draw attention to themselves. It makes me think for a second, what surely could they get out of this?

A way to talk to me. They said that I could tell my mum, now if they were going to hurt me surely, they would say 'don't tell your mother.' But they've asked me not to lie. And I don't lie.

As I reach my locker and put in the combination, I feel a sense as though someone is watching me. Although the hallway is filled with kids on their way to their last class of the day. I look over my right shoulder and I feel my heart race as lock eyes with the American boy who I feel is staring into my soul. I begin to feel nervous, but I turn my attention back to my locker. If I ignore him surely the staring will stop. I open my locker and I feel my stomach drop when I notice what is on top of my P.E. kit.

A brown case file. They broke into my locker. I

turn to notice the boy turn away from me and walk towards the other end of the school. Surely it's not him following me. I want to go after him. I begin to go to take the file out of my locker when Mrs. Holden, the new science teacher approaches me.

"Jules, come on get to class." She says sweetly. I watch her face as she sees the distress on my face. "Juliette what's wrong?" She asks, concern filling her voice. I swallow my heart back into my chest and give her a smile.

"Nothing, Mrs. Holden, I'm fine." I say with a not so convincing smile. She looks around my face for some sort of comfort but clearly the panic in my eyes says everything.

"Jules is something bothering you? Would you like to talk about it?" She asks. I hesitate for a moment, the only person that really knows about the presents ever year is my family, I never really told my friends.

I look at her for a moment, her short brown hair lays on her shoulders slightly and her minimal makeup makes her face look so fresh and bright, she couldn't be older than 25. You can tell she's a new teacher, she's lively and full of hope. I look down at the floor and shake my head. This would just cause a panic in the school.

"Honestly Mrs. Holden I'm okay. Just wondering whether or not I've passed my science test." I say to her with a slight smile. I watch as her body relaxes, and she places a hand on my shoulder.

"Don't tell anyone but I've already marked them all. You passed Jules, you never needed to doubt yourself." She reassures me. I take a deep breath. That does bring me some sort of relief, I was very distracted in my test since seeing the new boy in the hall.

"Thank you. That makes me feel better." I say with a smile before grabbing the book quickly from my locker and shutting the door, hoping she didn't see the file or ask about it. The last thing I want to do is explain it.

"Come on I'll walk you to your class." She says with a smile. I nod slightly as I clutch the book tight to my chest as I adjust my bag on my shoulder.

"Don't you have a class Mrs. Holden?" I ask as we begin to walk towards the History classrooms.

"I have a free class on a Monday. So, if you would ever like to talk Jules my door is always open." She says sweetly. Mrs. Holden has been one of my favorite teachers so far this year and I enjoy her classes. Purely because she keeps us interested, I may not be very good at science, especially chemistry but if I'm ever unsure she always makes sure she explains it to me after class.

"Thank you." I say to her after a moment of silence. I feel a lightbulb go off in my head. If anyone will know anything, especially about new students, it will be the teachers because surely, they gossip in the staff room.

"Mrs. Holden, I do actually have a question." I say as we reach the Mr. Wilson's classroom, my history teacher. She looks at me and raises her eyebrows slightly urging me to continue. "The new American boy. What is your opinion on him?" I ask. Her eyebrows shoot up and she thinks for a moment.

"I think he's a bright young man, he's intelligent and although he's very quiet. I think he will do well at this school." She says with a smile. I nod back at her before looking into my history class, I may only be 5 minutes late, but I really don't want to learn about the Victorian era. I take a deep breath as I look back and smile at Mrs. Holden.

"Thank you, Miss." I say with a smile. She scrunches her nose before opening the door for me.

"Sorry Mr. Wilson, I asked for Jules' help with something." She says before giving me a wink. I begin to walk to my seat which is next to Mikki who looks startled that for the first time ever, I am late to a lesson.

"No problem Mrs. Holden. Jules just take a seat, you haven't missed much." He informs me. I nod as I pull my seat out and take a seat next to Mikki who has concern plastered all over her face, and rightly so? I'm never late to a class.

"You good Jules?" She asks quietly next to me. I open my notebook and smile at her.

"Why wouldn't I be?" I ask her with a smile, a fake one. She just nods as she turns to pay attention to Mr. Wilson. I had just lied to my best friend, because in fact, I don't know if I am okay.

CHAPTER SIX

I take a seat in the library and begin to make a list of the homework I've got and set myself a timer. It's currently 3:30pm, school has just ended but I go to the library since my sister has netball practice, one of her many after school activities. She's the athletic one, I'm the one who pretends to be the brainy one. I'm not going to lie; I don't understand some subjects. For example, maths and geography. Two subjects I cannot screw into my head and have never been able to. I had a tutor for a little while and that was great, I think I was finally starting to understand the subjects. But then my dad died, and everything changed. I lost interest and my mum couldn't afford a tutor. So, I just decided to try and teach myself. I'd like to say it was going well, but I can't be so sure.

As I open my bag, I notice the case that was left in my locker earlier today. My mind wanders to that new boy, whose name I still don't know. All I know is he is American and he's 16. Not much to go off. I decide to look at it later, I've got homework to do and the last thing I want to be is distracted and focused on something else. As I look up from my bag, I feel myself freeze as I stare into possibly the most beautiful ocean blue eyes I've ever seen. I'm shocked, that he is sat so close to me, staring into my soul. After a few seconds of silence, he smirks before pulling out a book from his backpack. I decide to look at him, his mousey brown hair has flopped slightly since our meeting this morning in the hallway, and I can now see he has a dimple on his cheek. His skin looks tanned, like he'd just been on holiday, or better yet came from a hot part of America.

I break the silence between us first as he turns to look at me once more.

"Can I help you?" I say inquisitively. Thankfully, I managed to not squeak it, my mouth is so dry. He smirks for a second before leaning over his book and towards me, the scent of his aftershave fills my nose and can feel myself getting dizzy from his scent as I try and focus on anything but his eyes. I look down at his arm and notice there's a tattoo peeking through his white shirt which has been rolled up. A 16-year-old with a tattoo? Surely not.

"What's your name?" He asks. His American

accent is strong, and I didn't expect him to have such a broad accent. I can't even tell where in America he's from.

"Jules." I say softly, still watching his every move. I'm still fixated on his tattoo. How can a 16-year-old have a tattoo?

"That's a nickname, what's your full name?" He asks with that stupid smirk on his face.

"Juliette." I answer bluntly.

"Juliette." He repeats. *What is this guy a budgie?*

"Yep." I nod before looking away and down at my list trying to distract myself from the annoyance in front of me.

"Why don't you use Juliette?" He asks in the momentary silence. I look up at him startled for a second.

"I don't know, it's just too formal. I've always gone by Jules." I explain before looking back down at my homework. I look up at him lightly after a few moments and I catch him staring at me, not even hiding it.

"You do know it's rude to stare." I explain to him in my frustration. He laughs lightly before moving his tongue between his teeth in-between the smirk that I am now certain resides on his face.

He moves closer to me, so close I can feel his breath hitting my lips as he stops about 5 inches away from my face. My eyes are fixated on his. Those bright ocean blue eyes meet mine and I feel as though I'm getting lost.

"I can say the same for you." He says almost as a whisper. He moves away quickly and clears his throat. I feel myself go red immediately. Why am I blushing over this guy? I take a deep breath and hide my face from him while I try and contain the heat that is radiating off my face. I look over my notes trying to distract myself from the boyband American in front of me.

"So, Juliette." He questions breaking the silence at the table. I look up at him through my eyelashes slightly. He still has that never-ending smirk plastered on his face, and if he keeps looking at me like that; I'm on the verge of smacking it off.

"What homework have you got today?" He asks as he pulls a laptop from his backpack. I take a deep breath, clearly this guy isn't going anywhere. I pick up my history book and turn it to face him, still with a straight face. He nods as he types something on his computer. I place the book down and grab my pen, making notes of what I'll need to include in my small essay. It's only 500 words and I'd rather get it done and handed in rather than leave it till the last minute.

"Where abouts you from Juliette?" He teases in the moment of silence. I look up, confused at his question.

I narrow my eyes. "Here." I tell him. He nods in agreement before looking up from the screen and directly into my eyes.

"Where's here?" He asks. *Okay, is this guy for real?*

"London, you?" I ask him.

"South Carolina." He responds earning a nod from me before looking back down at my notepad. I'm hoping this guy gets the message soon that I would like to be alone in peace.

"You have an accent." He says which causes my head to jolt up.

"I have an accent? Have you looked in the mirror?" I respond now getting agitated. He's clearly doing this on purpose, trying to wind me up.

He begins to laugh, only a chuckle, but you can tell it has somewhat of an evil tone to it. "Oh! I know, I'm a strange creature compared to you British people. I talk funny. At least that's what everyone says." He mocks. I mean at least he's admitting he's the one with a funny accent.

"You do talk funny." I admit as I begin to write, something, whether it's English I haven't got a clue. He's distracting me. I like quiet and he's like a record player on repeat.

"I talk funny huh?" He questions. I roll my eyes and look up at him annoyed.

"Yes! What are you? A parrot?" I say raising my voice a little. Suddenly there is a *shh!* directed my way from the librarian of the school. I mouth *'I'm sorry'* before giving the American boy a look and stare back down at my work.

"Apologies, it's my fault." I hear him say to the

librarian which causes me to roll my eyes. I've never met an American, but I've never known one to be so annoying.

After what feels like a good 10 minutes of peace, I feel a slight breeze hit my face which causes me to look back at him. His hand is extended, waiting for me to shake it. I stare at his hand then back at his face. He smiles at him, hinting he isn't going to wait much longer. I extended my hand and shake his, it's warm and soft. I catch myself looking at that tattoo once more.

"I'm Damian." He says with a smirk which I join in with. "My full name is Damian Reece Williams." He continues. I can't stop the smile on my face now. I finally have a name. And it's very American, just as I'd expected.

"Well Damian Reece Williams, I'm Juliette Amanda Sanders." I say before pulling my hand away and picking up my pen. "But you can just call me Jules."

CHAPTER SEVEN

I can't help but sigh as I walk through the door of the house. It's been a long day, and I can't help but feel anxiety through my veins as I remember that the stranger had sent me a file to look at. I didn't want to open it in school incase a teacher asked about it and I would have to explain 'I have a stranger sending me files of God knows what and breaking into my locker'.

I didn't bother asking Damian, my new American acquaintance about the file and why he was looking at me earlier, more than likely it was just a coincidence. But deep down, as I try and convince myself of that, I know it's not true.

"Okay Ava, have a shower you're a mess." My mother says as she walks through to the kitchen. "I'll start making dinner, spaghetti bolognese alright?" She asks with a grin as she looks at me. I nod, words failing me because a sudden strobe of guilt hits my stomach as I look at my mother. I watch as her face frown before walking back through the door and towards me.

"Jules, you've been very quiet in the car. Is everything okay?" She asks as she gives me a hug. She's warm and as she's holding me, I feel as though the weight that is on my shoulders is almost lifted. Mum hugs are the best, they always make you feel safe.

"Yeah, just tired, it's been a long day." I say against her chest. I feel her kiss my forehead before pulling me from the embrace to look at her. She gives me a warm smile before pulling my hair out of my face and behind my ear.

"Well, I think you've done enough studying for tonight, don't you think? You work too hard Jules; I know you want a life where everything falls in to place. But taking a night off occasionally, doesn't make you less of a human." She says softly to me. I smile to her and notice her features; slight wrinkles are starting to form around her eyes and forehead and her freckles are starting to fade as we haven't had much sun yet here in London.

"I know Mum, don't worry." I reassure her. "I've got no homework to do anyway." I say to her with a grin. She shakes her head.

Most parents worry about their kids getting involved with a bad crowd, doing drugs, getting in trouble. All my mum needs to worry about is whether I've actually slept for 8 hours and not re-read my biology textbook.

"Well, go watch some TV like a normal fourteen-year-old or draw! You used to love drawing Jules; I'm so upset you didn't take art." She whines slightly while pushing some more hair behind my ear. I shake my head, although I used to draw a lot, I don't see the point in it now. I grew out of it, kids my age do.

"You know why I didn't, and I refuse to have this conversation again." I say before pulling out of her grip and making my way towards the stairs, my bag still on my shoulder. I hear her sigh loudly before turning to face me while I reach the stairs.

"Jules, you just work so hard. I wish upon a star that you would just get in trouble, just once." She says before walking into the kitchen. I'm hardly a rebel, most parents would kill for a kid like me. Hard-working, good results, I don't get in trouble. My mum is encouraging bad behaviour.

I walk up the stairs slightly laughing at her comment. I reach my bedroom and open the door encountering the MacBook I got for my birthday yesterday.

I sigh, I don't want to use it in case they are tracking what I'm doing. I shut my door hoping that this is the one night my sister doesn't decide to annoy me and leaves me be. I walk and place my bag on the bed pulling out the file which i have now noticed has my name on. A brown file, it looks new.

Clearly this is just a game to them, and they aren't getting me to look at a real case, or at least I hope not. My heart is pounding out of my chest.

What kind of case would they have sent me? Surely, they wouldn't have sent a murder case to a fourteen year old. That would be all kinds of dodgy. It could be anything, and I am thinking the worst.

I slowly open the file and to my relief there is no dead body on the first page, and I finally take a breather. I notice a letter, same calligraphy as the one from the previous cards and the letter that i received this morning.

"Juliette,
Since a little birdy told me that you wanted to be a detective once you're old enough, I wanted to see if I can put your skills to the test.

Over the past 9 months, undisclosed to the media, your school has been under scrutiny by the local police after drugs were being made in one of their science labs during the summer last year. Notice how Mr Dunston never came back this year and Mrs Holden arrived in September. Thankfully they have kept it out of the media, for now, but it won't be for much longer.

On Friday, the body of Georgia Howard was found in her room after a suspected overdose. Now this information hasn't been released to the media, but the school has been informed. Since she died of the drug that was originally being made in the science labs, the school is now once again under investigation by the local police.

Your task is to find the student who is making and selling the drugs. Now don't think this will be easy cause it won't be.

I know if you put your mind to it, you'll find out in no time.

Once you've found out who that is, leave the evidence in your locker and it will be collected and taken to the police. I understand that you'll not want your name mentioned, because there's nothing worse than being called a snitch in high school. Your name will remain anonymous when the evidence is handed to the police.

Please be careful. If you feel as though you are in danger, click the red button on the device in the file.

- Q."

I pull the small red device out of the file and stare at it. I'm stunned. They want me to find out who's selling drugs in the school? I don't know the first thing about drugs, where to find them and how to make them.

And Georgia is dead? She wasn't the kind of girl to take drugs, she cared about what kind of lip-gloss she was wearing and the biggest push up bra she could find. Although she is 2 years older than me, everyone knew her.

I think back, at lunch today her friends looked lost without their leader... they were no one today.

I sit on my bed speechless as I pull the

documents from the file. Documents from the original investigation into the school. The letter of admission from Mr Dunston, photos of the evidence they collected, fingerprint samples, statements from the school staff. Everything you'll need if you were doing a private investigation into the school.

But why do they have it? Why are they interested in what the school has been getting into? I'm out of questions, but they did say that I can ask questions every time I gather evidence. I decide to get a head start. I'm determined to meet this person in the flesh and if this is a way to show I'm dedicated, I don't know what will. I'm not afraid of the stranger, I know I should be. Yes, granted they have sent me on something that if I end up in danger, I could end up beaten or worse, killed. But this is what I'm wanting to do in my life.

I feel the adrenaline pulse through my veins. I'm not going to just solve this case for the stranger's benefit. But for my own, so I can prove to myself that I can solve this case.

CHAPTER EIGHT

The next morning is a blur.
Every person I look at I feel as though I'm suspecting them of a crime. My lack of sleep last night due to me reading the file has really made me on edge today. I feel as though I can't trust anyone, I think due to my lack of sleep, slight paranoia might be pulsing through my veins. No one seems to know about Georgia. Her sidekicks are walking the halls hanging their heads because they are without a fearless leader.

Surely the school should have informed us of a student's death. Unless they already know and they've been told they can't say anything. I stand at my locker fixated on the two girls who walk quietly through the halls. I suddenly catch eyes with Damian, who when he realises I'm looking at him, he smiles, before walking down the hall in the opposite direction. I roll my eyes; I will eventually slap that smirk that permanently resides on his face. I turn back to my locker and feel a body slam against the ones next to me.

"I was waiting for you to make a dramatic entrance." I say as I grab my book out of my bag.

"I'm acting." Katy says. I raise my brow to look at her and she rolls her eyes. "I'm you. Since you've been ridiculously quiet today." She says with a sarcastic grin. I roll my eyes again and shut my locker before tilting my head.

"I'm not quiet." I tell her. Katy scoffs and shrugs her shoulders.

"If you say so." She mocks before a confused look fills her face. I frown my brows before looking in that direction to notice Mikki, storming through the halls at us. Her black tight curls bouncing as she moves quickly through the crowd. She stops, her nostrils flaring before she swings and punches me in the arm.

"Ow!" I shout as I feel the effects of the punch. If this girl didn't want to be a teacher, she could certainly be a boxer.

"When were you going to tell us that you had a conversation with the American boy?" Mikki whispers loudly causing some students to look at us. I glare at her before turning and closing my locker.

"What is she talking about?" Katy asks as she looks at me wide eyed. As I open my mouth to begin to explain about my confusing conversation with Damian, Mikki buts in.

"She was getting cozy in the library with him last night." She says dramatically to Katy, which causes her to gasp. I groan in annoyance. Anyone listening in on this conversation is completely going to get the wrong end of the stick.

"Mikki, that isn't what happened." I explain to her. Before walking away and towards the dining hall. I hear the feet of Mikki and Katy running behind me, catching up.

"Okay so what happened then? We want all the details." Katy says as she begins to pull a notepad out of her bag and a pen to take notes. I look at her in disgust which causes the smile to drop from her face as we walk through the art corridor.

"I was at the library, and he joined the table I was sat at. That's it." I say casually, not playing too much into their fascination. They both look at each other and back at me and my eyes roll.

"But what did you talk about?" Mikki asks pushing for more information. I exhale loudly as we walk into the dining hall.

"He wanted to know my name, that's it. He's annoying you know; I don't see the fascination." I say as we take a seat. I watch as them two discuss the fact I called the new boy annoying. I watch as they turn their gaze to Maura and Holly, Georgia's pack. They smile as they walk through the hall saying hello to people they pass, people they would have given awful looks to if Georgia was here.

"I heard Georgia is on holiday in Dubai with her family." Mikki says to us before looking back at the twins. They walk over to Harrison Meyer, considering his parents are ridiculously wealthy, they sent him to a community school. I watch as Maura hugs Harrison slightly. She looks around before taking a packet of something from his hand. I feel my eyes go wide as they continue talking and gossiping like two friends.

Everyone knows that Harrison and Maura like each other, but it's because he was dating Georgia, they couldn't be together. Nothing worse than going out with your best friend's boyfriend behind her back. The only person that seemed to not notice it, was Georgia. And now she's out of the picture. Could Harrison and Maura have something to do with this? Harrison only joined the school at the start of Year 11 and because of his pretty face and great rugby skills, he made the bad boys table within a few weeks. Since then, he's the top dog, obviously because he's the one that's filthy rich.

"If Georgia was here, they wouldn't be acting like this." Katy says breaking the stare we were all in watching them. "Maura wouldn't even look at Harrison." She finishes. I look at her as she's talking before looking over at Holly who stands awkwardly next to her sister. Holly isn't normally quiet, between her and Maura, she's the one that is talking, or should I say flirting, with all the boys. But she stands there sheepishly, hugging herself like she's about to cry. I watch as Maura pull Holly in, whispering something in her ear which causes Holly to fake a smile and join in the conversation.

"Do you guys know why Harrison joined the school at the start of this year?" Mikki says looking at us both waiting for us to answer.

"Because he kissed all of the girls in his last school and needed a new sea to swim in?" I say sarcastically which causes Katy to laugh. Mikki slaps my arm lightly before leaning in. "He was kicked out of his last school. It wasn't because they couldn't afford it, no other private school would take him after something bad happened." Mikki says quietly before looking back at Harrison. I frown, what possibly could Harrison of done to get him kicked, and barred, from all private schools in London?

"Hey Detective Mikayla, any idea what he did that was so terrible?" I ask her. She narrows her eyes, out of anyone in our little group of weird, she knows everything about everyone.

"Ha! No, I don't. You're the one who wants to be a detective. You work it out." She jokes which causes Katy and I to laugh. Oh, don't worry I will.

I turn back to the table to think of reasons why Harrison would have been kicked out of his last school, only to be faced with a smug faced baboon, grinning like I had just uncovered his secret plan. I take a deep breath before taking my book out of my bag.

"What do you want?" I say as I pretend to look

uninterested at Damian's surprise arrival. He takes the book out of my hands; an objection almost escapes my lips, but I stop myself as I know it will just fall upon those deaf ears of his.

"Now is that anyway to speak to a friend?" He says as he places a hand on his heart like I hurt his feelings. I chuckle lightly before taking a bite of my apple.

"We are not friends." I explain. That smile on his face only grows wider as he knows that he's going to do everything to annoy me.

"You know we are." He taunts a little more. I roll my eyes before looking away at him and the other students. I'm a quiet person, keep to myself, have a small group of friends and this new American boy is really ruining my peace and quiet.

"Don't you have some poor unfortunate soul to annoy? Like a preppy popular girl?" I tease a little with a sarcastic grin. He does that thing with his teeth before clearing his throat.

"That's exactly what I'm doing." He teases. I roll my eyes before taking my book away from him and placing my arm over it.

"Ahem Jules?" Mikki says breaking the stare between Damian and me. I totally forgot they were here. I look at them their eyes are almost popping out of their head, like Damian and I have just been speaking *Klingon* for the last 5 minutes.

"You going to introduce us to your new friend?"

Katy jokes. I scoff before looking over at Damian who is already extending his hand out to Mikki.

"Damian Williams." He says as he shakes her hand, not forgetting to give a Katy a bright purely white smile. I swear a might be sick, he is such a flirt.

"I'm Mikayla Jackson, this is Katy Chen." Mikki introduces them both, Katy so red she could be sold as a tomato in Tesco. He smiles at them both before turning his gaze back to me, who is giving trouble one and trouble two a death stare.

"I wouldn't say anything else; you may find yourself in an arranged marriage by the end of the week." I say casually which causes him to laugh before leaning closer.

"You going to the library tonight?" He asks with a grin. I raise one eyebrow, surely, he's made some friends in the few days he's been here.

"So, what if I was?" I ask him as I take a bite of my apple. He watches my every move slowly.

"Well, I thought I could give you a hand with any homework you may have, you know with us being friends and all." He says with that silly grin. I must admit, although he is annoying, he is incredibly good looking. I sigh, even if I say no, he's going to help me anyway, and he may be able to help me with my maths homework tonight. That is one subject I can't do.

"Fine. But I'm only agreeing because even if I had said no, you would turn up and annoy me anyway." I say with a smile to please him. He grins wide before we all here his name called from behind us. We turn to see Harrison calling Damian over. I knew it wouldn't be long before the popular boys get a hold of him.

"Come sit with us." Harrison shouts. I turn my attention to Damian with a smile ushering him to leave so I can go back to my quiet with Mikki and Katy. He nods before taking half of my sandwich and standing up from the chairs.

"See you tonight, Juliette." He says with a wink before walking towards Harrisons table. I take a breath, thankful that he's given me the space I needed. I turn to the girls who just stare at me wide eyed.

"What?" I ask confused. Mikki scoffs before throwing her hands in the air and Katy shakes her head.

"You girl are going to fall deep for him too late and it's going to hurt like a bitch when you realise he wants someone else." Mikki says while poking me in the arm. I raise my eyebrow and look at Katy for support, but I get nothing, she's just nodding agreeing with Mikki.

"Do you guys seriously think I like him? He's two years older and let's not forget he's incredibly annoying." I say convincingly. Katy shakes her head while they both look at me.

"Now who's staring." I say as I close my lid of my lunch box and take a deep breath. "Guys, I don't like him, if you want a go, go ahead." I say with a smile. That comment seems to heighten their interest and they look at each other, possibly to work out who gets him first. I smile before looking down at my copy of *Alice in Wonderland*. I feel like Alice at this moment in time, high school is a place I'll never understand. I've always felt out of place, I never fit into any sort of group.

Between Damian and the stranger sending me on a case to uncover the schools drug dealer and maker, I feel as though I've just fell down the rabbit hole, and I've immediately been faced with the *jabberwocky*.

CHAPTER NINE

After lunch, it's that dreaded lesson, Maths. Although I have Mr. Anderson who is an okay teacher, he does try and help me. But I'm not the smartest, I just can't seem to grasp the numbers. Am I ever going to use Pythagorizes theorem? Absolutely not. Do we need to learn it? You bet.

As I pass the science rooms, curiosity fills my veins and I decide to take a quick detour to Mr. Dunston's old classroom. As far as all the students were aware, we were waiting for another new teacher to arrive in the school. But no one arrived. Mrs. Collins left on maternity leave and Mrs. Holden was her replacement, or so we were told.

After reading that letter from *Q*, I'm convinced that the teachers know more than what they are leading on. Does Mrs. Holden know what happened here last summer? Surely, she does. More than likely all of the teachers have been told that if anything gets out to the media, they will lose their jobs. I walk around the corner into the science block, it's quiet, most kids are in class now with the odd one walking through as there is only a minute till class. I peek into Mr. Dunston's old classroom, the lights are off, but you can clearly see that it's spotless. I can just imagine this place filled with police and forensics. Examining every Bunsen burner and every petrie dish, test tubes, and God knows what else. I stare into the darkness imagining what this place would have been like last summer.

My thoughts are quickly interrupted by the sound of heels, and I immediately move to hide, the nearest place being behind the door of the classroom. I shut the door quietly and listen to what sounds like bickering. And it's mainly coming from Mrs. Hadley, the headmistress' side.

"Elena, I can understand your concerns but as long as we keep our heads down and we keep the school out of the media, this will all blow over." Mrs. Hadley reassures. her. Who is Elena? I'm going to assume this person has some concerns about the drugs that were found last year.

"Susan, a child is dead! We can't just let blow over." The panicked woman explains. I feel my heart stop, that's Mrs. Holden. My breathing becomes rapid as I realise that the teachers might be in on this, and the thought makes me sick to my stomach.

"Elena, keep your voice down." Mrs. Hadley warns. I move closer to the door wanting to make sure I can hear everything. I go into my blazer pocket and pull out my phone before finding voice notes and hitting the record button. I know I shouldn't be eavesdropping on teachers' conversation but like Mrs. Holden said, a child is dead. If I can stop another child from dying then I will.

"The last thing we need is for this school to become a fiasco. We have observations all next week by the school board, and I need all of my teachers to act calm and cool. I do not need them to be losing their heads over something that can't be controlled." Mrs. Hadley says. I feel as though my breathing is getting heavier and I must cover my mouth so the phone can hear what is being said.

"Susan, you cannot tell me this is controlled." Mrs. Holden continues. "Even with Tyler in prison now, we have eyes all over us now. Let's not forget that suddenly the American boy, Damian has decided to join the school, I don't get a good vibe from him at all." Mrs. Holden finishes.

I can hear her voice getting shaky and my breathing is rapid. I mean yes, Damian turning up to the school midyear is suspicious. But he's a student, that needed a school surely there is nothing more to it? And besides, Mrs. Holden seems to be so panicked about Georgia's death that she'll jump to conclusions.

"May I remind you Elena, that if it wasn't for

me, you would have lost your job as a teacher last year when you were caught with Harrison Meyer!" Mrs. Hadley states. My eyes go wide, what was Mrs. Holden doing with Harrison? Surely, she wasn't having a relationship with a student, she's married! "Now I don't like that Damian boy either, I didn't even get a choice to accept him. It came from someone on the school board that he will be starting Monday, and that was that. It went over my head and then I had some American boy from New Orleans joining the school." Mrs. Hadley explains. I frown slightly, I thought he said he was from South Carolina.

I don't even have time to think about anything else when I hear my name mentioned. "He's hanging out with that, oh what's her name... Juliette Sanders girl from year 9. Keep an eye on them Elena. I feel as though they are up to something together." Mrs. Hadley whispers as a warning. I feel my heart stop. They are suspicious of me cause of Damian and the fact he's hanging out with me. Something doesn't add up here.

"Susan you are being irrational!" Mrs. Holden shouts. "Jules Sanders is a sweet kid, there is nothing more to the fact that Damian Williams is hanging out with her. You're overthinking it." Mrs. Holden comes to my defense. I feel a sense of relief that she isn't also the one accusing me. If anyone knows me, it would be Mrs. Holden.

"I am not being irrational, and I am not

overthinking. I know something is up with them both. And I cannot have them ruin the school and everything I am currently trying to keep together. Keep an eye on them. If you're wanting to keep your job, I suggest you do." Mrs. Hadley growls harshly before I hear the heel of her shoes walk away from the door. I decide that is when to stop recording. I lightly watch from the window and Mrs. Holden goes after her and I finally decide to take a breath when I know I'm finally alone.

This doesn't make sense. I haven't done anything. I mean yes, I am investigating the situation at the school but I doubt they know that. It might be that Mrs. Hadley is having some sort of mental break, because there is no way she thinks Damian has something to do with any of this.

But then, I don't know anything about him. I take a deep breath, my heart still beating out of my chest. This is worse than I had expected, but I don't have time to think about that. I'm already 10 minutes late to my lesson, the last thing I need is a detention. I open the door of the classroom and look both ways before making my way to my maths class.

CHAPTER TEN

I sit in the library, a bundle of nerves.

I lied to my Maths teacher and said I wasn't feeling very well, which isn't exactly a lie. I feel sick to my stomach and even more so when out of the corner of my eye I notice Mr. Green, the engineering teacher lurking at the other exit on the library. He joined me not long after I entered the library and I now know how it feels to be put under surveillance.

"Yo!" A voice startles me from behind. I feel my soul jump of my skin as I'm faced with the annoying baboon.

"You scared me." I say to him before putting my head down and trying to focus on this maths homework. Thankfully Mr. Anderson was totally fine with me being late, just advised me not to be late again.

"Sorry. So, what homework are we doing tonight?" He asks curiously. I look up at him, slightly shifting my eyes to Mr. Green in the corner before looking back at Damian. I take a deep breath; I might as well accept any help he's willing to give me instead of struggle.

"Maths." I say before showing him my homework. He raises an eyebrow before taking a quick look at my homework.

"You mean Math?" He questions. I frown, confused by his answer.

"Huh?"

"You said Maths, it's Math." He corrects me only causing me to eyeroll.

"No one here says Math, we all say Maths." I correct him, before pulling my homework away from him. I'm in no mood to have a pronunciation argument with him. Britain and America have different pronunciations for different things. This just so happens to be one of them.

"I'm not in the mood to argue with you Damian." I say annoyed. I move my eyes towards Mr. Green once more. This time, it alerts Damian who goes to look over his shoulder.

"Don't." I warn him before putting my head down. I can feel his eyes burn into my head. I still feel sick to my stomach about the fact the headteacher has eyes watching me. And I haven't done anything... yet.

"Why is the headteacher heading this way?" He whispers quietly. I feel my heart drop and panic begins to set in. He must notice because he softens his face before pointing at my homework.

"The answer is 45." He says before giving a smile to me. I frown slightly before remembering that I'm doing my maths homework and he said he'd help me.

"It's 45." I agree with him before noting it down. Funnily enough he is right for once. *I think...*

"Juliette, Damian" Mrs. Hadley greets us as she joins our table.

"Hello." Damian responds. I keep quiet, only giving her a light smile. She leans over, looking at my homework before looking into the eyes of me and Damian.

"What are you two doing?" She asks with a smile, a very fake one. As much as I would like to say, plotting the end of your career, I can only speak for myself, and I need more evidence that Mrs. Hadley is corrupt before I go pointing fingers at her.

"I'm helping Juliette with her math homework. She had mentioned she was struggling so I offered to give her a hand." Damian responds for me. For once I'm grateful for the charismatic American. I think if it wasn't for Damian, I would be a mess. I'm never in trouble, and even though I haven't done anything wrong, my palms are still sweaty.

"Juliette is this true?" She asks me. I feel my

heart sink back into my chest and I feel like I can speak. I don't know where my sudden courage has come from but it is currently flowing through my veins causing me to nod and smile at the corrupt headteacher.

"Yeah, I had mentioned when meeting Damian for the first time I struggle with maths." I begin to say before giving Damian a smile. "He offered to help me." I say before looking back at the headteacher. I watch as she moves her eyes between the both of us before nodding and looking around.

"I'm only here as there has been a couple of complaints about yourselves. I just don't want there to be any misunderstanding." She says before standing up from her chair. Damian and I exchange looks of confusion. How can there be complaints about us? That is clearly a lie.

"I'm sorry headmistress, but I don't see how me helping Juliette with her homework has caused for a complaint? Surely you should be encouraging your students to speak up if they need assistance, not belittle them into struggling in silence?" He questions her. I shoot Damian a 'shut up before I kill you' look which he ignores, still giving Mrs. Hadley a glare.

"I can assure you Mr. Williams, I encourage all students if they are struggling to speak up. I'm just concerned is all." Mrs. Hadley explains harshly. I'm hoping that the warning in her tone gives him the indication to shut up. But he doesn't. He continues.

"The only thing you need to be concerned about is that your students are happy and learning. The last thing you need is to come and threaten 2 students who are trying to study together. That would look terrible on the front page of The Mirror now, wouldn't it?" He warns, My eyes pop out of my head, did he seriously just threaten the headteacher of the school? If it didn't make him look suspicious before, it does now. I look at the headteacher who looks like she's going to have a stroke before she walks away from the table and out of the door next to Mr. Green. I turn my attention to Damian, who looks calm whereas I am furious.

"What the heck was that?" I question him. I watch as he begins to pack his things away, I watch his every move carefully as well as his facial expression never changing from a standard state of calm. "Damian!" I shout the whisper which causes him to stop.

"Why is the headmistress questioning us?" He asks me. I move back slightly trying to make sure my face doesn't give away the fact that I am slightly freaking out inside.

"No idea." I say casually. He scoffs as he puts his bag down and begins to carefully pack up my things.

I throw my hands up while watching him, stunned. "Damian what are you doing?" I ask him. He doesn't answer. He just reaches underneath the table and grabs my school bag and every now and again looking at the door in front of him.

I follow his gaze and notice yet another teacher standing by the main entrance of the library. What the hell is going on… "Damian!" I lightly shout which causes him to put the bag down and lean over the table towards me.

"Whatever that headmistress has in her head, it's clearly not good. We're leaving." He orders before handing me my bag. I'm too stunned to even move.

"Damian, I can't. My mum is picking me up in less than 40 minutes." I say to him, which by the looks of it he doesn't care about.

"Juliette, I will get you back here in time for your mom to collect you but if you don't get up out of your chair, I will drag you. Now. Get. Up." He demands and I listen. I get up and put my bag on my shoulder before he grabs my hand and walks me towards the high bookshelves. The library isn't large for the school, but it does have a number of high bookshelves with older editions of books on.

"Damian what are you doing? The door is that way." I state. He doesn't listen he just begins to walk even quicker looking down each row. "Damian stop!" I exclaim as I try and pull him off me. He stops before turning into me, suddenly the calm and collected Damian has a slight twinkle of worry in his eyes, although if I asked him, he would never admit it.

"Has this got something to do with the file that was left in your locker the other day?" He asks inquisitively. I feel the colour drain from my face, I knew he had seen something.

"What? No." I try and say but it comes out as a squeak. He laughs slightly before taking my hand in his once more.

"Lying doesn't look good on you Juliette Sanders. You have 10 seconds to give the real answer." He warns. I panic, the last thing I want to do is be left here when all the teachers are looking for us because of the headteachers overreacting. I look at him, his ocean blue eyes look into mine and I feel them pleading with me. He's right, I never lie.

"They don't know about the file and they don't know I know about what happened here last summer." I tell him. He looks around my face for a indication that I'm not telling the truth, but I am. I am telling him the truth.

"Well, whatever that is, it's got them looking at us like we are suspects." He states before taking my hand in his again. "I'm not going to let them get to you understand. You're safe with me." He tells me quietly. I can't find the nerve to move away from his eyes, they keep me entranced. And even though I have barely known this boy a week, I trust him. I shouldn't trust a boy who gives me some of the worst headaches I've ever had in my life. But he hasn't made me feel as though I can question is loyalty. Not yet anyway. I nod, which causes him to lightly smile before he becomes focused on distracting the teachers and getting us out of here.

He drags me through the high bookcases, and he notices that Mr. Green has left his post and to his left you can see him frantically looking for us through the other bookcases. He gives me a nod and encourages me to run, which I do, and he follows me. I pull the door and we run through the corridor and out towards the fire exit, still hand in hand. I begin to laugh; this whole week has been a mess. I'm becoming a mess. My mother may end up getting that naughty child she was craving for. He looks at me as we make our way out of the school gates.

"What are you laughing at?" He questions as he begins to laugh with me. I stop and take a breath, still little giggles every now and again.

"Never did I think I would be in trouble with the headmistress for something as silly as what she's accusing us of." I say not giving it a thought.

Oh god. He has no idea what I'm talking about, and I've just let it slip.

"What are you talking about Juliette? What have we supposedly done?" He questions. I begin to go quiet, hoping he will just forget what I said but that doesn't seem lightly as he walks towards me, closing the gap between us.

"Don't make me ask you again." He warns. I stay quiet for a second before looking away thinking of my next point of call. I've said it now, I'm going to have to tell him. And I can't lie to him.

"I overhead Mrs. Hadley say that she thinks we are suspicious. Well… mainly you." I tell him. As I watch his face not change. So, this guy really can stay cool under pressure.

"I see." He says calmly. "So how are you involved in this?" He asks. I take another deep breath and look around. If they are watching the last thing, I want to do is to draw suspicion to myself or to Damian, although, he seems to have done that himself with his little backtalk to Mrs. Hadley.

"Come on." He instructs as he takes my hand, and we begin walking. A frantic look comes over my face, which he notices immediately and stops before resting his hands on my upper arms. "Juliette, I am not going to hurt you. But we can't talk about it here. I live 5 minutes from here, we will go to my house." He says with a small smile to reassure me.

I know he would never hurt me, but after everything that's happened this week the last thing, I want to do is go to this boy's house. Now that would cause my mother to break out into hives.

"Damian I can't, my mum will be picking me up-" I begin to say before he puts his hand over my mouth.

"Juliette as much as I like the fact you are now talking to me; I am going to say this once more. Hopefully you will believe it. I will have you back here for 4:25, plenty of time for you to meet your mom, avoid the headmistress and I still have enough time to try and drill fractions into your brain." he tells me. My eyes are wide at how much he's got this all thought out, the only problem is his tone in his voice. It's not a request it's a command, and I don't have another way out of this. He removes his hand with the hopes that I don't argue with him.

I realise he's right, with the headmistress watching us like we're the suspects and I now can't go back to the library, I don't have anywhere to go. "I'll be your study buddy." He says in my silence. It causes me to smile and shake my head. I feel my bag falling off my shoulder and I move it, so it sits back comfortably.

"I'm going to get a bad name for myself if I'm seen with you." I tell him, it causes him to laugh slightly before walking backwards down the path.

"Good it means no one will touch you, come on." He ushers waiting for me to join him, and I do. If my mother found out I was going to a boy's house, even though it is to study, she would break out into hives and have a heart attack.

But right now, I feel as though the only person I can really trust, is Damian. And as crazy as that sounds - I'm not scared to trust him with my secret. Not one little bit.

CHAPTER ELEVEN

Jules Sanders

The walk to Damian's place is silent, but while walking through the city, it makes me realise that I am the poster kid for abductions. Between me messaging a stranger online and now walking to the house of a new boy who I barely know, I'm going to be the tale that parents will tell their children when they're older. *'Jules didn't tell her mum about the bad man, look where that got her.'*

Now I'm not a dumb kid, I know my rights from my wrongs, but this has to be the dumbest idea I have ever had. I'm possibly walking into my own murder.

"Jules." Damian's voice breaks me from my thoughts when I come to. I've walked past him, and he's standing outside the most beautiful townhouse I've ever seen. "We're here." He says with a smile before unlocking the door. I follow him, curious as to how the other half live. He's rich? More than likely if I asked him he would respond with 'we're comfortable.'

As we walk through the door, I am met with the most beautiful, pale blue and gold entry way I've ever seen. It looks like something you would see on TV, and I am looking at it in real life. My eyes wander, to the gold chandelier and the baby blue wallpaper with birds on. Now these people have some serious money...

"What the hell..." I begin to say as I look around, ignoring Damian's stares as I walk through to the sitting room. It's absolutely beautiful, light brown furniture compliments the white sofa in the middle of the room, It looks like no one has ever sat in here, but surely he spends time with his family in here. My thoughts are broken once more to the sweet sound of a woman's' voice. She sounds like Snow White, and I begin to feel as though I'm about to meet a real-life princess.

"Damian darling, what are you doing home?" The woman says softly as I walk towards the entry way to see what she looks like. As I come around the corner she gasps before looking at Damian and back at me. Her pale skin shows the freckles that brighten her nose and forehead. She's got the most beautiful auburn hair and blue eyes. I think I have just met a princess.

"Sorry Mom, I said to Jules we could study here instead of the library, it was busy tonight." He explains. I look at him, did he just lie to his mum?

"Oh – of course!" She says exclaims before extending her hand out to me with a warm smile. Of course, her teeth are perfect, complimenting the shade of red lipstick on her lips. "I'm Ginny, Damian's mother." She says softly while shaking my hand.

"I'm Juliette, but you can call me Jules." I say to her. Her smile only grows wider as she looks at Damian before letting go of my hand and clearing her throat.

"Well, welcome to the Williams house." She says sweetly moving her hand towards the staircase.

"Thank you. You have a beautiful home." I tell her. She smiles sweetly at me showing a dimple I didn't notice was there before.

"Thank you, sweetheart. You must be thirsty, let me get you something to drink." She says as she begins to walk down the hallway towards the door at the bottom. I look at Damian who only extends his hand indicating he would like me to go first. I nod to him following Ginny through the kitchen. My eyes widen as I walk through. The kitchen is bigger than my entire house combined. Sticking with the same colors of white gold and baby blue, the kitchen has a island in the middle with pale blue cupboards and gold handles. The dining room is attached with the most gorgeous marble table that matches the countertops on the kitchen. I stare in awe, and I suddenly feel someone push my mouth closed. I look at Damian who gives me a wink before grabbing us the glasses of juice from his mum.

"Would you guys like a snack while you study?" She asks as she begins to open a cupboard.

"Oh no , you. I won't be here long but thank you for the offer." I say softly to her. She smiles at me before walking my way and leaving through the kitchen door. I look up at the wall to my left to take a note of the time. It's only 3:55pm which mean I still have at least 20 minutes here before Damian is going to let me leave. He wasn't wrong, he only lives 5 minutes from the school. I could only dream. I live 30 minutes away from the school. But I don't mind too much. We live in a nice neighborhood.

"Sit. We have to get something drilled into your brain at least and you drooling over the house isn't my idea of studying." He says as he moves me towards the dining table. I place my bag and drink down on the table before taking out my maths book and a pen, as well as my homework.

Fractions. One of my many worst enemies. Damian sits next to me while taking out a pen of his own from his bag.

"Okay. Let's begin." He says with a smile and I feel a sense of relief. Suddenly I don't feel as though I'm going to get murdered anymore.

◆ ◆ ◆

The timer goes off and we both jump out of our skin, laughing nervously.

"Well considering you were useless at the start of this session, I think we are making slow progress." He says as I begin to pack up my things. I laugh at his joke but decide not to argue with him because deep down I know he's right. "So I was thinking I can be your study buddy? But rather than us getting stared at from all angles from the teachers, maybe you would like to come and study here when your sister has practice? Obviously speak to your mom first but the offer is there." He offers, I mean this has been peaceful, and God knows what kind of problems I'll get dragged into on Monday when we go back to school. "I'd like that." I say with a smile, he joins me and nods before picking up my bag and handing me it. "Parent approval dependent." I say with a smile, and he nods, not saying another word and he leads me out of the kitchen and towards the front door.

"Oh, tell your mum thank you for the drink and it was lovely to meet her." I say to him, and he nods as we reach the door. Suddenly the handle is pulled down and another man appears from behind the door and stares me right in the eye. He freezes not moving a muscle before looking between Damian and I, straight faced. What is it with these people staring? Suddenly, a smile appears on his face as he moves his eyes too look at me, up and down.

"Hello." He says in a seductive raspy voice. He isn't old enough to be Damian's dad, he can only be a couple of years older than Damian.

"Hi." I say back, not sure than anything else will come out normal as I don't trust my voice. He's just as godly sculpted as Damian, which can only mean one thing.

"I'm Rodger, Damian's brother." He introduces himself. *Bingo.* I knew it. I look back at Damian who is for the first time in his life, quiet and very pale faced.

"Damian never mentioned he had a brother." I say which causes Rodger to laugh as he looks at Damian with a look I can't exactly work out.

"He has two." Rodger says, still not looking at me. Their eyes burn into each other's, neither of them blinking. I begin to feel like I'm interrupting something, and I shift nervously.

"I better go. It was nice meeting you." I say with a smile to Rodger who suddenly breaks his look with Damian and gives me an unnerving smile.

"Wait! You have to meet the other brother then you've met the whole family!" Rodger says enthusiastically causing Damian to turn into a ghost. "Hey Spencer! You're going to wanna see this." Rodger shouts out of the door to who I'm assuming is the other brother. I watch carefully as the smile on Rodger's face gets bigger as another god like human walks around the door. It is taking all my strength not to let my jaw drop to the floor. This guy is tatted, head to toe, tanned with the occasional piercing on his ear. This is the kind of boy any mother would dread you brought home.

He doesn't say anything, he just stares at me. The longer he stares, the more I become uncomfortable.

"I'm gonna go." I say in the uncomfortable silence. I begin to walk towards the door to leave and the older brother, Spencer, stands in front of me, blocking me. He doesn't move but the longer I'm here, the more nervous I'm becoming.

"Let me drive you." He says in the silence. I look up at him, shocked by his offer. I turn my head to Damian who is still staring into his brothers' eyes, this time not with fear but with warning.

"It's fine, I'll walk her." He says to him before lightly placing his hand on my back and pushing slightly hinting he would like me to move. But Spencer stands his ground, looking into my eyes.

"It may only be 5 minutes away, but I want to make sure you get back safe. You can come Damian, but I'm not letting you walk it." He orders. I turn my attention to Damian who only nods. I'm assuming not wanting to argue with his scarier brother. The middle brother, Rodger moves out of the way and waves me goodbye, with the same smirk Damian gives me when he's annoying me. They really are brothers and I do feel as though Rodger is the joker of the family, Spencer the more serious one and Damian, well he is still a kid.

"Thank you." I say to Spencer as we leave the house. He doesn't say anything but gives me a nod as we walk towards his car. It's seriously fancy, I wonder what he does for a living. I'll have to ask Damian on our next study session, if his brothers allow me back through the door that is. "I'm Jules by the way." I say to the tatted brother who looks at me as he opens the car door for me.

"Spencer." He says before instructing me with his eyes to tell me to get in the car. Damian walks sheepishly round the other side and gets in. I smile at Spencer, but he doesn't return the gesture, so I just get I the car and do as I'm told. He shuts the door before walking to the drivers' side and he gets in. He turns around looking at Damian and raises an eyebrow.

I'm clearly missing something. Either they don't get on, or they are hiding something from me. Damian looks away from Spencer which causes him to turn around and start the car, in the car it will only take a few minutes.

The silence in the car is deafening, every now and then I check between Damian and Spencer. Damian quiet as a mouse looking out the window and Spencer gripping the steering wheel so hard, he looks like he's going to rip it from the car.

We pull into the car park, and I notice my mum isn't here and I have a few minutes until my sister finishes football.

"Thank you." I say to Spencer, and I receive a nod. I look at Damian; who looks back with a worried look on his face. "Thank you for helping me tonight." I say with a smile, and he returns. The once cocky, annoying Damian sits in a shell afraid to speak. The last thing I wanted to do was get him in trouble. Between the headmistress now looking at us like we are suspects, and now his brothers giving us unnerving stares – I'm unsure as to whether or not I'm being told the truth.

I begin to walk towards the school debating whether or not to just call off this whole study buddy thing with Damian as it's clearly going to cause him problems.

"Jules!" I hear him call after me. I turn to see him running in my direction. "I'm sorry about them, they just –" He begins to say before he takes a deep breath. I take a moment to look back at the car and see that Spencer is now standing, leaning against the car. I turn my attention back to Damian's face. "They have always teased me about girls and how I'll never have a girlfriend or be able to talk to a girl. When in reality I just didn't want to." He says quietly between us. My heart sinks and i feel it break for him. Brothers can be cruel, I never had one but I have a sister and surely it's the same thing. Teasing comes with the territory and since Damian is the baby brother, I reckon he gets teased a lot.

"Don't worry about it, your brothers seem…" I begin to say before darting my eyes back to Spencer as I say this. "Unnerving." I say before giving him a reassuring smile. "I know it's harder said than done, but don't let them get to you, okay?" I say to him reassuringly. He smiles for a moment, before looking back at Spencer who still has a straight face. Does he ever smile?

"I know. I will." He says softly before turning to look at me once more." Have a good weekend. See you Monday." He says with a smile before walking towards the car. I watch as they get into the car. Just as they pull out of the car park, my Mum pulls in. I put my bag on my shoulder and give her a soft smile as the pulls in. I open the door and throw my bag in the car.

"Hey cherub, how was school?" She asks sweetly. I look at her and notice there are bags under her eyes and her skin isn't as bright as it usually is.

"It was okay, are you alright Mum? You look tired?" I question her. She opens the sun visor of the car. "I do not!" She exclaims horrified before lightly pushing me. I laugh at her before the door opens in the back of the car and I smell the sweaty muddy stench of my sister.

"Hi." She says as she slams the door. We exchange a look between each other before back at Ava.

"What's wrong grumpy pants?" I tease. She sticks

her tongue out at me before sighing and putting her seatbelt on.

"Danielle kept pushing me over today." She says as she looks out of the window. I frown as I look at my mum who is just as shocked as me.

"What? Danielle is your best friend. Are you sure she wasn't just playing?" I ask. Ava shakes her head as she looks down at her knees.

"We can talk about it when we get home okay?" Mum asks softly before rubbing Ava's leg but gets no response. I exchange a look with my mum before turning back around and taking a deep breath. Danielle is Holly and Maura's younger sister, the friends of Georgia. My heart beats a little bit quicker when I remember that I can tell the stranger about the evidence I've gathered once I'm home.

I mean I could wait, the last thing I want to do is drag Damian into this mess with the stranger, what if they get curious? As my mum pulls out of the car park, I think of ways I can tell the stranger about the conversation I overheard.

I take my coat off and head upstairs to start the rest of my homework. The only thing that is on my mind is telling the stranger about the conversation I overheard. I have decided not to tell them. They want to know who is selling and making the drugs. Right now, I am not sure as to how they are involved in this whole situation. But what I do know is that they have a say in some of this.

◆ ◆ ◆

After I finish my homework and with what Damian taught me, I feel a sense of accomplishment. I've always struggled, and he showed me a way I can understand it. I decide that I'm going to spend the rest of my night looking at what evidence I already have. I go over to the box and get the case file. I thought that was the best place to put it so my mum doesn't find it. I had decided earlier today that I would tell her, just not yet. I place the case file on the bed and go over to my desk and get the laptop.

After opening it up and putting in the password I notice there is a message waiting for me. I haven't given them any new information on my end and I feel myself become anxious. I move the cursor and click on the icon which opens up a message.

"Juliette,

After further investigation, I located a case that was made against Mrs. Holden last year at her previous school. Now, you and the rest of the students were told that Mrs. Holden is a new teacher, and this was her first school when in reality that isn't true.

Mrs. Holden was a Science Teacher at Middlestone Prep. She had been a teacher there for 2 years before being transferred to your school. The reason for her instant transfer over the summer as there was a investigation into her relationship with Harrison

Meyer, a student a few years older than you that I'm going to assume you will know.

Now there was no charges pressed against Mrs. Holden, but what I did gather is that there was a large sum of money floating around and then suddenly Mrs. Holden got to keep her job, as long as she transferred to a new school, but little did the Meyer family know, they transferred their son to the same school.

I'm not going to tell you the reason why he was transferred, but I'm going to assume that little brain of yours has a good idea-"

"Yeah, a relationship." I say out loud. Now hearing what Mrs Hadley had said to Mrs Holden earlier today, that makes more sense.

"Now if you have any information you would like to tell me about what you have found so far, I look forward to hearing it. This is your case but remember a fresh set of eyes always helps."
-Q.

I look at that last sentence again, maybe I should tell my Mum. Like the stranger said, a extra set of eyes would help. I decide to type a message back, not telling them about the recording just yet, but I will just say I have a few people in mind that I will discuss once I have some evidence. Maura handing Harrison a packet of God knows what isn't enough evidence.

So far, believe I have sussed out 3 potential suspects.

There. That should make them happy I've started the case. I watch anxiously as I get no response. Minutes feel like a lifetime, until a message appears on my screen.

Good. Since you've started making progress, I will allow a question of your choice.

Well then, that is not what I was expecting as a response. I think hard, my heart beating out of my chest, and I can feel my hands become shaky as I think of a question. I take a long deep breath; I doubt they will answer this question honestly.

How come you always come across case files that have been hidden from the public eye?

As I press send, I feel my heart bash against my rib cage. I had given it a thought that possibly they worked in the police force, or one of them did. Like the note on my birthday said, *'all our love.'*

Even if I did want to go out looking for this person I wouldn't even know where to start. Every time my mum went to the police, nothing ever came of it. It wasn't that they weren't bothered, it was more that they couldn't find anything.

I have friends in the police force.

I feel my heart sink. That's why we couldn't get any answers. They possibly paid them off to keep quiet or they are hinting they are in the force.

Although I feel frustration running through my veins, I also feel a sense of relief that I do have some sort of answer as to why I never got answers and leads as to who the stranger is.

Thank you for telling me.

I decide that I don't want to answer anymore messages and I doubt they would tell me anything else anyway. I click the attachment and grab my notebook and pen to make notes. Tonight, is going to be a long night, and by the looks of it this case file is over 100 pages long. I really know how to have a wild Friday night...

CHAPTER TWELVE

Damian Williams

I'm in some deep shit.

On the drive back, Spencer's silence and his heavy breathing was all I needed to know about the situation I'm going to deal with when I get home. His knuckles were white as they gripped the steering wheel.

I know what he's going to say, and I know the way he's going to say it. But it still doesn't calm my nerves. My brother, calm and quiet – that's until you do something that's stupid. And I... I have done something stupid.

Spencer parks the car and turns the engine off. He still hasn't said anything, and my guess it's because he wants to wait until we get in the house. I don't look back at him as I feel him turn his gaze to me. I don't need to look at him to know he's staring right into my soul. I can feel he is, ripping apart my heart from my ribcage with his mind. He takes a deep breath before opening the car door and I do the same. I knew this was coming, did I expect it to be so soon? Maybe… honestly, I don't know.

I walk slightly sheepishly behind my older brother. He may only be 21 but he is one of the scariest people I know. He opens the door and I follow behind and into the hallway. The door slams behind me almost causing me to jump but before I can react, he grabs my jacket at my shoulders and shoves me into the door. His eyes are dark, and his breathing is manic.

"Have you lost your fucking mind?" He grits between his teeth. "You had one fucking task Damian, what you going to do when he finds out what you've been up to? Huh?!" He continues to shout. I look at him dead in the eyes, I know I'll be in the shit with him.

"Don't worry, I'll dig my own grave." I say with a slight smirk. He doesn't find me funny and shoves me into the stairs. Spencer runs his hands through his hair, clearly trying to calm down otherwise he will put me in that grave himself.

"I see you've made a friend Damian. What was her name again?" My brother Rodger stands above me with a smirk, more devious than the one that was on my face 3 seconds prior. "Josie? No… that's not it. Ah! Jessie! No... that's not it either." He continues to tease. I hear Spencer growl in front of me which causes me to turn my head.

"Rodger shut it." He warns before looking over towards the kitchen. I turn my head to find Ginny, staring quite worried at all 3 of us. "Ginny, go back into the kitchen, this doesn't concern you." Spencer demands as calm as he can which causes Ginny to scatter. I snort before looking back at Spencer who is currently killing me with his eyes.

"You think this is funny?" He threatens as he moves quickly towards me. "He warned you not to talk to her, you're there to keep an eye on her. You were not meant to interact with her! Does this conversation ring any bells at all?" Spencer questions loudly. With the way he's looking at me, I decide sarcasm isn't going to get me further than 6 feet under so I decide to agree, leave the sarcasm up to the other brother.

"Yes, it rings bells. But I have my reasons." I say in my defense. He scoffs before running his hands once again through his hair. Rodger moves from behind me and sits next to me on the stair.

"Oh please! Pray tell!" He encourages enthusiastically. I glare at him. Rodger always has to be the sarcastic one no matter the situation.

"Can you be serious for two fucking seconds Rodger?" Spencer asks through his teeth. Rodger gasps horrified.

"I am being serious. I am concerned about

whether or not Damian's little activity has caused you to finally break before our fearless leader. It's not the first time he's done something he wasn't meant to when we were sent away. Do you remember New York? With the wanna-be model?" Rodger jokes. I roll my eyes at his response to my brother.

"Not the time Rodger." Spencer shouts causing a grin out of Rodger. He really is a narcissist. "Damian, you better have a very good reason at to why she was in our house less than 20 minutes ago." Spencer says trying to rationalise the situation before he kills me.

"I do. On Tuesday I saw someone put something in her locker. It looked like a case file. I couldn't get a good look at their face, but it was a man about 6ft, black hair." I explain to them. Spencer's reaction is still the same, anger but also trying to remain calm.

"Why didn't you mention this the other day?" He asks. I look at Rodger whose smile is still plastered over his face, no surprise there.

"Because you two would go all undercover. Look I have this controlled. Or I thought I did." I say as I look back at Spencer whose expression has now turned back to anger after my last sentence.

"What do you mean?" Rodger asks.

"There was a situation with the headteacher, which is why we ended up here. The headteacher was suspicious of me helping her and was trying to say there was complaints about us studying together." Rodger and Spencer's eyebrows raise at my comment. "Then when I asked her about it, said nothing was going on, I had to tell her I knew about the file and her face went white. Like I wasn't supposed to know." I tell them. I watch as they exchange a look between each other, more than likely filled with curiosity.

When we were sent to watch Juliette, I was given 2 instructions.

1.Don't talk to her.

2.Don't interact with her in anyway.

I was told to stay clear, but make sure she was safe. That was what I was sent here to do. Spencer was running surveillance on the house at night and Rodger watched her mother. That was the deal. We made sure they were safe, until we were told that the threat had been handled. They were extremely vague on what that threat was.

When that was going to be exactly no one knew. Spencer, a man of very few words, wasn't best pleased about being sent to babysit our fearless leader's obsession. When we were brought into this family, he made sure that we felt protected. If we did what he asked, we always had a home to go to. And for 3 kids who didn't have parents. He became a father to us.

Ginny was hired to make us look like a normal family. She was a acting graduate from Nashville. So, she was hired to act like our mother, at parent - teacher conferences and school events. She was about 35, did something different with her life. And ended up working with the likes of us.

"So you didn't think to mention the file when you watched it being placed in her locker. I mean that is one of the many things we were sent to watch for! What the hell is in that file?" Spencer questions while pacing the hallway.

"Let me hang out with her, I think I was close to her telling me what was in that file. She said that the headmistress is involved. Let me see if she will open up to me." I beg him. He looks at me with warning eyes.

I know he doesn't like the idea. But right now, he doesn't have a choice. And what he decides to tell the boss, well that's up to him. I'll take my punishments like a man, but I was sent here to protect her, and I told her I would. They don't need to know that, so I think I'll keep that one to myself.

"Fine. But you need to go upstairs and explain to him what you've done this week. He wants a update. But Damian for the love of God, do not tell him you've been hanging out with Juliette." Spencer warns before walking into the living room not waiting for my answer. I feel a hand reach my shoulder as I look over at my brother Rodger, that wicked grin still plastered on that face.

"Well good luck little bro." He says before standing and walking down the stairs and into the living room, he stops as he reaches the door. "Spencer owes me $50. He said you would be able to stay away from her and I said no way I give it a week. Guess who's a winner." He says with a wink. I roll my eyes; he always knows how to push my buttons.

I take a deep breath before walking up the stairs to the study. If he finds out later that we have lied to him, he will put a bullet in all of our brains. But I understand that

I'm about to lie to Robert Quinten, the leader of the American mafia, who is also happens to be Juliette's birth father... now I'm even deeper in the shit.

CHAPTER THIRTEEN

Jules Sanders

The weekend went by way too quick. But apart from look at the cases, I didn't do much else. Grandma and Grandad came for Sunday lunch which was nice since I hadn't seen them since my birthday party the week before.

After looking at all the evidence, I've concluded that Mrs. Hadley and Mrs. Holden have to be in on the same deal as what was sent into place before Mr. Dunston went to prison. Mrs. Holden was accused of having a indecent relationship with harrison Meyer in Middlestone Prep, except those charges disappeared.

My question is who is making the drugs? I would

like to think it isn't Mrs Holden for a few reasons:

1. She wouldn't want to risk her job, again.
2. It seems too simple to be Mrs. Holden, yes; she maybe a science teacher, but that isn't a good enough reason to accuse her.

But in order to prove that, I need evidence. Apart from the breakdown I listened to on Friday between Mrs. Hadley and Mrs. Holden, I don't have any physical proof. So that is what this week is about – hiding in the shadows to try and get some leads.

I can't be asking around; it would cause too much suspicion. And since I'm already a walking problem for the headteacher, I need to keep my head down but also keep my ears open for conversations that might happen.

As I say goodbye to my mum and sister, I begin to walk towards the art classrooms to meet Mikki and Katy, who are going to want to know everything about what happened on Friday with Damian. To be honest, I don't know what to tell them. They will jump over hurdles of conclusions if I mention I went to his house and met his brothers and mum. But also, I don't want to lie to them, so I think I'll keep the update small.

As I walk round towards the science rooms, I feel someone pull my wrist and I feel my back pushed into the pillar. My shock is suddenly subsiding when I see the American baboon.

"Hello." He says with a smile. I laugh trying to

calm my racing heart.

"Hi. What's up?" I question him. I begin to look around and notice people starting to stare at us as they walk to their form class.

"How was your weekend?" He questions, ignoring the stares around us.

"Erm, yeah good. I didn't do much." I say which is clearly a lie. I look into his eyes and for some reason I can feel as though he can sense that.

"So, you didn't look at that file that was put in your locker last week?" He teasingly questions. I huff, I thought he may have forgot about it, but how could he? He is the center of the conversation between the headmistress and the science teacher. "Did you talk to your Mom about studying at my place?"

I nod. "Er, yeah. She said she will need to talk to your mum first. But other than that, it's okay." He looks around quickly before pulling his phone out and hinting I do the same.

"I'm going to give you my Mom's number so they can speak on the phone. Does your sister have practice tonight?" He asks. I nod as I type in the number as a message to my Mum with Ginny's number so she can talk to her.

"Yeah, she has netball." I tell him. I click send on my phone, before putting it back in my pocket before a teacher spots me on my phone. I look up at him and smile before catching a glimpse of the troublemakers walking towards us.

"Oh god." I say as I try and turn my head away, but I lock eyes with Mikki as I watch her move quicker, her afro bouncing as she makes her way towards us, Katy following behind.

"I thought we said we were meeting – " She begins to say, until she notices Damian and she quickly shuts up and looks at Katy who ignores her stares and glares at me. I smile, Mikki runs her mouth 24/7 so it's very rare that she's speechless.

"Sorry, I just wanted to check on Juliette." He says with a smile, and I nod. Katy's mouth drops open and I roll my eyes.

"Okay, well thank you again. I'll see you later. Come on." I say as I link arms with my two gawking friends pulling them away from my American study buddy.

As I turn to walk back the way I came, I'm immediately stopped in my tracks by Mrs. Hadley who has a devious smile on her face.

"Hello girls, good weekend?" She asks. I internally roll my eyes.

"Yes." I respond and she nods back before her gaze looks behind us. I follow her gaze only to realise that Damian is no longer there, lucky.

"Well, get to form class girls, don't be late." She instructs, stepping out of our way and begins to walk in the direction of Damian. I finally take a breath after a moment, but I do earn some inquisitive looks off my friends and I huff out loud before looking at my watch.

"Come on. I've got something's to tell you." I say dragging them towards the empty art classroom. The teacher that was in there never returned this year and they couldn't find a replacement in time, so they just left it empty.

As we reach the door, I push it open before placing my bag on the table and looking at my concerned friends, who don't have a clue what's going on.

"The headteacher came to Damian and I on Friday in the library and said there were complaints about us studying together." I explain them, earning a very confused look from both Mikki and Katy.

"Jules, that doesn't make sense. You and Damian have only been studying together a few days, he's been at the school a week? Does she have something against him?" Mikki asks trying to figure out the situation that's been playing in my mind since Friday.

"No idea, what I do know is she had no say in him joining the school. It came from the school board." I begin to say before Katy interrupts me.

"And how do you know this?" She questions which causes me to pause my next sentence. I've kept too many things from them this week but if I want to find out who's selling and making the drugs, I need to keep it to myself for now.

"I overheard her." I speak. Which is the truth, but

in reality, there is so much too it. Like our science teacher on a Tuesday is possibly connected to this.

"Okay, so who is more suspicious, Damian or Mrs. Hadley?" Mikki questions.

I barely know Damian, and I don't know Mrs. Hadley at all. But since she wants to start throwing accusations into the air, I might as well do the same, because unlike her I have proof. All she has is speculation.

"Honestly right now, they are both as suspicious, but it doesn't matter." I say as I pick up my bag and walk towards them quickly.

"So what are you going to do?" Katy asks.

"I'm going to Damian's house because he's going to help me with maths." I tell them causing their eyes to pop out their head. "I'll do some digging before I can positively say I can trust him." I watch them exchange a look of pure shock. I just admitted to going to Damian's house and tomorrow, they are going to need all of the details. "I've got this under control." I reassure them. My tone is harsh, hinting I don't want them to start asking questions. To my surprise they keep quiet, and I decide to leave them in silence as I make my way towards my form class.

CHAPTER FOURTEEN

The day drags, just like most Mondays. I feel like I've barely focused today. I've been too busy looking over my shoulder to see if Mrs Hadley was going to give me detention. Thankfully, I've avoided her so I think I've saved myself for today.

The question that is buzzing around in my mind is do Holly, Maura and Harrison know about Georgia's death? I can't seem to work out whether they are grieving or they simply having got a clue.

I also can't help but feel bad for them. If they don't know, then that's absolutely heartbreaking. They are going on living their life, thinking that Georgia is going to walk through the doors of the school, but I'm the only one who knows that that will sadly not happen.

As I come out of History I begin to make my way towards my locker to get my maths book. I will need for Damian's house; I notice someone in a black hoodie moving quickly to my area of the lockers. I stop in my tracks. Am I overthinking? as I slowly walk around the corner wanting to see their face. I watch intensively, no one seems to be bothered by a man in a hoodie. Except my fellow my American acquaintance who I notice is now standing at the other end of the hall.

I feel a wave of confidence as the hooded man struggles to open my locker with the combination. I look at Damian who shakes his head hinting at me to leave it as he walks towards him, but I don't listen.

"Instead of struggling you could just give me it?" I taunt, breaking the silence, he doesn't turn round and stops for what feels like a lifetime before he pulls the file out of his coat and hands it to me still not looking at me.

I take the file carefully out of his hands not breaking my gaze from him in the hope that he turns around and he does. His eyes meet mine as they burn with anger, but the expression on his face is smug. Like he meant to get caught.

"Thank you." I say in the silence. He only nods, which somewhat surprises me. He moves to stand with me rather than be hunched over. "What is it?" I ask. He doesn't break his stare, not even a blink as he looks down at the file then back up to my eyes.

"Look for yourself." He encourages a slight smile

appearing on his face which instantly makes me nervous. He's American, and I'm not sure why but that surprises me. I don't want to break my eyes away from him as he nods once more hinting that he wants me to open the file. I look down briefly and open the file hoping he doesn't run away. First thing I notice is a photo of Holly, Maura and Harrison outside the school. The photos look recent, I can tell because I notice a watch on Holly's wrist that she got as a present from her parents last week. She was showing it to everyone in the food hall the day before Georgia died. I glance at it before looking back up at him, trying to show the least bit of emotion.

"What do they want with me?" I ask not thinking. I don't break my stare from this stranger. I can't help but feel like if I blink, he might disappear and I'll be once again searching for answers in a never ending pool of questions.

I don't think for a second that this person is the one who has sent me presents for the last 14 years. He's too young, maybe late teens and I get the feeling he must just be the messenger. I can feel eyes on me now, whether it's Damian's or the other students; I can feel as though I'm being watched as I can feel my heart begin to beat quicker but I'm attempting to keep my cool.

He's standing before me now, maybe 5 inches between us, and I can smell his cologne, dark, musky and warm. I inhale it as it's the only thing I can breathe. He smiles at me, not a creepy smile but a reassuring one.

"Just do as they ask, okay? You'll be able to prove your worth it. Worth all of this although, I don't see the fascination." He says with a cheeky wink before walking off and not giving me a chance to ask another question. He walks in the direction of Damian with his head down not wanting to make eye contact. Damian watches him carefully, the hooded man lifts his head slightly and the anger that resided on Damian's face, is now plastered with realization, as though he knows the hooded man. I feel my heart sink. *Could they know each other?* I finally break my stare from Damian and look around to the students who have stopped to watch. Some with confusion, some with curiosity and I don't even blame them. I would be. But then you know what they say... curiosity killed the cat.

I quickly go to my locker and pick up my books before walking towards Damian avoiding all stares from other students, even some teachers who don't know how to react. Out the corner of my eye, I notice the headteacher, Mrs. Hadley, staring us down as Damian leads me out of the corridor and towards the nearest exit. My heart is pounding, and I feel sick to my stomach.

Damian thankfully doesn't say anything, just keeps quiet as we leave the school to head to his house. I'm thankful because I really don't know how to respond right now as I process what has just happened.

When he opens the door, I'm greeted by his strange brothers who sit on the stairs like they were waiting for us to arrive. I look at Damian who I now notice has a face full of anger as he shakes his head at his brothers and leads me towards the kitchen. I watch as Spencer and Rodger exchange a glance of confusion.

As we enter the kitchen, Damian goes into the cupboard to grab two glasses and then fills them up with water and hands me one with a smile. His brothers enter the kitchen in silence, I watch as none of us say a word but I can see Damian about to snap. I walk over to the kitchen table and take out the file in silence.

"You two are awfully quiet. Did you get into a fight about fractions?" Rodger teases which cause's Damian to snap. He slams the glass on the counter with such force it shatters. I gasp, he's always had such a calm demeanor, what am I missing?

"Shut it Rodger." Damian warns, which only causes Rodger to laugh. My eyes turn to Spencer as he moves away from Rodger, ignoring Damian's outburst and makes his way towards me. His walk intimidates me, and I stand frozen as he approaches. His broad shoulders covers my view of the two boys in the corner. His gaze follows down to file and then back up at me.

"What's in it?" He asks in the silence. I shake my head at him, and he doesn't like that answer. He grabs a hold of the file himself and places it on the table showing the of the contents of it. I look at Damian for a answer hoping he will give me one, and he seems to be as speechless as me.

I turn my attention towards Spencer who looks inquisitively at the photos and the documents fanned out across the kitchen table. His brow raises as he picks up a photo of Holly and Harrison. He turns the photo to me, his now jet-black eyes staring into mine searching for answers.

"What the hell is this?" He questions. I feel my voice get stuck in my throat. And this isn't because I am afraid of Spencer, yes, he is slightly frightening, but not enough to scare me away and to make me cower. I'm afraid to answer him due to the fact I don't want to admit this to anyone else. Although Q said I could ask for some help, they also said I could tell my mother. I really didn't want the brothers to know about this. I still feel as though i can't trust Damian, and I can not trust the other two brothers because I don't know anything about them. I wouldn't trust the sarcastic brother as far as I could throw him.

"Juliette, I asked you a question." He demands in the silence.

"Nothing you need to include yourself in." I say sheepishly, afraid of how he will react. I don't want to trust them with this case.

"I don't care what you think right now. I want to know who these people are. And you're going to tell me and not give me any sass." He says coldly and I feel a chill go down my spine. The look he is giving me right now, is the look of I need to hand over everything. But I'm going to be stubborn and selfish.

"I don't have to tell you anything." I say confidently in the hopes he just drops the whole thing and walks away. But I couldn't be more wrong. He begins to walk quickly towards me, breaking the space between us.

I turn my head slowly to look at Damian and as I do, he steps in front of me, as if he is a shield, my protector and I'm slightly confused by the gesture.

"Their names are Holly Vanwald and Harrison Meyer." He says so I don't have to. I exhale loudly, clearly annoyed. But am quickly met with angry eyes by all 3 brothers, even the creepy one.

"Now why do you have these?" Spencer asks as he lifts the photo to show me. It shows Harrison and Holly in some sort of argument. My eyes narrow while I take in the photo. Harrison is screaming at Holly while she seems to be crying. She's holding something in her hand, and I turn my head ignoring the stares from the 3 boys to look at the other photos, hoping to see if they took a photo of the item she's holding.

I move myself to scatter the photos taking in the details of each one. Maura is in some of these too, clearly trying to protect her sister from whatever Harrison is screaming at her, but even she is visibly upset. I place the photos down so I can see them clearly and I feel eyes following my every move.

Then, underneath some sort of letter, I see it. *Bingo.*

The tension in the room only heightens as I pick up the photo to see what Holly is holding and I feel my heart sink. My eyes flash back to the other photos laying on the table. The hurt in the twins faces, the anger in Harrison's, the tears falling down their cheeks. It all makes sense.

I look back at the photo of what Holly is holding, my breathing is heavy as I place it back on the table ignoring the stares.

"Juliette what is it?" Damian says breaking the deafening silence in the room. I take one last look at the table as I back away, looking briefly over the date on the photos. *11.06.2014.* That was the weekend.

"They know about Georgia."

CHAPTER FIFTEEN

"What do you mean they know about Georgia?" Damian asks before picking up the photo from the table. "Know what?" He asks once more. I turn to look at him and the boys all of whom have confused expressions plastered all over their faces. I sigh. Clearly, I'm not going to be able to just explain it to just Damian, I'm going to have to settle for the fact all 3 of them will know.

"Georgia died of a drug overdose last Friday." I say looking over the documents on the table. Damian's eyes almost pop out of his head whereas Rodger and Spencer exchange a look of confusion.

"Who's Georgia?" Rodger asks.

"She's one of the popular girls." Damian says before picking up the letter and reading it. I didn't

even know what it said before his brows frown.
"Juliette, what's this?" He asks while handing me the letter. I raise my eyebrow as I begin to read it.

"Juliette,

I thought I would give you a helping hand. I had a friend of mine who works in the police department, who is also looking into this case capture these photos. He said both Harrison and Holly, as well as Maura were visibly upset when they had learnt of Georgia's sudden death. There should be a file sent to your MacBook with images that were caught on the Sunday. I thought these would be better to see in person.

The rest is down to you now.

-Q"

I stare at the note once more, feeling the stares from the boys forcing me to look up and meet their confused faces. My mind wanders back to when I received the file from my mysterious stranger. His complexion tanned and lightly freckled, like he had come from somewhere sunny. I think back for a second, trying to remember anything but those emerald eyes. I close my eyes trying to remember anything else from the man as I do a play by play in my mind. I feel my heart stop as I suddenly remember.

"He had a tattoo." I say in the silence, causing them to look at each other.

"Who had a tattoo?" Spencer questions, intrigued.

"The man who gave me the file." I begin to stay before I shake my head. "No, not a man. A boy, a teenager. He looked young." I recall as I look at Damian. "You knew him." I say almost as a whisper as his face of realization begins to replay in my mind. I make my way towards him, and he doesn't move a inch. "You can't tell me you didn't because the realisation on your face told me everything I needed to know." I say, now angry. I'm being lied to, and I don't like liars. Not one bit.

"Juliette, I don't know what you're talking about-" He begins to blurt out before he stops, and I pull up the sleeve of his flannel to reveal the same tattoo that the mysterious boy had. For only a second, I thought I might have been mad, that surely the mysterious boy doesn't have the same tattoo as Damian, but now that I'm looking at it in the flesh, I begin to wonder, who are these people? I know nothing about any of these brothers. I know nothing about someone claiming to be my friend.

"I am not a idiot, and I don't like being painted as one. I know that that boy had the same tattoo as you." I say pointing at it causing the boy's faces to drop. Damian's eyes meet mine in a simple plea before Spencer grabs a hold of his brothers and forces them into the hallway and slamming the door, leaving me in the room; baffled as to what's just happened.

A lightbulb goes off in my head as I realise I'm not

going to get any answers out of the boys. I pack up everything in the file and place it in my bag. This is possibly the most stupid idea I've ever had. Trusting someone I barely know with something so sacred to me. He can not deny that he doesnt know the hooded boy. His face told me everything.

I notice a gate in the back garden and decide that I'm done being lied to. I'm done being told one thing, and I am done trusting the Williams brothers. I open one of the French doors closing it carefully before running up the garden and unlocking the gate and heading down the back alley hoping it leads to the main road so I can make my way to the school. I keep looking over my shoulder, waiting for one of them to come after me, but none of them do.

I make my way towards the road. I have every intention to go back to school and ignore any questions Mrs. Hadley may have. If I'm on my own, she can't accuse me of having any complaints. That is another lie. What is it with people lying for their own benefit recently?

As I turn the corner on the main road back to the school, I'm caught off guard by Harrison Meyer. He stands tall in front of me, annoyance clearly plastered all over his face.

"Can I help you Harrison?" I ask slightly startled. He ignores the fear on my face and instead looks me up and down.

"You've been sticking your nose where it doesn't belong Juliette." He smirks slightly. I can't help but laugh. *Is he for real?*

"I don't know who your source is, but I think you should get some evidence." I smirk back as I begin to walk away. Just as I feel as though he is going to leave me alone; he grabs my arm, forcing me to look at him.

"I have questions, and you have the answers." I try to pull away from him but it only makes him grab my arm harder as he pulls me towards a black car against my will. "You're going to tell me everything you know." He demands before pushing me head first into the car.

CHAPTER SIXTEEN

Damian Williams

I don't agree to being forced out of the room after what Juliette just said. I want to explain everything to her, but I know I can't, and that in itself is torture.

"What does she mean by he has the same tattoo? Who gave her the file?" Spencer demands. I meet his eye and I sense a little bit of frustration in his voice.

"Marcus." I say to him and watch his face drop, disbelief filling his face as he doesn't believe the name that just fell from my mouth.

Marcus is one of Robert Quinten's children. One of 7. 4 boys, 3 girls. One of those girls being Juliette Sanders, his first, and only, blood daughter, and the youngest.

Marcus is one of the middle brothers. He's witty, and easily convinced which means that Robert knew exactly who he wanted to help with his little scheming plan. What that is I'm not so sure yet. But all I know is that this is going to send Spencer into a spiral.

"You better be joking." Spencer warns, looking for any indication I'm lying. When I don't give him one, he takes a deep long breath before he continues. "Why the hell was Marcus at the school?" I only shrug my shoulders, feeling like if I was to make a joke right now, I may find myself against the wall with the knife against my throat that he carries in his boot.

"Maybe he misses you?" Rodger jokes, causing us both to look at him in disgust. Spencer ignores Rodger's joke, only for us to meet eyes once more.

"One of us should stay with her." I speak in the tension and Rodger shakes his head.

"She'll be fine for a minute; she'll be looking through those letters. She will keep herself busy." Rodger reassures me. But deep down, I know that she would rather be out there searching for answers. She's the type of girl that isn't going to let this slide, and we need to get our stories straight.

"Did he talk to her?" Spencer askes and I shake my head.

"Yes. He encouraged her to look in the file. It was if he was taunting her." I say to him as he runs his hand through the light stubble on his chin trying to grasp the information.

"Wait, I thought we weren't allowed to talk to her?" Rodger asks and I look to Spencer for an answer.

"We aren't and neither is he." He begins to say as he runs his hands through his hair and exhales loudly. I look to Rodger, who for once in his life is quiet; not sure as to what to say and if I'm going to be honest neither am I.

My mind begins to race and ask questions. Like what exactly were we sent here for? Our task was to keep Juliette and her family safe. Making sure that no harm comes to them and wait until the threat we were told existed, left.

There were rumors circling in Robert's group of acquaintances that he had a daughter 14 years prior, to a woman, even we don't know her name. I know that whoever she was she left a long standing pain on Robert's heart, because he has never dated or married since Juliette was born. But even saying that, with Robert's reputation, she's either dead or living the life of luxury. It's a question we probably won't have the answer to.

"Why would he send Marcus? He knows we are here?" I ask after a moment of silence. I see the anger on Spencer's face and decide that I'm not going to open my mouth anymore because any question is going to tip him over the edge.

All Spencer has ever done or ever tried to do

is prove to Robert he is capable of being included in his family. We were never officially adopted, but Spencer always has to prove to Robert he is good enough to be included in Robert's family.

"I don't know, but I want to find out." Spencer growls clearly more annoyed as he rubs his hand over his face and through his hair once more. "You two go and speak to Juliette and get her to tell you everything, everything she knows so far on that case or whatever it is."He instructs before running up the stairs, two steps at a time towards his office. "Wait what you going to do?" I shout.

He then turns around slowly, so slowly you would think it was in slow motion. "I am going to locate that bastard who as decided to get involved in our task." Spencer says in a sort of calm manner. But his tone is vey harsh, almost hinting we should hurry up and do what he asks. Rodger listens, surprisingly and as we walk into the kitchen; we find it empty, no sign of Jules, her bag or the case.

"Oh Jesus. She really is Robert's daughter." Rodger jokes. His narcissistic grin plastered all over his face as I punch my fist into the wall.

"She's gone Spencer!" I call after him and I hear a bang from upstairs.

"Find her!" He demands from upstairs and I exchange a look with my brother as I turn on my heel and walk into towards the front door. She can't have gone far, we were only away for a few moments. We have dug our own graves and as much as I hate to admit it, this is 100% my fault.

CHAPTER SEVENTEEN

Jules Sanders

I sit in the back of the car and wonder how I got myself into this situation. Now granted, I didn't want to be in the same room as my annoying so-called friend and his peculiar brothers and leaving them, I now have made a mistake. But I'm feeling betrayed more than scared which is also unsettling me because I've just been kidnapped by 2 of the popular group.

I watch how Holly fiddles with her fingers next to me. She's nervous, her leg is shaking and the atmosphere in the car is unsettling. She has clearly been roped into this against her will. Maura is the more demanding type to get things done whereas

Holly is the social butterfly, not the deceiving one.

Harrison's expression is emotionless. He doesn't care he just kidnapped a fourteen-year-old and forced her into a car. My question is where are they taking me? Because although it has only been a few minutes, the road is incredibly familiar.

We pull into the school and I can't help but feel uneasy as I notice y Mrs. Hadley, and I instantly feel sick. She makes me nervous, and it isn't because she's my headteacher, it's because she's got something to do with all of this.

I'm dragged out the car by Harrison who pushes me towards Mrs. Hadley who stands tall, in her bright white suit with a floral blouse staring down at me like I'm something she's stepped in.

"Now Juliette, I feel as though we should have a little talk now, don't you?" She speaks clearly with a smirk slowly creeping on her face which makes me unsettled. I can't run, that's not an option, I have nowhere to go.

"I don't think you should." A voice behind me speaks up and I turn to find the hooded man standing in front of me with those emerald, green eyes once more and I feel myself freeze, unsure of what's happening. He avoids my stares, keeping his entire focus on Mrs. Hadley who I hear laugh behind me.

"And who might you be?" Mrs. Hadley questions as she walked towards him. He doesn't move, his face stays the same.

"Well, I don't think that matters right now. But where I'm from, questioning a child without her parents present, or without their knowledge is a criminal offence." He speaks clearly, his body language bold and unbothered by Mrs. Hadley's dominant demeanor.

"Well, we aren't in America sweetheart, so how about you walk away this doesn't concern you." She stands tall, trying to show her dominance, but he laughs. A spine-chilling laugh that even makes Holly and Harrison look at each other.

"Where would you be having this conversation exactly? Your office? Or the classroom that was once used as a drug den?" He taunts Mrs. Hadley. I watch as her dominant demeanor begins to fade very slowly and it makes me question, what else he knows.

"Now Juliette and I are leaving, and if you follow us, I may be obliged to go to the school board about your extracurricular activities. I mean imagine bringing in your own school kids that you are under a duty of care to protect and make them into criminals?" He teases and I turn to see Mrs. Hadley visibly shaking and Harrison and Holly looking to the headmistress for some sort of answer.

"You don't know what you're talking about." She expresses, panic starting to fade over her face.

"Don't I?" The hooded man taunts with a grin slowly creeping on his face. He eventually meets my eyes, and although I'm still frozen, I feel him ease me slightly with the reassurance in his eyes. Why is he protecting me? "Juliette let's go." He orders and I don't even hesitate to follow him, moving myself well away from my fellow classmates and crazy head teacher.

I've only had this case over a week, and everything seems to be falling apart. I follow behind him like a puppy as we get to his car, and he opens to door indicating me to get in and this is when reality hits me and he notices.

"I'm not going to murder you Juliette, get in the car for god's sake." He orders once more and this time I do as I'm told. I put my seatbelt on, unsure on how bad his driving is. He joins me in the car, the scent of sandalwood fills my nose, and it causes me to look at him. His aftershave smells expensive, and just with that alone I can say for certain he's part of whatever this is. He isn't just the messenger.

He speeds away from the school, taking a right out of the school gates and begins to head towards the city.

"How did you know where I was?" I ask breaking the tension in the car. I watch to see his hands grip the steering wheel just a little tighter and he stares out into the road, ignoring my direct stares.

"You activated the device you were given. It gave me a location." He says calmly which causes me to panic for a moment. I quickly pull out the device I got sent with my last file and look it over to notice it's flashing red.

"So, you came to my rescue? How sweet." I joke, which he doesn't laugh at, and only grips the steering wheel tighter. At this moment, I have never felt more like a idiot. I'm in a car with a stranger, who although says he wont murder me, he is certainly dressed like one.

"I didn't have to. I didn't want to be a babysitter but here I am, doing someone else's task." He says bluntly as he focuses as we turn onto one of the busy streets.

"You mean the Williams brother's task?" I question. His eyebrows raise and for the first time in about 5 minutes, he looks at me and I stare into those emerald eyes. He looks me up and down, taking in my body language that clearly states, I'm the least bit impressed with what is going on and quite frankly, I'm sick of being lied to.

"What do you know about that?" He questions with a slight smirk on his face. I think that he's hoping I would land them in some sort of trouble, but the truth is – I don't know anything.

"Nothing, so how about you tell me." I demand, which causes him to laugh once again, his dark laugh fills the car and makes me slightly uncomfortable as he goes round a round about with a smile on his face.

"I don't need to tell you anything." He states.

"I think you do. For starters, you all know each other. Damian's face gave it away when you passed him after handing me the file. Also, you have the same tattoo. Are you all part of some cult?" I question, causing laughter once more to fall from his lips.

"Depends on who you ask." He jokes and I roll my eyes. It's infuriating and I feel as though I'm talking to a brick wall.

"I'm starting to feel like I'm running in circles because no one wants to give me a straight answer. Not you, or the Williams brothers!" I shout. I feel so out of loop, like I don't get the running joke that everyone else seems to understand.

We are silent in the car for a few moments, I don't even bother to ask where he is taking me, although it seems to be the most scenic route of London, but also making sure we avoid all the traffic.

"I knew him sending you on this case was a mistake." He mutters underneath his breath, and I quickly turn my head and narrow my eyes.

"How!" I shout. "I haven't been able to look at the case because everyone has been getting in my way." I explode, which his calm demeanor ignores.

"Juliette, he sent you on something that was so dangerous, and he didn't even realise it." He expresses as he runs through a red light, and I roll my eyes.

"What are you talking about?" I ask and he exhales loudly, clearly frustrated by me but I have no intention on backing down.

"Forget I said anything." He mutters once more, and I scoff in anger and look out the window. I can feel his eyes watch me every now and again, but I don't feel like being the first person to talk with the tension in the car being so thick.

"What do you know?" He asks which does cause me to look at him. I don't want to say anything but I know I have no choice, because right now – I've gone willingly with a complete stranger. I really am the poster girl for missing kids.

"One of my other teachers was panicking the other day and I overheard the conversation and I recorded it." I say and he looks at me every now and again meaning he's listening for once. "I never mentioned it, well not yet. I was going to. But it sort-of proved, that both Mrs. Hadley and Mrs. Holden are involved in some way or other." I explain and he listens carefully before he takes a very quick U-turn and I hold on for dear life.

"Where are we going?" I ask as he speeds away in another direction.

"We're going to see some friends of mine."

CHAPTER EIGHTEEN

We pull up to a familiar street and immediately roll my eyes as all the houses start to look the same. I look to my hooded driver, and he ignores my judgmental stares as he parks right behind Spencer's car.

"What are we doing here?" I question and he merely ignores me and slams the door in my face. I exhale loudly before my car door opens and he undoes my seatbelt and drags me out of the car and to the path. "You know you could have asked me nicely to just get out of the car." I state and he looks me dead in the eye while raising one eyebrow causing me to move back and the uncomfortable lack of space that is between us, that awful clearly expensive aftershave filling my nose and I'm trying hard not to sneeze.

"Would you have moved without a fight?" He

asks, a hint of humor in his voice. I avoid all eye contact and exhale, hard. "See, my actions have reasons." He says before he walks towards the door, and I sigh in frustration as I follow him like a puppy to the door. "I don't want to be here as much as you. So whatever remarks you have. Save them. I am not in the mood to deal with your childish behaviour. " He warns.

I roll my eyes at his comment. "You don't know anything about me." I state, annoyed. Which he laughs at causing me to turn my head.

"Keep telling yourself that sweetheart."

He rings the doorbell and within a second, we are greeted by Rodger, who as always appears to have that sadistic grin on his face as he looks between the both of us.

"I believe this belongs to you." My hooded acquaintance says, and I look at him in pure disgust which he notices and smiles.

"And I'm childish?" I ask and he laughs just a little harder. Rodger still stands in the doorway, taking a sip from a can of what I'm assuming is alcohol, that smile still painted on his face.

"Delivery!" He shouts with humor in his voice as he moves aside, taking another sip of the can. I look up the stairs to see Damian and Spencer greeting me with a look of disbelief.

"Where did you go?" Damian expresses as he runs down the stairs and towards me. I swat him away and begin to walk to the kitchen.

"Away from you, since you all clearly don't want to give me a straight answer." I say as I take a seat on the counter.

"But instead, after she left here, she was forced into a car with a guy. Care to explain why I'm doing your job?" The hooded man says before looking to all 3 brothers. Rodger is the least bit bothered as he goes to get something from the fridge, I'm assuming another can.

"You know you aren't supposed to be here." Spencer warns as he walks towards me and pulls me off the counter and drags me to a seat. The look he gives me is a warning to stay, but by the looks of things they are about to give me some answers to the questions I have and they don't even realise it.

"Oh! So, you have this under control, do you?" The hooded man taunts which earns him a growl from Spencer out of what I'm assuming is frustration.

"Do you not know what he's going to do to us, all of us, if he finds out you're here and talking to her!" Spencer shouts and I begin to listen carefully, hoping one of them will slip up and tell me who 'he' is.

"This isn't my fault. You couldn't stick to the task of babysitting Spencer. How was your task so difficult? Protect her and stay away from her. That was your task." He mocks and Spencer is becoming more and more angry as the seconds tick by. The hooded man points to me and looks to Spencer who stares through me. "Now look who is sat at that table." Spencer exhales as he looks at Damian who I'm going to assume had the same talk and I press my lips together trying to hold in a laugh, which fails miserably, and a light giggle escapes my lips causing all of them to look at me at once.

"So, you don't know each other then?" I tease, mainly to Damian, who only an hour ago told me he didn't know him.

"We work together." Damian explains and I nod as I stand up and walk towards him.

"I see." I taunt slightly. He ignores me as I lean over onto the counter ignoring the burning stare from Spencer.

"Juliette is about to play us a recording she got of two teachers the other day. Isn't that right!" My hooded friend exclaims as he grabs my arm and forces me back to the chair.

"I'll only play it if you tell me your name." I ask as I'm being forced to the seat. I think after our conversation in the car, I should at least know his name. I turn to see the brothers stare at the hooded man waiting to see if he will tell me his name, or will he tell me to go and off myself. I'm unsure.

"That's all you want?" He asks and I smile to him.

"For now." I taunt causing me to get a huff from him.

"My name is Marcus." He says as he takes a seat next to me and the smile on my face only gets wider as pull my phone from my blazer pocket.

◆ ◆ ◆

After I play the audio for the boys, they all seem as stunned as each other. The 3 brothers, unsure on where to start and Marcus is just quiet. I decide that I should just get out the file that Marcus gave me earlier.

"So, Mrs. Holden has some part in this too? But isn't she new?" Damian asks and I shake my head as I place all the contents of the file on the table.

"That's what the school wanted us to think, she used to work at the school that Harrison Meyer was expelled from." I state smugly because for once I know more than the rest of them in this room, even Marcus. And I know this by the way he looks at me, shocked by my answer.

"And how do you know that exactly?" He questions, the humor fills his voice as he takes a seat next to me. I turn to him and smile to meet his.

"Are you forgetting I already have a case file at my house?" I question.

"You already have a case file?" He responds and I begin to become confused. Damian looks to his brothers, who meet his look with confusion as well. Something isn't right here.

"You didn't put it in my locker, did you?" I query. He shakes his head while looking to Spencer. I begin to think that they have all been played against each other.

The silence in the room becomes deafening, none of us knowing what to say. I turn to look at the clock noticing my mum will be picking me up any minute, secretly I'm hoping that she might be a little late so I can get the boy's opinion on the case. But if I know my mum, she's probably going to be on time.

"Okay, since you lot don't know you've all been played against each other, I'm going to go home and look this over and see if there is any indication as to who might be making the drugs." I say as I begin to gather up the case file and Rodger stops me.

"You're clearly too young to be looking into this." Rodger says protectively taking the case from me and placing it on the kitchen bench.

"Oh, I'm sorry, you clearly can't stick to your own task so your going to take mine instead?" I question, frustration slightly in my voice.

Within a second, he sits me back down onto the chair with force, although the anger is burning in his eyes, his face has a psychotic grin. Like he enjoys trying to frighten me.

"Don't make me regret protecting you, Juliette." He warns calmly which makes me uneasy, his hand still heavy on my shoulder. Damian gets in between the small space between Rodger and I and backs him up giving him a warning look.

"You're scaring her, stop it." Damian warns his

brother who pushes him off as he still looks at me, that grin still plastered to his face like a mask.

"Good. She should know how dangerous we can really be." Rodger provokes him. I see Spencer roll his eyes and take a deep breath and when I look at Marcus, he seems to be giving the same look as Damian, warning Rodger that the next words out of his mouth, he should choose carefully.

I stand up once more, feeling all the boys stare at me. I look to Damian, who almost gives a 'I'm sorry look with his eyes.'

"I can't trust any of you, you've not given me any reason as to how I can. You all lie." I say almost as a whisper. I'm not upset they don't want me to look at this case, I understand the dangers, I'm not stupid. "All my life all I've wanted is answers. Why I have gotten presents every year on my birthday and then money for Christmas. It's the most bizarre thing, my mum is beside herself because no matter how many times we go to the police, we are always told there's nothing they can do." I shout. "You all know who he is or who they are. So, either, you give me that case and we can solve it together. Or you leave me alone, because no matter what any of you tell me, I'm never going to get the truth – and that's all I've ever been searching for." I say.

Silence fills the room, not one of them trying to say a word, they begin to look at each other waiting for someone to speak up.

In the midst of the silence, a light chuckle

erupts from the kitchen bench and everyone turns to Rodger, who seems to be laughing at me plea to be involved.

"You are so naïve." He laughs, causing me to frown. Damian almost stands in front of Rodger in a indication for him to shut up. But Rodger only keeps laughing, a sadistic laugh that bounces off the walls.

"How am I naïve?" I question as his laugh slowly begins to get quieter. "How is it that when I'm searching for answers about something, not one of you can give me a straight answer?" I shout. Rodger moves past Damian in one very swift move and is now standing before me, a grin on his face waiting to push me over the edge.

"Because, you're stupid to think that this hasn't been about you. The reason we're here, it's to protect you." He explains. I burst into laughter.

"Protect me?" I laugh. "Protect me?" I question once more as a light chuckle leaves my lips. "What could you of all people have to protect me from?" I shout at Rodger while looking to the boys for answers, as I'm clearly not going to get one off their brother.

"Jules." Spencer warns me. I ignore his warning.

"Come on then." I encourage Rodger. "Since I'm so naïve what could I possibly need protecting from?" I question him once more and this time I'm not met with silence, I'm met with the same level of anger as I'm feeling.

"You really wanna know?" He taunts me and I nod, encouraging him along. I briefly look to Damian as panic begins to fill his eyes and I watch him try to tower over his brother pleading that he doesn't say anything else.

I started this. I started the fire, but do I have any indication to put it out until I get my answers? Absolutely not.

"Don't you dare." Damian warns his brother who's playful smile gleams across the room.

"Rodger, don't." Marcus also warns him, but nothing seems to get through to him as he barges past Damian and is now standing in front of me, tall, showing his dominance. And I, a clearly naïve fourteen-year-old couldn't care less.

"Juliette, have you ever looked at yourself and then your family and notice how different you all are?" He questions as he walks me towards the table, clearly indicating I should be frightened, when I'm anything but scared. I would like to slap that grin off his face, but I feel like he would like that, and I shouldn't encourage him anymore. I'm unsure on his line of questioning so I ignore his taunts. I am my mothers daughter. "God you're so stupid, so is your Mom. Surely, she could have put two and two together?" He taunts and I feel myself get slightly angry at the mention of my mum. But I'm quickly silenced by Spencer who attempts to push Rodger away from me but fails as Rodger stands his ground and ignores the pleads from his brothers and

Marcus.

"We were sent to protect you because there are so many people in this world that would prefer you were 6 foot under that out living your life to the fullest." He taunts attempting to push his brothers off.

"Rodger stop!" Marcus pleas once more.

"Why would I need to be killed?" I shout. He aggressively pushes past his brothers and stands before me. The only thing is see in his eyes is a ton of crazy and it makes me slightly nervous.

"Because you're adopted."

CHAPTER NINETEEN

I laugh.

I can't help it. It's the most ridiculous thing I've ever heard. I'm not adopted. My mother is Amy Sanders and Paul, who sadly died, he is my father. I look like my younger sister, everyone says it. So, this is the most pathetic attempt to get a reaction out of me.

"Funny Rodger." I joke. Pushing him off me and looking at Damian who is as white as Casper the Friendly Ghost. I instantly become sick because Damian's facial expression isn't giving me any sort of comfort, it's only causing anxiety.

"Damian, he's joking. I'm not adopted." I reassure him as I shake my head trying to ignore the worry that is starting to build in my stomach. I am not adopted.

"Sure, you are." Rodger pipes up and I roll my eyes. He really knows how to get under my skin.

"I'm not. So whatever reaction you were hoping for with your little lie. It didn't work." I smugly say, and he meets my grin with his psychotic one and I instantly drop my smile feeling his dominance radiate.

"Oh, you are Juliette. Think about it." He says stepping towards me once more. This time, Marcus stands in front of us, but that doesn't stop Rodger. He only ignores Marcus' dominance. He's taller than Rodger, only by a few feet, but that doesn't matter, it doesn't stop him. "Every year on your birthday you get a gift." He reminds me and I feel it hit me like a truck. The presents. This card. The expensive gifts. The whole mystery behind this person called Q.

"That's enough Rodger you need to leave." He warns, only earning a laugh from him. I am trying to shake this uncertain feeling that I have but I can't seem to get rid of it. The longer I stand here, the more realization is trying to seep through my veins.

"Oh Juliette, have you met your older brother?" H jokes and I freeze and dart my eyes to Marcus who is trying hard to ignore my burning stares. "Well one of your older brothers, you have 3 others." He grins. In a flash I watch as Marcus punches Rodger and he falls to the floor. I gasp as I step back away from the boys. This isn't happening, I'm not adopted. I keep repeating it in my head, I'm not adopted.

I'm not adopted.

"You had one fucking task Rodger." Spencer mutters under his breath. I move my tear-filled eyes to Spencer who sits forward his elbows on his knees as he plays with the rings on his fingers. He meets my broken gaze which is about as empathetic as Rodger is right now. He's angry and the way he's looking at me, I feel like I'm part of the reason why.

I feel myself begin to sink to the floor as I'm trying to comprehend what is going on. I feel eyes on me and I'm not sure which brother, whether that be the brothers or my potential new brother but someone's watching me crumble.

I also jump out of my skin when I hear the doorbell, but I feel frozen to the floor, frightened that if I move something else will come out and I'm starting to become overwhelmed. I suddenly feel the tears that I didn't even know were falling. The only person I turn to is Damian, for some sort of answer, to tell me this is a joke. But the only thing I'm met with is sad eyes and I feel my heart sink even further. I quickly wipe me eyes and grab my bag, throwing it over my shoulder and moving past the boys grabbing the file off the kitchen bench in the process.

I hear someone shout my name and I ignore them, quickly going to the front door and I am met by my mother standing with a smile that quickly fades when she sees what I'm assuming is distress in my face. And as I meet my mother's eyes, I can't help but my heart begins to ache. Why wouldn't she tell me? Why would she keep it a secret, we had no secrets in our family? I feel like my heart is going to explode because now although I'm numb, I feel the tears falling onto my cheeks. As much as I want this to be a joke, the one thing that I can't seem to shake that makes this all believable, is the fact I got presents every single year.

Everything moves in slow motion. The movement of my mother as she cups my face and pleas for me to tell her what's wrong. But I'm numb, my mouth is dry. The world around me crashing and burning and I'm using all my strength to not collapse to the floor. My ears are ringing, and I don't hear her shout, but I can see she does as my world around me begins to fade so slowly and she grabs my face again.

"I'm adopted?" I manage as a whisper to her before I collapse to the ground.

CHAPTER TWENTY

Robert Quinten - June, 2000

The door opens suddenly and we are met with 3 new people. I lock eyes with the couple holding hands so tightly they may be cutting off eachothers circulation. That's them. Julianna's new parents.

I can't help but hold Julianna tighter. I'm not ready, I know I'm not, and I'm sure as hell not ready to be a father. But she's my blood. My daughter and I feel like I need more time. Forever if that's possible.

But I know that's not fair on the parents who I have agreed can take her but also to Julianna. They are good people, who come from hard working class families. That's what I want. I want her to have a normal life.

"Mr Quinten, I'm Susan Fisher." The older lady introduces herself with a smile before turning to the couple standing beside her. "This is Paul and Amy Sanders."

All I can do is smile at them as my way of saying hello. I don't trust my voice right now. I know it will fail me. I turn my attention back to my little human. She's making little noises and I can't help but smile as I rub my thumb gently across her little cheek.

"Mr Quinten, would you like to let the new parents hold her?" Ms Fisher asks. I turn my head to notice the couple staring at her in awe, I can't say I will judge them. It's all I've been doing since I held her. I can only nod, still my words will fail me. I am not an emotional person, I never cry. However, handing my daughter to two complete strangers may just send me over the edge.

I begin to walk in their direction, holding Julianna very tightly in my hands so she's safe. I look up to the gentleman, Paul I believe Ms. Fisher said his name was.

His eyes meet mine and for a moment we have an understanding of eachother. He can tell that handing over Julianna is going to kill me, so instead he places his hand on my shoulder as a form of comfort.

"Mr Quinten, I know this isn't what you want to hear. But I can assure you she will have the best possible life. She will be loved, cared for. She will smile, laugh and I will never let her heart get broken and will kill any man that tries." He reassures me which only causes me to start to cry, my emotions getting the better of me. "She will be happy."

I can't control my emotions as I begin to sob. I pull Julianna closer to me and hug her softly hearing those little noises in my ear and it makes my heart hurt. It is too hard, letting her go to some strangers.

I pull Julianna away from me and look back up at the Sanders, who are both crying now. That wasn't my intention, making her new family cry. But there is so much emotion in one room, both happy and sad. It's bound to be emotional for everyone.

"I called her Julianna." I say quietly as I hand her gently over to Paul. Amy looks up to me with her sad eyes but I meet her with a smile. "Of course you don't need to call her that. She is your daughter." As I say that last sentance I feel my heart break even more. Amy hugs me unexpectedly and I am taken back for a moment. I here gasps come from beside me as my family all process the fact that this is the first hug I've had since my Mom died. I hug Amy back, tight as I begin to cry onto her shoulder. She welcomes it, and doesn't let go until she knows my sobs are almost gone and I compose myself.

We exit the embrace and for a moment, I thought it would be awkward, but instead she holds my hand, tight. Almost to reassure me that it was okay to name her. "Mr Quinten, she's your daughter too." She says softly while squeezing my hand once more. "You have every right to name *your* daughter. All you are doing is letting us raise her. She's still your blood." She explains sweetly and I manage a nod.

"She can't ever know about me. Or her mother. You have to make sure she never finds out." I plead with them and she shushes me, hinting she would like me to stop talking. I know that they know the terms of the adoption. Julianna is never to find out about me, the organisation and they are to give her a new name, one that doesnt have the name Quinten attached.

"We know. But Robert, although we are thrilled that you have given us something we have been dreaming of for years we have to ask whether this is what you want? Are you sure you're ready to give her up?" She asks, her tone is harsh almost but I get the sense that this is so she has some security on her end.

I gently rub my finger over Julianna's cheek as she begins to make small noises again. I shake my head at Amy as I look at her, my eyes full of tears on the verge of another breakdown.

"No, Mrs Sanders, I'm not ready to let her go. But I can't protect her no matter how much I'd like to think I could. She'll never be safe." I heartbreakingly explain.

I'm grateful when she doesn't say anything apart from embrace me into another hug. I know I've chosen wisely with this couple. Both of them are great and have dealt with this a lot better than I have. But I guess that this is their gain, they have always wanted a family, and they are the perfect people to raise Julianna.

"Would you like to hold her one more time?" Paul asks as I share a look of sadness with my siblings, apart from Oliver who is long gone.

"I don't think I would hand her back Mr Sanders." I explain honestly. He smiles to me before handing Julianna to Amy and pulling me in for a hug which I gladly accept. "I'll protect her till the day I die."

CHAPTER TWENTY ONE

Damian Williams

I have never seen reflexes as quick as Spencer's. As Juliette fell backwards, he was there and caught her with such elegance that you would think it was a scene from a movie. There is silence for a few moments as we all try to grasp what has just happened. Amy now is completely distressed as Juliette lies on the floor unconscious.

"Jules baby?" Amy pleads trying to shake her daughter awake. But Juliette doesn't budge. Spencer moves so she no longer has her head on his lap and moves to check her pulse.

"Her heart rate is through the roof but she's

stable." He reassures Amy, but that does nothing. She looks to my brother, about as angry as we all feel towards Rodger who is no where to be seen, possibly out celebrating his win of ruining a young girl's life.

He hated this task the second we were sent on it, and for him to, in a feud with Juliette, tell her she's adopted it only angers me more. We were supposed to protect her from the people that were going to hurt her. Never did we think that it would be our own brother to be the one to break her heart.

"Who told her!" Amy shouts. I cower slightly, even though I was young when my mother died, I am now feeling suddenly frightened by the way Amy shouted at us all.

"He's gone." Marcus reassures Amy by sitting next to her and placing his hand on hers gently. She looks to him, her tear-filled eyes broken as she moves her hand quickly away and begins to sob.

I feel for her, she was given an instruction and that was to make sure that Juliette never knew about her birth family. Her Dad's side anyway, we don't know anything about her mother and what happened to her.

I blame myself that this happened, or should I say happen so suddenly. I think both Spencer and I know, even Marcus, that sending Rodger on a task to protect Robert Quinten's daughter that doesn't know that he exists was a dangerous game. Rodger is impulsive, he acts out, he's a psychopath. But for him to tell her in the coldest way possible, really shows he is what we all call him.

"Amy, I don't want her near Rodger. We need to get her somewhere comfortable. Are you capable of driving or do we need to drive your car?" Spencer asks softly. He's always had a soft spot for woman. He was very close to our mother before she died, and I think that's why he took the task of protecting Amy. Amy nods and she staggers to her feet grabbing onto the railing of the stairs and looks to me with disappointed eyes. She doesn't say anything. But I know. I know she knows I screwed up.

Spencer carefully picks up Jules and cradles her bridal style to the car and we all follow, even Marcus who only a few hours ago, was trying to break into her locker to give her a file he didn't even understand the contents of, well not properly anyway.

"Damian you're with me, we will meet you at her house." Marcus instructs and I follow behind, climbing into the passenger seat and watching as Spencer carefully get into the back of the car with her and Amy get into the driver's seat. Marcus jumps into the car and watches as they drive away before I feel his fist collide with my jaw and after a moment, I finally can shake it off, placing my hand on my jaw and rubbing gently.

"That is for bringing her to the house." He shouts as he starts the car and I still stare at him in utter disbelief that he has just punched me in the face. "Jesus Damian, all of you had one task, stay the fuck away from her. What is so hard about that?" He shouts again while hitting the steering wheel.

I come up empty, and I don't say anything because I know he's right. I shouldn't have introduced myself, I shouldn't had offered to teach her math. He's right. This is my fault.

"I know." I agree and he looks at me, the anger enraged on his face as he speeds away from the side of the road to follow Amy to their house.

"Why Dad sent Rodger on this task still baffles me. Every single one of us, even Ezekiel for god's sake, the quietest out of us, even piped up and he said he agrees that Rodger shouldn't have been sent on this task with you and Spencer. He even said you shouldn't go after your last incident that proved you weren't capable of being apart of the organization." He shouts through the car. I don't fight him on it because I know it's true, and although Ezekiel, the youngest brother even said he didn't agree, I'm surprised that Robert went ahead and let us do this.

"Is it some sort of test?" Marcus continues and I turn look at him. He is now just as confused and angry as Amy probably is right now in a few cars in front.

"I mean why did he send her on a case that's what I want to know?" I respond ignoring Marcus' question. He shakes his head at me, and I know he already knows the answer I'm looking for.

"It was to prove her loyalty. Which I found strange considering he was never going to meet her." Marcus says as he turns the corner quickly to follow Amy and catch up so there isn't any distance.

"But that doesn't make sense, why would he send her on a case and promise that if she solves it, she could meet him." I blurt out causing a very quick look from Marcus who glares at me, almost horrified by what I had just said.

"What the hell are you talking about?" Marcus slams the breaks as we come to a red light and quickly turns to me, the frustration growing quickly on his face, and I know that's my queue to start telling him what I know and no bullshit.

"Juliette said earlier that the reason she's solving this case is because Q, who I'm assuming is Robert, told her that if she solves the case, she gets to know who he is." I explain. I am met with a very confused glare from Marcus.

"He told me that if she was to solve the case, he had already got her a place to be an apprentice in the Major Crimes Division in the London Police Force." He continues and curiosity begins to fill my veins as none of this is making sense to either of us.

"So, who's he lying to?" I ask, the curiosity now fueling my veins. I know we have a mutual agreement and that is that Robert Quinten is sending all of us on a wild goose chase. If this is a test, the only thing he is testing is our patience.

◆ ◆ ◆

We arrive to Juliette's house, I watch as they carry her into the house. She's still unconscious, frail and I can't stop the guilt that's beginning to build up within me.

I did this. She had this reaction because I brought her back to the house where he would be. Granted I never thought Rodger would stoop so low and tell her the way he did and right now I don't think he cares. He took off through the back gate when she seen her Mom.

As we enter the house we are met by Jules' Grandfather, Norman. He looks to us with a plea in his eyes that this can't be happening. And believe it or not we greet him with the same look – more so me than Marcus.

I turn to see Amy, Spencer and Jules' grandmother walking down the stairs together. She must still be out and rest is probably best until we work this all out. Amy looks to me with sad eyes and walks straight to me, the grief and heartache painted on her face. I don't blame her, no one wanted this to happen.

"You better tell me what the hell happened." She warns, trying her hardest not to burst into tears. She walks away from me and into the kitchen, only to be followed by her father and her mother leaving myself, Marcus and Spencer to try and grasp what has just happened.

"She's out like a light." Spencer explains. "It

must have hit her like a truck and seeing Amy..." He begins to say but pauses, looking to Amy who welcomes a hug from her mother while sobbing gently into her shoulder. "I think it only made her believe him more. They don't look that alike." Spencer says clearly his throat straight after. Spencer took the task of looking after Amy because he was close to our mother, and it broke him when she died. In fairness, the best person, although he shouldn't have been here at all, to look after Ava was Rodger. He hates kids. Despises them and when we were all given our tasks, we knew he would do it. Just very badly.

"Where's Ava?" I question looking to Spencer who turns towards the staircase.

"Upstairs, that's why I'm being quiet, last thing we need is for her to start asking questions." He snaps to me causing me to nod. I don't want to piss him off more, so I decide that from now on, I'm going to keep my mouth shut.

"What the hell do we do now? We can't leave her." Marcus asks looking towards the kitchen to see Amy and her parents are coming back through.

"We aren't going to leave her." Spencer snaps to Marcus causing him to frown. "This wouldn't have happened if you had just got her locker open quicker." Spencer erupts. Marcus turns, rage filling his face as he gets close to Spencer. I stand in the middle, hoping that they don't kill each other.

"Okay if you're going to blame anyone blame me,

then Rodger, then Marcus." I say quickly hoping he will stop the death glare to Marcus, and it does… but only turns it to me.

"If you had just listened to his instructions. We wouldn't be standing here having to explain to her mother why the hell we are here." He snaps again. Just as I'm about to say something a thud from the table startles me and I turn to see Amy placing 3 bottles of water on the table and giving us a 'you better start talking look.'

"Take a seat boys. You've got some explaining to do." She says coldly as she takes a seat herself at the table. I look to Spencer and Marcus who all have the look of run in their eyes. But we all realize there is no point. Juliette knows, and now we're going to have to explain who we are to the one woman who has been through more than all of us combined.

CHAPTER TWENTY TWO

Jules Sanders

I wake up groggy and confused. *How did I get back home?* I was at Damian's house. Trying to remember the events becomes difficult as I look around, my school bag with the case is missing and I can hear noise downstairs. I look outside to see it getting dark outside meaning I've been out at least a few hours or so. Last time I checked it was getting close to 5 o'clock, my mum –

My mother...

Then it hits me like a truck. The conversation at the Williams house, the argument, if you would even call it that, with Rodger. *"Juliette, have you ever looked at yourself and then your family and notice how different you all are?"*

I feel that one sting as I try to come to terms with how my head is feeling. He was saying so many awful things. I may have provoked him a little. But it didn't give him to right to tell me …

I'm adopted.

Little things start coming back in slow motion, opening the door to find my mum standing there, a smile on her face, and then it quickly changing to distress. My heart pounding, it's all I can hear and that sick feeling. I start to feel dizzy and sit on the floor next to my bed.

This is insane, and as much as I don't want it to be true, I can't help but know it is. Just seeing my mum, how I look nothing like her except we have the same hair colour, it makes it more real. I look up to my desk and catch the photo of Ava and I and crawl up to it, not realising that I'm crying once again as the tears hit my hands. I can't help it; I feel as though the earth around me has shattered and I'm standing on the last shard of glass before I plummet into a black hole.

Although I am feeling betrayed, it isn't by my family. I have had an amazing life. I have amazing parents, who although may not be my parents by blood, they are still who I will call mum and dad. They have given me a roof over my head, so much love, and have encouraged me to go for anything I want in life. I may not be their daughter by blood, but I'm a Sanders through and through and no one, not even Rodger Williams, the Williams brothers, or Q will take that from me.

I hold the photo of Ava and I tightly, clutching for it as I lightly weep now noticing the differences between us. I wouldn't say they were massive differences, but once you realise, they are there.

I hold the picture frame of my family too, with my dad Paul just a year before his diagnosis when we were on holiday in Spain. The happier times, before a year later he took such a turn we didn't know if he was going to survive the night.

They were some of the dark days, the not knowing. I was only 10 and my dad was dying. They talk about the 7 stages of grief in grief counselling that we had to go to, Ava too young to understand and me? Well I was forced.

Auntie Alison always talks about us needing therapy, and right now with how much my heart hurts and I feel betrayed and angry – I'm considering calling her. But that will do nothing but give her the satisfaction she's craving.

She always argues with my mum about how we should be in private schools and always looks down on my mum. My mum does a fantastic job as a single parent, she gives her too much grief. I wonder if she ever gave her grief about adopting me? The curiosity fills me, maybe she has or maybe she hasn't and I'm painting my Auntie Alison as a nasty witch.

I'm not sure how much time passes as I go

through my life and play out everything that's happened to see if there were any instances where I could of said, *oh well I should have noticed then...* but there's none. Not one. I can't help but feel frustrated and it's at myself because I don't have the answers. I had managed to stop the tears for now, only feeling angry and stand up and place the frames back on my desk, ignoring the Macbook. Last thing I want to do is tell whoever is behind that screen about me almost being kidnapped by the headteacher, that my potential brother had to rescue me, god knows what else. I reckon they probably know I'm adopted too and they sent Marcus as a test. I look at myself in the mirror. My bed hair messy with my tear filled eyes is only making this harder but I want to talk to my mum, I want her to know I'm not angry with her. I'm angry with the boys who are probably long gone.

I open my door gently, hoping to hear something, but it goes quiet. I make my way down the staircase, and no matter how quiet I try to be, our staircase has always been creaky.

"Everything we did, we did to protect you all." I hear a voice say and I stop instantly. *Why are they here?* Why can I hear Spencer's voice coming from the dining room. Anger fills my veins quickly, but I take my time towards the dining room hoping that I'm just hearing things.

But as I get to the last stair, I notice Marcus, sitting next to my Grandad Norman and Grandma, and lastly I notice my mother sitting at the top of the table. She's been crying, her eyes are puffy, and her cheeks are red.

"Well, you did a great job didn't you?" I mock. Everyone's eyes are immediately on me; no doubt being met with the anger that currently resides on my face knowing they are in my dining room and not on a flight back to whichever part of America they are from.

"Go home." I instruct coldly to the boys as I walk past them. Damian desperately tries to get me to meet his eyes as I walk to the kitchen to get a drink.

"Jules." I hear my mother plead as I grab a bottle of water and walk back through, greeting her with a small smile.

"Mum, I'm not mad, I'm not upset at you." I explain giving her a warm smile before looking at my Grandparents, a look of shock on their faces and I give them the same smile as my mum. "Or you." I reassure them hoping to ease their worry.

I then turn my attention to Damian who meets my angry eyes with broken ones.

"Go home. Like home, home. Back to America." I instruct before turning to walk away.

"Juliette, please let me explain." Damian begs. I quickly turn to him cutting him off.

"Explain what?" I mock almost, humor is in my voice and my anger is turning into frustration. "Explain how your brother has just unveiled one of the biggest secrets ever in my family like he was telling a joke? Where is he by the way?" I joke pretending to look around for Rodger. "Out ruining another young girl's life?"

"Probably." Spencer scoffs and I turn my attention to Spencer with a glare that could kill. He meets my eyes and I almost see fear running through him as he shakes his head. "Bad joke, Sorry. Not the time." He coughs and sit up before taking a sip of his water.

"Also, answer me this. Is Ginny your mum or is that another lie?" I shout.

"She's a actress who was hired to play our Mom." Damian says quietly, unsure on how I will react. My eyebrows raise as I am stunned by his answer.

"Juliette, please listen to them. I know your angry-" my mum pleas to say before I cut her off.

"Why didn't you tell me?" I ask. She's taken back by my tone and I quickly change it. "I mean, I just thought we had no secrets." I say in a calmer tone, not as calm as I would like, but, I'm hoping she can understand why my tone isn't as nice as it should be.

"Because I was told I couldn't in the adoption." She says calmly to me. I hear what was left of my heart shatter the minute she mentions the word adoption. It makes it more real and she notices how I begin to get upset and points to the chair in front.

"Your dad and I had been married for 3 years and were struggling to have a baby. We had tried for a year and a half but, nothing was happening. So we decided to down the route of adoption. We wanted to raise a family, and adoption was a great idea for us. We were on the list for about a year until one morning we got a call from the agency saying that there had been a baby just born to a young couple who wanted a very private adoption." She explains and the more she talks the more my heart hurts a little.

"We waited just under a day and then we got the call saying we could pick her up at 3pm and we were so excited. It was a girl. We wanted a little girl and when we met you, gosh Jules you were perfect." She begins to cry and my Grandma hands her a tissue and rubs her back. "It was like all of our dreams had come true and we were so grateful to this young couple." She lightly weeps and I can't stop myself from crying too.

I quickly wipe my tears away and look to my Grandad who only gives me a weak smile.

"We met your birth father." She blurts out causing me to direct my gaze to her as does everyone else, even the boys. "He was so young, and the distress on his face when he handed us you was so raw, he couldn't stop crying." Mum explains in a sob. "I asked if this was what he wanted and he shook his head as he stroked your little face and said 'I can't protect her, no matter how much I'd like to think I could. She'd never be safe.' And that broke my heart even more." She sobs. I quickly wipe my tears away from my face and try to compose myself.

"So how do you know I was adopted?" I turn to

the Williams brothers, who try to stutter and come up with a explanation. "And don't lie." I instruct. Damian hangs his head in shame letting Spencer do the talking. I get the feeling that because Spencer is older that Damian always has to watch what he does incase Spencer loses his head. Spencer leans forward placing his hands together tightly and looks into my eyes.

"Because we work for your father." He says honestly. "Our task was to protect you and your family." He explains, although Spencer can be too dominant, I do feel as though he's trying his best to be empathetic.

"I see." I quietly say. "So, what exactly does he work as?" I question causing panic to fill Spencer's face.

"He's a businessman, he owns lots of companies." Marcus responds, but I know that's a lie.

"I don't wanna know what he actually does for a living do I?" I query and all 3 boys shake their head. I exhale loudly processing the information, my mum at the other end looks so guilty and so upset with herself.

"Mum, I understand why you didn't tell me. It's okay." I reassure her which causes her to smile. I pause for a moment debating whether to ask the question that is floating around in my head. I decide i might as well, I feel like they aren't going to lie to me, not tonight anyway.

"So what's his name?" I ask and I feel the whole

room go silent, no one takes a breath as the boys look at each other debating whether or not to tell me the truth. "Just tell me." I demand and Spencer gives Marcus a nod.

"His name is Robert Quinten." He says and I feel my whole body go into shock.

CHAPTER TWENTY THREE

I instantly feel sick when I hear his name, *Quinten.* That last name. Something about it doesn't sit right with me one bit. But eventually the cogs in my brain begin to work and the sickness feeling only gets worse.

"Q." I breathe out barely audible, but Spencer hears it and nods.

"It's the name of the organization that Robert runs along with his siblings." Spencer slowly explains and I begin to nod my head not wanting to hear anymore. I get up and slowly begin to pace trying to digest the information that's just been given to me.

"Siblings?" I ask while pacing.

"He runs the organization with his 4 siblings. Your aunts and uncles."

"So are you really my brother?" I ask Marcus who looks at me with a smile and nods slightly.

"I'm one of your brothers. You have 3 others and 2 sisters." He begins to explain which takes me by surprise. "There is 7 of us, including you." He says with a smile.

"So wait, why did I get put up for adoption?" I ask slightly annoyed, and he sees this and shakes his head.

"Juliette we are all adopted, you are his only bloody daughter." He explains.

"Wait, so because I was actually created by him, I had to be put up for adoption?" I ask, clearly annoyed and I don't know why. It's not like I didn't have anything; I have a family but that just makes no sense.

"No Juliette, we were adopted after you were born." He says softly trying to ease my annoyance that I'm assuming is clearly on face. "After dad gave you up, he was a mess. They had to pull him out of a very dark place and when they did, the first thing he did was adopt a teenage boy... who is your older brother Nathaniel. I think it was because he felt like he could incorporate Nathaniel into the organization somehow." He begins to explain before taking a quick sip of his water. "Don't get me wrong, he loves us all dearly, even your sisters. But we knew that we weren't you." He says softly while leaning forward. The reassurance in his eyes tries to ease me but all I end up doing is pacing as I try to swallow this mountain of information.

"When did you find out about me?" I ask softly. He takes deep breath and he shifts uncomfortably.

"It was Nathaniel who found out about you. He was in dad's office about a year ago and he had noticed a photo of dad holding a baby so he asked him about it. Dad was very honest and told him who you were. Obviously Nathaniel was upset so he came to us. And that is how we found out you existed." Marcus explains. I feel like there is something else he isn't telling me.

"Go on." I encourage as I can see this wasn't the end of what he wanted to say.

He takes a deep breath, shifting nervously before clearing his throat. "We said some awful things about you. Dumb, cold, immature things that should never have been said. You didn't know, and once we had got the jealousy out, we realised that you probably didn't even know or care who he was." He explains honestly and although he clearly said some hurtful things, that is in the past. And I'm hoping that now he has spent sometime with me, that he knows that I'm not what he probably said.

"So, if he didn't want me to know who he was... why did Q – I mean Robert send me on a case?" I question and immediately my mum becomes alert and looks to me for an answer.

"Q? What?" My mum pipes up and I stop pacing and instantly I regret opening my mouth. I never told her about the case. Although they encouraged it, I held off telling her because I would only add to her stress. This, this is where I get grounded.

"You remember my birthday? When the MacBook arrived?" I question and she nods her head before realisation hits her like a truck and she shrieks.

"Oh my god the note!" She exclaims not knowing how to control her reaction. She quickly composes herself while wiping her tears. This must be difficult for her, having to listen to all this. But weirdly enough although I'm hurt and I'm feeling angry, I'm very slowly just trying to come to terms with everything. I will deal with this in my own time and in my own space, but right now I have a lot of questions, and I feel like this one is about to send my mother into orbit.

"Did you know he had sent me a case to solve?" I question Spencer who shakes his head. I hear my mother almost hyperventilating at the top of the table and before I can get my mouth open to explain, she's standing up in her chair, concern plastered over her face.

"The note we saw together wasn't the only note that he sent." I tell her and her mouth drops open, the shock causing her to sit back down. I decide that I very quickly will have to finish the story otherwise I'll never get a word in, ever. "There was another note inside the MacBook case, it was almost like a taunt. Someone had told him that I wanted to be a detective when I'm older and he wanted to know if I wanted to work a case in order to find out who he was." I explain.

My mother is beside herself by this point and rightly so, I was talking to a stranger. Yes, it may have been my birth father but that's beside the point I was having a conversation with someone she didn't know and that I didn't know, that's the dangerous part.

"Juliette!" She shouts and I throw my hands up in defense.

"This is entirely my doing, he told me to tell you." I stutter which only causes her to almost have a heart attack. "I'm sorry I didn't tell you; I just didn't want to add to your stress." I explain and that somewhat starts to ease the anger in her face, and I'm pleased that I'm stood at the other end of the dining room table.

"You were talking to a complete stranger online!" She exclaims and I fall quiet, words failing me cause she's right.

"To be fair, it wasn't a stranger, it was her father." Marcus pipes up earning a death glare from my mum who clearly has steam coming from her ears. Marcus decided to slide down his chair instead of arguing with my furious Mum

"Juliette Amanda Sanders, I am so disappointed!" She exclaims and I nod, still not knowing what to say no matter how many apologies came out of my mouth. "What if you were kidnapped?" She shouts and Marcus coughs uncomfortably.

"Er, Juliette – want to tell her about your adventure today?" Marcus pipes up, not helping and Spencer, Damian and I all shoot him a glare.

"What is he talking about?" My mother shoots me a 'you better start talking' look and I almost cower under the pressure.

"The case that Q – I mean Robert sent me on was to locate and find out who is making and selling drugs at the school." I explain to her and watch slowly as her eyes almost pop from her head.

"Mrs. Hadley seems to think Damian and I are getting a bit close and she sent Harrison and Holly, two year 11 students who she is clearly working with to collect me and bring me back to the school." I explain to her, and her mouth falls open in shock, as does my Grandparents.

"He sent you on a task to locate a drug ring?" My grandma asks and I pause. Well since she's put it like that, it's a lot worse than what it originally was made out to be. My mother looks to the boys in anger.

"You let him send my fourteen-year-old daughter to locate a drug ring!" She shouts but not loud enough to startle Ava.

"In our defense, we didn't know it was going on." Spencer says holding his hands up and Damian nodding in agreement. "That was until we caught

Marcus putting another file in her locker." He says in defense earing a death glare from Marcus.

"Dude!" He exclaims and Damian panics.

"I'm sorry! She frightens me." He says sheepishly causing me to roll my eyes.

"Oh, look, my great protector." I mock before taking a seat and taking a sip of my water. Damian looks to me with a look of shut up but ignore it.

"I didn't know what he had sent me on until I looked in the file, I thought it was something innocent, I didn't realise it was to locate and dismember a drug ring." He defends himself but my mother's anger doesn't shift. "If I hadn't of delivered it, god knows what would have happened to me when I got home." Marcus explains earning a look from everyone.

"So instead of protecting my daughter, who happens to be your younger sister, you instead endanger her by giving her the file that then caused her to be kidnapped?" My mother query's sarcastically and it throws Marcus completely off his game, but he nods.

"Not my finest moment, I'll admit. So, I apologise." He says sheepishly while he folds his arms and sinks back into the chair.

"He does redeem himself though." I tell them and I watch my Grandad raise an eyebrow.

"Oh! Do tell." He mocks causing me to laugh just a little. Marcus sits up and leans over the table but giving my mum direct eye contact.

"When Juliette was taken from the Williams house tonight, they had put her in a car and when she got in that car, a device that Robert had given her in the last file. It sent all of us a location." Marcus explains but what catches my eye is the look between Spencer and Damian.

"It tells everyone, but the people who were sent to protect her?" Spencer mocks and Marcus nods in agreement.

"I'm starting to think he's played us like a fiddle." He jokes which causes a laugh out of Damian.

"You think?" He mutters under his breath, humor filling his voice.

"I'm starting to think this is some sort of test and we've all failed." Spencer says coldly and I feel a lightbulb go off in my head.

"Not necessarily." I say softly causing a look from everyone, especially a eyebrow raise from my Grandad. "He doesn't know that I know." I explain to them, and they all begin to look around at each other waiting for someone to get it but no one does. I scoff annoyed at their incompetence. "He doesn't know, unless he's bugged the house?" I question to Marcus who simply shrugs his shoulders. Well, he's useless. "He doesn't know that I know who Marcus is, or who any of you are. All he knows is that I accidently activated my locator device." I explain hoping they will understand, and Damian is the first one to get it and quickly looks to Spencer.

"Did you ever tell him I screwed up?" Damian almost jumps out of his chair and Spencer ignores his reaction.

"No, I was going to but after I heard he was in the city I decided against it." He says while giving Marcus a sarcastic smile which he returns.

"So, we can use that against him. He doesn't know anything. So, let's do it together." I say as I take a seat hoping that they will agree but I'm startled when I see my mum stand up from her chair shaking her head.

"No." she says in the silence, and everyone turns to her, even my grandparents. "It's too dangerous, he's already put you at risk what's to say he won't do it again?" She expresses harshly and I think about and deep down I know she's right.

"Actually, Juliette has a point." Spencer speaks up which makes us all turns our head. "The headteacher and the science teacher are both in it deep, we heard that on the recording. We know who's a part of it, there's proof. We just need proof of who is making the drugs." Spencer explains to my mum who listens carefully and instead of arguing she gives him a signal to continue.

"Juliette, go and get everything he's sent you so far on the case, we're doing this together and no one is going to get hurt." He reassures my mum who only agrees.

"No one tell Rodger. I want him nowhere near

me." I tell them as I turn to head towards the stairs.

"Trust me, you'll not see Rodger for a while. He's done his damage." Marcus reassures me and I smile as I make my way up the stairs to gather the evidence.

CHAPTER TWENTY FOUR

Damian Williams

Spencer, Marcus and I almost crawl through the door of our house. It was a late night, however we do have a understanding of the case that Jules has been sent to solve.

I still feel sick to my stomach, how could I not? My actions caused a girl to find out one of the biggest secrets in her family and she found out because our very own brother has never been able to keep his cool in a arguement.

Spencer places his keys on the entry way table and Marcus sits on the stairs looking up at me. His eyes aren't angry which does surprise me. He seems calm, but also tired. However when I look over to my older brother I see a look of rage. Like he is trying his hardest to calm down from the spiral he is about to unwind from. I know what this is about, and I know who this is about.

Rodger. Who, is probably off ruining someone else's life. He is good at that. Marcus exchanges a look with Spencer, who storms up the stairs no doubt looking for my older brother.

I hear the door fly open and Spencer shout some vile language while things come crashing to the floor and items begin to shatter.

"He's not up there." I say in the silence between Marcus and I. He catches my gaze and frowns slightly, unsure on how I will know this. "Rodger would have been thrown down the stairs by now. He's just doing damage to his room."

Marcus nods slightly laughing a little while he takes a deep breath. "I never wanted to meet her like that." He says honestly. I tilt my head slightly unsure on what he means. "I always had this vision of her finding out from her parents, and her looking for us." He says almost as a whisper. The sounds of glass shattering has stopped and I notice Spencer now standing on the landing listening in.

"She took it like a boss." I say softly and Marcus nods with a smile.

"Yeah she did." He says with a grin. "I don't think I would of handled it half as well as she did." He admits.

"She's got so much courage." I say quietly as I

lean against the entry way table. Spencer comes into view by standing and leaning against the wall on the stairs.

"More courage than I would of had at her age." He says while staring at the door. I exchange a look of confusion at Spencer for a moment.

"Dude, you're only five years older?"

"Doesn't mean I had half the courage she does. I was a coward at her age. I would of hid away from the world forever if it meant I didn't have to deal with my feelings." He admits and I'm slighty taken back by his answer. Marcus is very protective of his siblings, especially Alexis the oldest girl sibling. She had came from a terrible family before Robert adopted her. Marcus was too protective sometimes, but that was because he's had siblings before and sadly he couldn't save them from their own demons.

"You did your research on her before you took the task, didn't you?" Spencer asks him and he nods instead of turning round.

"She's my sister, what would you expect?" He says almost as a whisper. We all stand in silence now. He is right, Marcus had every right to look into his sister and get to know her.

We don't move for a few moments until we hear keys in the front door and a very tired, sneaky son of a bitch tip toes through the door shutting it quietly behind him. Rodger gets a shock when he sees us standing there and looks to us all with a look that can only be described as a deer in headlights.

"Is there a family meeting? Am I late?" He jokes with a grin. I can't stop myself as I lunge towards him and collide my fist with his jaw, causing him to fall to the floor.

"How could you do that to her!" I shout as he wipes the blood from his mouth. Marcus stands in front of me as if he is a shield between Rodger and I. But the only person he needs to stop from killing Rodger is Spencer because within a second, Spencer grabs Rodger and throws him up against the wall.

"You had one task!" Spencer shouts in a fit of rage ignoring the coughs of blood coming from Rodger.

"Okay, get away from him now! Go. Now!" Marcus instructs while we watch Rodger gasp for air. "I know we are all angry, but if we kill him what would that do?" Marcus asks.

He's right, no matter how angry we are at Rodger, he will never learn. He likes destruction, he likes to break hearts and he likes to enjoy the aftermath. He gets a high from causing problems. He's always been the same. He is just wired like that.

"You know if she hadn't of pushed me I wouldn't of told her." He says smugly wiping the blood from his mouth. Marcus turns to Rodger slowly, the once almost calm look on his face is now a filled with rage and not one of us knows what he is going to do.

"You fucker." He says almost as a whisper. "You son of a bitch. How dare you say that? You shouldn't of told her in the fucking first place you could have ruined any relationship she had with her Mom!" He shouts as walks towards Rodger slowly.

"Oh boo hoo, she'll get over it." Rodger jokes and Marcus punches Rodger so hard he falls to the floor once more.

"That wasn't for you to decide!" Marcus shouts before storming through to the kitchen.

The silence in the room is deafening as we all arent sure what to say as it will only come out in anger. Marcus returns with cans of beers for myself and Spencer but doesn't get one for Rodger.

"Where were you?" He asks in a calm demeanor. Rodger rolls his eyes but grabs the bag that had fell to the floor the first time he had been punched.

"None of your business. But you'll soon find out." He taunts as he pushes past us towards the stairs.

"Don't go near her." Spencer instructs which only causes Rodger to laugh as he makes his way slowly up the stairs.

"Yes boss."

CHAPTER TWENTY FIVE

The next morning as I walk through the school gates, I can't help but feel as though I'm being watched from every angle. Paranoia seeps through my veins and I can't help but keep looking over my shoulder.

I walk towards my first class and decide that apart from Katy and Mikki, I need as much time away from Damian as physically possible. He can do whatever he needs to from afar, but I don't want him near him as I don't feel as though I can trust him, or his brothers. They may be helping with this case, but I want them to help me do the bare minimum. But finding out I'm adopted and the man that sent me the case is my father, it makes me feel sick to my stomach as I'm still trying to process it.

The boys stayed until 12am, so did my Grandparents who really want to help and they did. Grandma worked out that there was a lawsuit taken against the Mrs Holden, the details of the lawsuit were blanked out but I'm sure I could work my magic and find out.

As I walk to my next class, I catch the eye of Harrison who gives me a glare, almost as a warning. All I can do is smile at him, in the hopes it gives him a hint that I have worse things on him than he has on me, but i think he knows that.

I come round the corner and almost jump out of my skin bumping into Mikki and Katy. "Jesus!" I exclaim while grabbing my chest. They both laugh as they each grab an arm each as we walk to our next class. Thankfully we are all together.

"How was your little adventure to Damian Williams house?" They ask and I instantly feel sick. I'm not one to lie and as much as I love both of my friends; they are the biggest gossips in the world. By the end of the next class everyone would know I'm adopted and that Damian and his family work for him.

"Fine." I lie. "He helped me out with my maths homework and then I left." I continue. But in reality, I found out I'm adopted, Harrison and Holly forced me into a car, there is a drug ring at the school. But they don't need to know that as I feel like they couldn't keep it a secret.

"Well, that's boring." Katy whines as we reach the

English class. "I thought at least something would happen." She huffs. Yeah, like I want to strangle him for lying to me.

"Sorry to burst your bubble, but nothing is going to happen." I harshly say before pushing past them and taking at seat at my desk.

"Okay, settle down." My English teacher shouts before pulling up a PowerPoint presentation. "Today we are going to be reading Romeo and Juliet." She exclaims with a smile and the whole class groans. "Miss why?" A boy, Matthew, cries from the back of the class.

"Because I say so, grab a book from the middle of the table and open to page one." She instructs and we all do as we are told, except some students whine while opening the page.

"I love Romeo and Juliet." Katy exclaims next to me and I watch as Mikki nods, who sits in front of me causing me to roll my eyes and shake my head.

"You two don't need another dysfunctional fictional love to fan girl over." I mock and Mikki sticks her tongue out at me. They know I'm right. They read some much romance and watch so many movies that when they do get a boyfriend their high expectations are going to plummet when they realise that men or woman, aren't like they are in the stories.

◆ ◆ ◆

As the end of the day approaches, I start to feel some sort of relief that I haven't been pulled by Mrs. Hadley, Holly, Maura or Harrison. But just as I thought we were free; my history teacher stands and explains that everyone must go to the food hall after school for a talk. Conversations start floating around the room as to what the talk could be, and my mind goes to two different options:

1. Georgia's death,
2. The way Georgia died.

But then I quickly come to the realisation that it won't be the second option because they wouldn't want to have someone sniffing around their drug ring that clearly exists amongst the school. This will however put a dint in my plan to find out who is making the drugs.

My mind starts to think back to the car ride I had with Marcus yesterday, one of many strange things that happened. A flashback of him telling me that this is bigger than Robert originally thought gets me thinking that maybe he's right. What if it is bigger than Robert originally thought, and he thought it was just something petty that was just an in school thing. What if they are selling the drugs online but also buying the stock there too.

As all these thoughts come rushing to my brain the bell goes and I almost jump out of my skin.

"Right class, grab your bags and head to the hall please." The teacher instructs and we all do as we are told.

We walk side by side, shuffling like penguins as we head to the hall. It looks like the entire school is heading to the hall and the more people I see, the more I start to think that they will be telling us all about Georgia.

"Thinking what I'm thinking?" A voice, and an annoying one at that almost whispers in my ear. Instead of turning to Damian, I nod in agreement as we head into the hall, and I find Katy and Mikki who look at me just as confused as the rest of the students who are piling into the hall.

"What do you think this is about?" Katy asks as she looks around. I shake my head as an answer because I don't feel like giving her a verbal one. However, I do look to Damian who is only thinking the same thing as me.

Slowly but surely the amount of people who are piling in begin to reduce and after a while the hall is filled with students from year 9 – year 13. What has caught my eye, is two people holding each other so tight you would think they were looking for warmth rather than comfort. But what also catches my eye is the casually dressed police officer with his badge standing

"Okay shush! I need people to listen please!" Mrs. Hadley shouts from the front of the hall. Little by little, the hall becomes quiet as everyone turns their attention to her. "I have some news I need to share." She expresses, sadness in her voice. All I'm thinking is how fake it sounds, and I instantly start to feel my blood boil. After overhearing her conversation with Mrs. Holden and how she saw Georgia as nothing more but a problem my respect if I had any is now nonexistent,

"Last Friday, Georgia Howard was found unresponsive by her parents in her bedroom. Paramedics tried everything to keep her alive her but unfortunately nothing more could have been done and she was pronounced dead at the scene." Mrs. Hadley explains. Gasps and cries begin filling the room from her friends and classmates and hearing it out loud even it brings a tear to my eye. Katy and Mikki both look at each other and at me who tries to act like I haven't known about this for weeks, Damian does the same.

"Counseling with the Pastoral team will be available from tomorrow onwards. We will be sending a letter home to all parents to explain to them the situation. We encourage that everyone please be present in school, we do understand this is a shock – but Georgia would want you to continue your learning and not mourn her death. We should be celebrating her life." Mrs. Hadley encourages, and I watch as Georgia's parents hug each other and nod at Mrs. Hadley's speech.

"How long do you reckon it took her to draft that up?" I whisper to Damian who tries not to smirk.

"And to make it sound compassionate." I murmur and he bites the inside of his cheek trying not to laugh.

"Police Officer Bradley is currently investigating Georgia's death and will be conducting interviews with her close friends over the next few days as they begin their investigation." Mrs. Hadley explains before handing the stand to the police officer who looks around.

"I understand this is a shock to everyone and I can't even begin to process how you are all feeling right now. I'm so sorry." He empathizes as he speaks clearly on the stand. "Like your headmistress said, we are currently in the early stages of our investigation into Georgia's death. We do however believe that drugs are involved as a large amount of MDMA was found in Georgia's system." He explains. "Obviously, we are still looking into how she died but it does look to be a overdose." He finishes and people begin looking around. Like me, we never thought that Georgia was the type to do drugs. She always cared that her hair looked perfect or that she didn't have a eyebrow hair that was out of line. Since it is a London based school, the effect of taking drugs is drilled into your brain. Drugs are a massive problem in London, granted not as much as knife crime at the moment – but it's a huge problem that the government are trying to contain.

"Over the next few days like she said, I will be conducting interviews with people I have been made aware of. You may be pulled out of lessons so teachers just so you know this will be going on." He says speaking to the teachers who all nod their heads.

"They took their time telling people. What do you think they were waiting for?" Damian whispers in my ear and I shrug before turning away from him and focusing on Katy and Mikki who are clearly distressed about the whole situation. I gently link my arm with Katy who leans her head on my shoulder not bothering to stop her tears from falling. Although I knew about Georgia's death and she may not have been a friend, she was still someone I saw and for her to die in such a heartbreaking way. It hurts my heart.

◆ ◆ ◆

Since my mum found out that Mrs. Hadley has a vendetta against me, she and my grandparents decided on a new pick-up plan. Damian and I go to the school gates where we are met by Grandma who will take us back to our house. I finally got a house key which I should be excited about as it shows freedom but also trust, but I only got it because my mum is worried about the drug ring in the school.

I hear a whistle come from the side of the school gates as I head towards my grandma's car. I turn to find the one person I was hoping to never see again. I continue walking ignoring the destructor who currently stands near a bunch of bushes.

"What do you want?" I exclaim after he whistles once more, and I lose my temper. Rodger smiles as he walks towards me, that stupid grin only growing as he now stands inches away from me. I don't feel scared of him, I never really have. But right now, I'm angry and he was the last person I want to see.

"I want to talk." He says with a joker like grin residing on his face and I roll my eyes.

"What happened to your face?" I ask as he comes more into the light. He has a black eye, bruised cheek and a cut lip, I don't care if he is okay, I just want to know what he did to deserve it.

"Oh you know. Girl's boyfriend found out about me, thought he would teach me a lesson." He jokes with that smile. I can't help but laugh.

"The boys beat you up when you got home didn't they?" I ask smugly. He rolls his eyes but doesn't say another word.

"You know there is a name for someone like you." I tell him as I tilt my head showing that I'm not afraid of him which is what he wants.

"Funny? Handsome? Charming?" He jokes.

"Pedophile. You're hanging round a school talking a fourteen-year-old." I say bluntly which catches him off guard and he stutters. "Oh wait, I don't know you. You're a stranger!" I exclaim and I watch the fear flash in his eyes. "I'm going to scream!" I shout before he lunges at me and places his hand firmly over my mouth, the look of fear turning to blazing anger.

"*Ah. Ah. Ah.*" He taunts as he shakes his head at me. "I would hate to tell your father I had to kill you because you couldn't keep your mouth shut." He says still holding me against my will. I move to push away but he holds me still. "Snitches get stitches." He warns me before I use all my strength and push him off me once I feel him loosen his grip on me.

"You're despicable." I say as wipe my face trying to get any essence of Rodger off me, God knows where he's been. I begin to laugh. "First you ruin my life, then you threaten to kill me. No wonder you're always alone you clearly can't keep friends." I say as I begin to walk away but he keeps me there by grabbing onto my arm causing me to look at his once smug face that is more disinterested than anything.

"You had a right to know." He tells me, avoiding my eyes at all costs. I instantly feel rage boil inside me.

"And who are you to decide that? Didn't think that my own mother should be the one to tell me?" I ask him, clearly enraged and for once he doesn't argue or smirk, he just nods like he's admitting defeat almost and the sight makes me nervous. This man has no empathy for anyone, I maybe the daughter of his employer, doesn't mean he has to have any empathy or feelings for me.

"Jules, I don't regret telling you one bit you know why?" He asks as he gets close to me, towering over me. I'm about 5ft 5 and this man stands over me attempting to intimidate me. "Because it's better you hate me than think you can trust me." He says coldly and I ignore it only giving him a smile in return.

"Oh, I know I can't trust you." I joke to him, and he searches my face for answers not expecting me to laugh at him. "But now that you've ruined my life, I can easily ruin yours." I taunt and his face never changes as he waits for me to continue. "I could easily tell Robert Quinten that you screwed up on your task and to deal with you accordingly." I continue but no change apart from a slight twinkle of something in his eyes, but I can't place what emotion that is whether it be fear, or anger either way I'm really asking for a death wish.

"You wouldn't dare." He growls and I tilt my head with an annoying smile.

"Wouldn't I?" I taunt and his face becomes neutral as he realises I'm dead serious. "You want to make sure I keep my mouth shut? Do me a favor and stay well away from me. I don't need you ruining anything else in my life." I tell him before walking away not wanting to hear an answer, but I do anyway.

"Done." He shouts my way and I stick my thumb up as I walk towards the car park to meet Damian and my grandma.

When I eventually meet them, they are both as panicked as each other as I'm clearly later than I said I would be.

"Where were you?" He says concern filling his face but quickly changes to confusion when he sees the expression on my face that is no doubt anger.

"Arguing with your lovely brother." I say as I get into the car, I see a slight bit of confusion reside on his face for another moment before I roll my eyes. "Rodger came to see me." I say as I put my seatbelt on earning looks from both my grandma and Damian. I shake my head to them ignoring their worrying stares.

"Trust me he won't be bothering us." I say reassuringly before my grandma hesitates as she begins to look around for him but inevitably decides to start the car and drive away from the school. I'm grateful but my mum is not going to be happy I spoke to him, she's still not happy about doing this case, but after the boys explained why this would be beneficial, she ultimately agreed if there was someone over 18 that she trusted helping us. Those people being Grandma, Grandad Norman or her. Which makes the most sense.

The drive back to my house isn't long, but I feel as though today, these past couple of days have been so draining. I'm still not coming to terms with the fact I'm adopted. It doesn't sit right with me that I'm not, by birth, a Sanders. I feel a little bit disappointed,

TORRIE JONES

and I can't seem to place as to why.

CHAPTER TWENTY SIX

I feel myself being lightly shook and I'm woken up to Damian shaking me eagerly trying to wake me up.

"We're back." He says before he takes his seatbelt off and proceeds to get out of the car. It takes me a second to grasp my surroundings but then I notice we are back at my house, and I feel somewhat safe knowing I'm here.

I get out of the car and grab my bag and make my way towards the front of the house where I watch my Grandma greet Spencer and Marcus who stand waiting at the top of the steps, giving her a small smile. I catch Spencer's eye and he walks to meet me. I'm still groggy from my little nap and he takes my bag from my shoulder which catches me by surprise, and he notices.

"Damian said you've just seen Rodger." He says as we walk towards the front door and Marcus who stands there checking his phone. "He was at the school?"

I nod at him, words failing as I'm feeling slightly exhausted.

"I wouldn't provoke him anymore if I was you. It will end badly." He says to me, and I slowly turn to him showing my slight annoyance and he quickly changes his tone. "I'm serious Juliette. Don't do anything stupid when it comes to him. If you do something idiotic, I'll be more than angry." He says as a warning which I ignore, and he notices. As I turn to walk away, he grabs my arm firmly in front of Marcus causing me to wince.

He's harsher than Rodger is and I get he's frustrated , but that doesn't mean he gets to talk to me like I'm some little kid acting out. "Just because I've been sent to protect you Juliette, it doesn't mean I have to like you." He says harshly and I move my eyes that were somewhat fixated on his hand around my arm to his eyes that are filled with only rage as he looks deep into mine. "Don't make me regret protecting you." He warns harshly. We stay like that for a moment before something collides with Spencer's arm and he winces in pain grabbing his forearm in the process.

"Touch my Granddaughter like that again and I

will shove my stick where the sun doesn't shine. Do you understand son?" That booming southern London accent speaks from beside me and my heart instantly feels full. My grandad, my great protector. He gives me a wink while he takes my school bag off Spencer's shoulder pushing past him as we make our way inside.

"Don't know what it is with the Williams brothers feeling like they can just grab me when they want. I'm not their property." I say as I rub my arm, no doubt there is going to be a bruise in the next few days.

"Unfortunately, you are their life insurance policy darling." He says almost as a sigh. He turns to me, and before I even bother asking what he means, it dawns on me. He's right. I am their life insurance policy. They need me alive in order to stay alive.

"Do you need to get anything from upstairs?" Grandad asks as I place my bag in the dining room and think about it. "Oh yeah I need the MacBook." I say to him before giving him a quick kiss on the cheek.

"Juliette, she wanted to tell you." He whispers softly and it takes me by surprise. My grandad is not one for genuine conv never has been. So, this is a definite shock. "But she had made a promise to your birth father. She knew deep down he wasn't a good man, that's why they had such a private adoption." He tells me as he looks to my Grandma who starts placing all of the evidence on the table. "When your parents said they were bringing home a girl we were overjoyed. We didn't care that we weren't your original grandparents. We knew we would love you just as much as any of our other grandchildren." He reassures me.

My grandad is never this honest or raw with anyone. Not like this. If he wants to be brutally honest, he will find my Auntie Alison. But this is new for him, to open about the past, especially something so new and deep for me.

All I do is smile at him, not being able to find the words. Granted I haven't started processing any of it yet, but I will in my own time. He knows that words are failing me, while giving me a smile back, he walks over to Spencer and smacks him on the back of the head with his stick. Spencer winces while rubbing his head and Marcus and Damian begin to laugh. Spencer turns to him, and he gets very close to him, not as tall as he would like but he is trying to make a point.

"I will dismember each of your fingers if you touch her again. You never place your hands on a lady, or a child. Understand?" Grandad warns making the place fall completely silent. My eyes dart to Spencer who, would never admit it, is intimidated by my Grandad.

He nods, not wanting to say anything and quickly moves away from him so Grandad can't hit him again. I laugh as I go up the stairs, to collect the MacBook from my desk. I open my bedroom door and place my bag in the corner of my room and begin walking over to collect it, but something catches my eye.

A new file.

I feel my heart sink as I look around trying to work out how someone would have got in. Doesn't help that my heart is beating out of my chest, and I feel like I'm having a heart attack. Something isn't right and I can't place my finger on what it is.

"Spencer! Marcus!" I shout as I feel like my heart is about to explode. None of this is making sense and how did someone get in my room?

Within a few seconds I feel Spencer and Marcus stand beside me looking around.

"This a joke?" I ask pointing at the file. They exchange a look before Marcus takes charge and picks up the file and begins to go through it.

"I never left this." He says. But the glare I give him makes him panic. "Jules I'm serious. This isn't me and it isn't your father either." Marcus reassures me and I look to Spencer who doesn't move only stares at Marcus wanting to believe him.

"Then what's in it?" I ask. Marcus begins pullingout photos and blueprints. Who would want to send me blueprints?

"What the hell?" Spencer questions as he looks through the photos his brows frowned as he looks through one by one. "These were taken last night." He says pulling one from the file and pointing to the timestamp.

"We were all together when these were taken." Spencer points out and I take a deep breath. This is insane. "Everyone who knows about this case was in that room." He explains. But then it hits me and I groan in annoyance.

"Not everyone." I say as I go to lie on my bed. Why is it that he suddenly wants to help? He ruined my life last night.

"So that's where he went." Marcus groans while rolling his eyes before joining me on the bed.

"You think Rodger did this?" I laugh, as I sit up on my elbows. I get a look from both boys. "Also which one of you beat him up?" I ask with a smirk. They all look down to file ignoring my question for a few moments.

"It was a joint effort." Marcus pipes up after a moment which causes me to laugh lightly.

"First, he ruins my life then wants to help? Is he okay?"

"No." they say in unison which only makes me flop down on the bed.

"Come on, grab the MacBook." Spencer instructs and I do as I'm told.

As I follow both boy's downstairs, I see the look of worry on my Grandparents face, and I go over and give them a hug while Spencer places the blueprints on the table. Grandma looks to me in confusion as she watches Spencer one by one place the photos that are of each building on the outside and places them on top of the blueprints.

"We believe Rodger left this for Jules. It was on her bed." Marcus explains earning a look from both Grandparents and Damian.

"Why would he do that?" Damian asks confused. Everyone shrugs their shoulders.

"Who cares, he's given us something to work with... I think." Marcus pauses. "What that is I don't know." He says while tilting his head. I keep looking at the photos hoping that something will pop out, but it doesn't. Whatever Rodger is trying to tell us, I can't work it out.

"You reckon he's just toying with us?" Damian asks Spencer who shrugs clearly just as baffled as the rest of us. But suddenly he has turned his head, more so like he's found something in the sea of nothing.

"Juliette, do you know if the school has a basement?" He asks and I shrug.

"I don't know." I say honestly. It more than likely does but I've never paid attention. He signals me over to stand where he is and begins to point at the blueprints. "What am I supposed to be looking at?" I ask and he exhales quite loudly.

"Where is that in the school? What section of classrooms?" he asks, and I begin to look around the blueprints to understand them. "Erm." I mumble finding my bearings. "It's the science block." I tell him which then puts a thick cloud in the air as we all realise.

My sister comes through the door like a bat out of hell with my mum before Spencer can ask another question. Ava looks startled as she just stares like a deer in headlights at the boys and my grandparents.

"You made new friends?" Ava sarcastically says to me which earns her a eye roll.

"Ava, go upstairs and start your homework. Your sister is doing her project down here." My mum explains while giving me a long hard stare to go along with it.

"Yeah Ava, sorry I really need to focus." I say playing along, but instead of Ava listening, she walks up to Spencer causing him to back up, frightened like he's looking at a monster.

"He looks like a criminal but okay." She says before making her way up the stairs. Laughter fills the room from all of us. Ava has always had a funny side to her, she's brutally honest but in the best way possible.

"She's a character." My mum says laughing while placing her bags into the kitchen. "What happened today?" Mum asks opening the fridge. I walk into the archway and lean against the door handle. "Mrs Hadley told the school about Georgia's death." I tell her and she turns to me shocked. "The whole school was told we had to go to the hall after the last class."

"No way." My mum says dumbfounded.

"Yes way. A police officer was there and explained

they are treating Georgia's death as a drug overdose." Damian tells her as he joins me in the doorway.

"No doubt they will start doing presentations on drugs and the dangers." Marcus says from the dining room table and I nod to him.

"Georgia's parents were there too." I tell her and she looks at me with sad eyes.

"Those poor parents." She says softly while holding her chest, the tears beginning to fill her eyes. "They lost a daughter. It's just so sad."

We all remain quiet for a moment cause we all know it's true. Although we are investigating Georgia's death, the principle is a girl still died, and we need to get her some sort of justice.

"The police officer will be doing interviews with Georgia's friends and people she interacted with from tomorrow." Damian says to my mum who nods slowly. I watch as she gets the juice from the fridge and place it on the kitchen bench before heading to the cupboard to get some glasses.

"You didn't know her though, did you?" My mum asks me, and I shake my head.

"Never spoke to her, but I'm curious as to what they will ask them." I go over to help my mum with the glasses for the juice which I then place on the table and start pouring everyone a glass.

"So, what's all this?" Mum asks as she looks over the photos and I can't help but take a deep breath as I know how furious my mum is going to be when I tell her what happened.

"We think Rodger broke into your house and left these on the bed." Spencer says so I don't have to. My mother then begins to choke on her juice and Damian gently pats her back as she gets her breath back.

"I'm sorry what! Did you not think to start with that!" She exclaims in between the coughs as Damian continues to pat her back before she places her hand on his shoulder. "I'm fine now thank you." She smiles to him. "What do you mean you think he broke in?" Mum exclaims as she looks to Spencer for an answer but I butt in.

"Well, we don't know it's for certain it was him but he knows about the case and he was the only person not here last night when we were working on this. Look at the time stamp on the photos." I explain and she picks up a photo to verify what I'm saying. She looks at Marcus with eyes full of rage and he shakes his head at her, stuttering.

"I promise it wasn't Robert, I'm the only person he sent to London." He exclaims earning a look from Spencer and Damian. "Minus you two of course. And our lovely psychopath." He jokes which causes me to roll my eyes.

"Can we please work out what these blueprints mean, thank you." Spencer says as we all gather round.

"Jules, you said this is the science block." He says as he points to that area on the blueprints. "Do you know if those stairs are in use?" he asks, and I close my eyes, and begin to try and find my bearings. I follow the corridor on the blueprints, and I'm met with the original drug den classroom, I turn left and turn around but frown.

"There's a wall there, not a door." I say as I open my eyes and back at the blueprints.

"You sure?"

"Positive." I tell him and he huffs.

"Maybe these are old blueprints. It's showing a door there." He tells us and I begin to look around to the other buildings, the English block, the geography section... but then I notice it. "That's the new sports hall, it was only built last year. It's new blueprints."

"Probably to hide the fact that there was a drug den going on in one of the science rooms." Marcus mutters under his breath and we all look to him as we all realise he's more than likely right. It was probably a cover so they wouldn't locate the drug den.

"Look." Grandad Norman says while pointing to the basement section of the blueprints and we all follow.

"There's another staircase, there would have to be to fit in with guidelines. It's probably the main entrance, they just boarded up the other exit." He explains and we begin trying to place where in the school it's underneath.

"What's next to the English block and the cafeteria?" Marcus asks looking to me and I look to Damian.

"The library!" We both say in unison. Suddenly it all starts to make sense. The extra control around the library after school, I didn't know why but now I'm starting to realise why there was always a teacher walking backwards and forwards in front of that door.

"Everyone thought it was a extra staff room." I explain looking to mum who is almost as white as a ghost.

"What kind of school did I send you to?" She exclaims taking a seat at the table, holding her face in her hands in a moment.

"A dodgy one by the looks of it." Marcus mutters a little too loudly earning a scowl from my mum and I begin to laugh.

"Let me guess? Private school?" I ask him and he hesitates. His silence is the only answer I need

"I'm going to say this once." Spencer pipes up before turning me gently to face him. "Do not go looking for the potential drug den in the library at the school." He instructs both me and Damian, I roll my eyes.

"Spencer, I'm not stupid. I already know who's making the drugs." His eyes widen at my answer as does everyone else.

"Care to explain?" He asks softly and I nod.

"Well, it's just a theory at this moment in time. But-" I begin to say before I'm rudely interrupted by Marcus.

"Theory isn't good enough Jules; you need evidence you should know this."

I exhale loudly at his unwanted comment. "Well, if you would let me finish, I'll explain. So, shut it." I pipe up causing him to throw his hands up in defense.

So, I know for certain there are 5 people involved:

1. Mrs. Hadley

Now I believe Mrs. Hadley is the ringleader, that Mr. Dunston, the teacher that was caught last year I feel he went down for her crimes. It never stopped when Mr. Dunston was caught. It just moved location.

2. Harrison Meyer.

Now I feel as though he's the seller. It goes way beyond this school. He originally went to a private school which means more than likely he will have contacts there that he will sell to. Not to mention his parents friends kids, he has so many people he can sell too.

3. Maura and Holly.

I do feel like Maura is more involved than Holly. I get the feeling she doesn't agree to any of this, but they are the ones who package everything so they can give it to Harrison who sells it.

4. Mrs. Holden.

I believe she's the maker. She's the science teacher, so it would make sense. Maybe she's in some debt and needs the money which is why she's a part of this.

As I explain this to them, they all look around one another processing my theory. Granted it is a theory, but I'm not done yet.

"But I think we are missing one more person." I say which then has all eyes on me. "Something about this makes me feel like we are missing someone out of this little group. Now my theory is they have someone who buys the material, and they bring it to the library if that's where we are thinking the new drug den is."

"You reckon it's someone on the outside? Maybe one of Mrs Hadley's friends or something?" Marcus asks and I shake my head.

"I really doubt that Mrs. Hadley would want to incorporate her friends into her little scheme. I mean she might, but that doesn't seem likely. A lot of them will be parents themselves." My mum says.

"What if it's another student?" Damian pipes up. We look to him and that theory doesn't seem too bad. Neither does Marcus' but for some reason another student does seem likely.

"Possibly. But how would they get their hands on the ingredients to make - what drug is it again?" Mum asks.

"MDMA, molly, ecstasy. There are tons of names

for them now." Spencer pipes up and my mum nods while taking a deep breath.

"Grandma, Grandad, what's your theory?" I ask. They've been quiet. Probably taking in everything.

"Would the science teacher not be able to order the ingredients through the school?" Grandad asks and Spencer shakes his head.

"Very doubtful, they would want to do it under the radar." Spencer explains before taking a sip of his juice.

"Besides, with the amount they might be going through, it would cause severe suspicion if they are ordering it like once a month?" Marcus says and I nod. He's right, it would cause too much suspicion.

"They are more than likely getting the ingredients from the black market." Damian says. I look to him as he runs his hands through is hair. "If you take a look on the black market-"

"I can't say I've had a recent browse. Are there new items?" I mock and he shoots me a look. Everyone else begins to laugh which only frustrates him more.

"You're forgetting that we know nothing about any of this." My mum points around to my grandparents and I. "That's more your area of expertise."

"Well, it's not mine. But it is someone we know." He tells us while his eyes fall to the Macbook.

"Robert." I tell my mum who sighs loudly, her head falling into her hands.

"Of course." She murmurs. "Does your brother not know anything?" She turns to Damian who shakes his head.

"Believe it or not, Rodger is very against drugs." Damian explains and I whip my head round to Spencer who is nodding.

"You're right. I don't believe you." I say before grabbing the laptop off the middle of the table.

"Wait, Romeo, do you have any questions left?" Grandad asks and I shake my head.

"No, but because we have a some evidence, even though some of it is just speculation at this point. It means I've earned a question." I explain and he nods.

"Better get this over and done with." I say opening the MacBook and clicking on the message icon. I suddenly hesitate. I don't know what to say but also messaging this person now has a whole different feeling to it.

"Jules?" Mum says rubbing my shoulder gently, I suddenly feel emotional, granted this last 24 hours have been hard. I've found out life changing news and I'm currently looking into something dangerous. I can feel my chest tightening as I try to come to terms with the changes.

"This whole thing has a totally different meaning when it turns out you're related to the person who's on the other side of that screen." I say quietly. My mum coos and places her hand on my knee squeezing gently. I take a deep breath before typing to him.

I have collected new evidence.

Silence fills the room as we wait for an answer. I look to Marcus who is staring intensely at me, not giving me any other emotion. I look back at the screen hoping that soon we will receive a message.

What have you found out?

I look to my mum who takes a long deep breath but nods to me giving me the go ahead. I know she doesn't agree with any of this deep down, but I know what I need to do.

I begin typing, giving him a rundown of everything that we know so far, including sending over my recording of Mrs. Hadley and Mrs. Holden, explaining there is a room underneath the library that might be used as a drug den, giving names and roles in which, we think they have. Anything we had, we handed over.

Once I finish sending over the last bit of evidence, I fall back into my seat and exhale loudly. This is draining and I'm probably not going to be hearing from him soon, or even tonight.

I feel my mum stand up from her chair and pat her legs. A very English thing clearly cause the boys look startled.

"Right, mother come give me a hand while I make

tea, dad I'll make you a dicky ticker." She says as she walks through to the kitchen. "Would you boys like to stay for tea?" Mum asks and they exchange glances to one another.

"If it isn't too much trouble." Damian replies. She simply smiles at them through the archway, and they return the gesture.

"She's a good woman." Marcus says with a smile while finishing off his juice. I nod in agreement, seeing Spencer smile does warm my heart a little. He's always got such straight face, it's nice to see him relaxed.

"Your dad chose well." He smiles to Marcus who nods with him. I sit in silence taking in the sight, that my potential new brother and newfound friends. Marcus rolls up his sleeve revealing some of the tattoos he has, and the one on his forearm piques my interest which is the one I noticed Damian had when I met him in the library.

"What does that tattoo mean?" I ask which causes him to look down not knowing which one I'm talking about. "The one you all have on your arm."

Marcus laughs realizing that it's the one I'm probably referring to. "It means family." He says putting his arm out to show the tree that's in the middle of his arm. The detail is incredible, and I look round to see Spencer trying to locate his. I mean to be fair, the man is covered head to toe in tattoos. Another one that catches my eye is a 'W' on the side of his ear, no doubt for Williams.

"Did you lose it?" I laugh. He nods as he holds his arms up trying to find it.

"I think it may have moved." He says which only makes the boys and I laugh harder.

"Dude it's on your upper arm remember?" Damian laughs and Spencer opens the inside of his arm and nods.

"Found it." He says with a smile causing me to laugh, as do the rest of the boys. "Robert wanted us to have one. He may not legally be our father, but he has taken care of us since we were younger and has given us a good life." Damian says which causes me to smile at him. It's nice, that he gave them a good life, and Marcus too.

"You seem so much more relaxed. You had an angry face when we first met." I express and he laughs.

"I've came to the conclusion Robert is going to kill me anyway because Rodger told you, so I'm just trying to enjoy what little time I have left on this earth." He jokes, except I don't find it funny. I look to Marcus who only pulls a face which doesn't give me any comfort. I decide that until I get to speak to Robert in person, if I do decide that's what I want, I'll tell him to go easy on the boys.

"Is it the same artist and tattooist?" I ask changing the subject quickly.

"Your Uncle Peter is the artist, but the actual artist who drew the tree is your brother Ezekiel."

Marcus explains and I start to feel a little nervous.

"Creative." I say almost as a whisper which causes him to snort.

"He is, but not as creative as dad is. Dad is an amazing artist." Marcus admits which makes my heart beat a little faster.

The rest of my family struggle to draw stick people, whereas I have always been creative in that way. Art was always a passion until my dad died. He used to encourage it, but it was hard after he died to continue having the same passion.

"He likes to draw?" I ask almost as a whisper. Marcus nods with a smile as he pulls up his other sleeve to reveal the most beautiful and detailed portrait of a boy and a girl. I stare in awe as I admire the detail and and the colours that have been used on the tattoo.

"Dad drew this last year for me. It was a 18th birthday present. It's one of my favourites." He says with a smile.

"Who are they?" I ask softly. But i realise i probably shouldn't of as the smile on his face turns to a one of pain as he pulls his arm away and rolls his sleeve down.

"My brother and sister from another life." He says quietly but with a smile of reassurance that it was okay to ask.

Since Marcus told me I have other siblings, all who are older. Every time I get the thought, I feel sick and

I'm not sure if it's because I don't know whether I'm not going to be able to fit into the family, or what but I know I'm nothing like them. Whatever they are like.

"You said I'm the youngest. The oldest is Nathaniel, what are the others called?" I ask and he begins to smile.

"Nathaniel is the oldest, then there is Tommy, then yours truly." He says with a grin pointing to himself. "Then Alexis, Ezekiel and Clarissa and you of course." He continues to smile. "You're a lot nicer than Clarissa."

I frown. "How so?" Spencer scoffs before running his hands through his hair.

"Clarissa is a nightmare." He says with a light chuckle while Damian agrees.

"She had a baby 6 months ago." Marcus says and I feel my eyes slightly pop out of my head.

"Wow. How did Robert take that?" I ask and I earn another scoff, this time from Damian.

"He was furious obviously."

"But what made it worse was that he was willing to accept it, buy her a house, let her have her own space away from the mansion to raise the baby." Marcus begins to explain but stops. I move my head forward hinting that I want him to continue.

"But?" I ask.

"But, we never actually saw the baby after she went into labor." Marcus says and I look around. The same expression on both Spencer and Damian's face.

"Did she lose the baby?" Mum asks behind me and Marcus shakes his head.

"Nope, they spoke to her doctors, and they confirmed she had a happy and healthy baby girl, who according to them she was calling Sapphire. But then that's the end of it. When she returned home, there was no baby, and every time the subject is brought up she will either leave the room or change the subject completely." Marcus explains. I feel like my jaw is about to hit the floor. How could anyone just get rid of a baby?

"Do you think she sold the baby?" My mum asks but this time only earns a shrug from Marcus and the boys. My mum gasps horrified. "We wouldn't put it past her. But we know the baby isn't dead as there hasn't been a death certificate filed but we also don't know if the baby is alive because she never filed a birth certificate."

"What about adoption?" I ask trying to think of any sort of possibility but all I'm met with is shaken heads.

"She knew what it was like to come from a broken home, Tommy and Clarissa are blood brother and sister. Their parents were crack addicts and sadly died one night. Tommy was 15, Clarissa 11. They were then put in terrible foster homes until dad found them. Tommy was about to leave the system and Clarissa was an absolute nightmare at 13. It's 3 years later and she's still as psychotic as the day he brought her home." Marcus explains. "We've all had it rough, and I would like to think that Clarissa wouldn't want to subject her kid to whatever she went through."

"What about the baby's father?" My mum asks hoping for a possibility. Marcus smiles to her. "Trust me Amy, Uncle Peter has went down every route to try and locate Clarissa's baby. It's still one of his many tasks. But even he can't find out who the father is."

I sit back in my chair, absolutely stunned by what I'm hearing. "Does she even care about the fact that you all lost a niece?" I ask trying not to cry. My heart is breaking for that baby.

"She doesn't care about anyone. That's why her and Rodger are friends." Damian says too quickly, and everyone darts a look to him.

"Well that explains a lot." I say as I get up from the table.

As I turn to go and help my mum in the kitchen to avoid the possibility of a conversation about Rodger, a ding goes off on the MacBook causing me to immediately stop in my tracks. I look to my mum who meets my eyes with fearful ones, and I turn on my heel and wake up the computer.

"What does it say?" Grandad shouts from the kitchen.

Well, that is some very good evidence Juliette, I am impressed.

You have earned yourself a question.

I turn to my mum who has her eyes fixated on the screen, unsure on how I should respond. I begin to think, on what we would need to solve the case.

"Juliette ask him what you want." Marcus encourages. "Forget about the case for a minute. I'm sure you have tons of questions for him. Ask him one, without giving it away that you know he's your father."

I hesitate my answer. Not because I can't think of a question, I have plenty of those floating round in my head. But I can't seem to find the right one to ask with regards to a personal question.

"I can't think of one." I lie and Marcus looks at me with pitiful eyes.

"If I ask him about the black market maybe we can solve this case a little quicker." I say to my mum who looks at me with the same eyes as Marcus. I quickly turn to Marcus once again, my fiery eyes meeting his sad ones as I decide on my question.

"The quicker we solve this, the quicker we can get back to having some sort of a normal life." I say before typing.

I have a theory about an extra person possibly being involved in the drug ring. I get the feeling that you're into some illegal underground operations. My question is, can you find out if there have been any shipments of the drug needed to create MDMA that has been bought on the black market and delivered to anywhere in London within the last 6 months?

I click send and look to my mother who seems impressed with my question. I'm just pleased she's no longer giving me the puppy dog eyes.

"I wouldn't of been able to word a question like that." Spencer laughs. "Bravo." I smile at his reaction only to be caught off guard once more.

"Jules." My mum says in a serious tone which makes me walk back to the laptop.

Leave it with me.

Well, that was easy. I take a sigh of relief as I hold my head in my hands. Until he can get me that list, I can't do much more tonight. But I'm quickly silenced at a gasp coming from my mum.

"Jesus Christ that was quick." My mum exclaims which causes Marcus to chuckle.

"He probably knew what she needed and had the list ready." He says as he gets up from his chair and begins to put the photos that we assume Rodger had sent back into the file and Spencer and Damian help.

"Let's have dinner then look it over briefly. I think we all need a relatively early night tonight." Mum says as she rubs my back and walking back into the kitchen to greet my grandparents. Before closing the laptop, I type a quick message to Robert.

Thank you.

But within a few seconds I am met with another message.

Please stay safe. Take your evidence with you to school tomorrow. You will know why when you get there.

-Q.

I roll my eyes at the last message and shut the laptop. God knows what he has planned tomorrow. More than likely he's expecting Marcus to collect it. But until then I will do as I'm told. But I can slowly feel this start to take a toll on me and I'm not sure how much more I can take.

CHAPTER TWENTY SEVEN

When Robert sent through the list, we each took a section and went through and crossed off anyone that didn't seem to fit the bill. Because there was 7 of us going through it, it only took us an hour to get through it all.

We calculated that there are 27 potential people or companies that could be buying it to potentially distribute it somewhere else. We worked out that the people that are buying it are buying it every few months. But we still managed to get it to 27 names out of about 300.

After we went through the list they read out names and companies to me and my family since we all lived or worked in London, no one stuck out like a sore thumb for any of us, so that was a dead end.

I walk the school halls constantly checking over my shoulder. I am not one to be afraid, but since I don't know what to expect with Robert today, I am feeling on edge.

The first two classes went by so quick I didn't realise it was break time until Mikki and Katy dragged me outside. They talked about a movie they had both went to see called *Kingsman* and were gushing, of course, over the lead – Taron Egerton. I know his name after they told me 6 or 7 times to watch it and how amazing he was. I will watch it, just not when my brain is currently a plate of scrambled eggs.

As we walk through to go to our English lesson, I catch a glimpse of that police officer and Mrs. Hadley walking through the school and no other than Harrison Meyer walking behind them. He must be the next person to be interviewed. Everyone is talking about it, how people speculate that because they said hello to Georgia in 2012 at the beach, they are going to be called in for a talk with Officer Bradley.

I exchange a look with Mikki and Katy and we all head to our next class. I keep my school bag very close as underneath I have all of my evidence that Robert had asked me to bring to the school. I feel as though I can't leave it in my locker as Mrs. Hadley would go snooping so my best bet is to keep it with me today.

"Did you hear?" Mikki says as we turn the corner to the English block. "They have already conducted all interviews apart from one. Harrison is the last person to be interviewed since he was her boyfriend or whatever you want to call it." She says under her breath as we enter the English class.

My interest piques, who else would they need to talk to as long as he's spoken to the main people. It's only 11:15am, how has he managed to get through all the interviews with people already? If he has and that rumor is true, he is a very thorough man, or I would hope he is.

"I wonder who the last person he needs to talk to is." Katy says while taking a seat next to me. "She only had like 5 actual friends. It's weird."

I nod in agreement, not wanting to say anything as I feel mentally drained from the past few days. Not only am I feeling slightly paranoid, but I'm also feeling wiped out. The adrenaline of working this case and trying to solve it but also finding out that my family isn't my own, I'm still coming to terms with it and today it has hit me like a brick.

"Okay class, open your books to chapter 15, we will be resuming Romeo & Juliet." The English teacher says. Mikki does a giddy little dance as she enthusiastically opens her book.

English class is a drag and when the teacher

excludes us, I feel a wave of excitement flow through me as I realise it's lunch time and I can get some fresh air. The English classroom is stuffy and I feel grateful that it's quite cold in London today.

I follow Mikki and Katy down the stairs towards the food hall and I feel my stomach grumble. All this crime solving has made me hungry.

As I'm about to leave the building, I feel someone grab me and pull me into a classroom. Just as I'm about to scream I see who my kidnapper is, and I grab my chest.

"Damian!" I exclaim and he puts his finger to his lips to tell me to be quiet. "What?"

I watch as he pulls his phone out of his back pocket and begins looking for something as I calm my racing heart. He then turns the phone round to show me, and I feel my heart fall like it's just fell off a building.

"Jesus." I say as I grasp what I'm looking at. A MDMA pill. On the top of a toilet in what I'm assuming is the boy's bathroom.

"It was in the locker room bathroom; I've just had gym." He says as he zooms in on the pill. I ignore his American lingo as I can't be bothered to correct him as much as I would like to.

"Look at the engraving on the pill." He points out as he turns the phone once more. I squint my eyes slightly as the quality isn't great. Damian could never make a career as a photographer.

"Is that a *H*"? I ask which I get a nod as a response. "What the heck does *H* mean?" He shrugs.

"No idea, but I might be able to find out." He says as he puts his phone in his back pocket.

"Damian…" I begin to say, and he quickly shushes me.

"Harrison asked me to sit with them at lunch. Without causing too much suspicion to myself. I'll ask him if he knows anything about it." He exclaims with a smile. It causes me to narrow my eyes.

"Remember when you were given the task to stay well away from me, and that lasted all about 2 days. The same task that Robert gave you apparently evaporated in your eyes, and you ignored all instructions? Remember that?" I mock. He doesn't find it funny I just get an eye roll as a response.

"Trust me Jules." He says and I begin to laugh.

"Trust you? Look where that got me last time." I say harshly but it's true. If he hadn't inserted himself into my life, I wouldn't be feeling the way I do about my identity. I've never had to question it before and the whole feeling is so unsettling.

"Look, we still need to talk about everything that's happened. I'm sorry Rodger was the one to tell you. I really am. It wasn't ever meant to happen. But I need you to trust me, just this once." He pleads.

I stare at him, not knowing whether to trust him. I may not have trusted him for long, but I was foolish to believe him last time and I ended up with earth shattering news.

"Fine." I agree. I know deep down this will go to hell, but he would probably do it anyway.

"I promise you; you won't regret it." He says squeezing the side s of my arms gently before making his way out of the door.

I really hope I don't regret it.

◆ ◆ ◆

I leave the classroom and begin to take a very slow walk to the hall to get some food and give a little white lie to my friends as to why I disappeared. I walk through the English block and towards the food hall but catch the image of my mum talking to Officer Bradley at Reception.

"What the-" I begin to say to myself before quickly making my way to Reception.

"Mum?" I ask causing her to look at me with a surprised reaction.

"Hi darling. You okay?" She asks as she gives me a kiss on the cheek, and I nod.

"What are you doing here?" I ask and she turns to Officer Bradley who greets me with a smile. I take a quick glance at him. His white shirt is very well ironed, and his brown tailored pants fit him to his ankles. He has light stubble and only a small amount of hair on his head.

"Hi Juliette, I'm Officer Bradley how are you?" He asks while extending his hand. I hesitantly take, but my mum brought me up to be polite and I will be. Especially to the police. "I gave your mum a call as I wanted to discuss with you about your friendship with Georgia Howard." He says softly and I look to my mum, confused.

"I didn't know Georgia, well I knew of her. But I had never spoken to her." I explain and he frowns to me.

"Well I was told by multiple people today that you were friends with her." He asks with a frown and I feel my eyes dart to Mrs. Hadley who stands with Holly and Maura no doubt discussing another elaborate scheme or the one they are currently doing.

"I was just wanting to have a talk and ask some questions is that okay?" He asks and I nod, barely hearing the question. I could of agreed to be arrested that's how much I was staring into Mrs. Hadley's soul.

"We will go upstairs then." He says as he instructs me to go first, exchanging a glance with my mum who looks easily as confused as me right now. She knows I'm barely a people person anyway so why would I be friends with a girl 2 years older than me, that clearly had her own group of friends.

"Jules, Mrs Sanders. Please take a seat for me." He instructs as we reach one of the derelict classrooms up in the language side of the school.

"Now. Can I get you a drink of water at all?" He asks softly and we both shake our heads. I'm beginning to become nervous. I've never been in trouble with the law or had to talk to a police officer before.

"Juliette, I know you were never friends with Georgia Howard, or that you had spent anytime in her presence." He explains and I turn to my mum confused but I'm met with the same expression.

"So why am I here?" I ask which earns me a smile from his pearly white teeth.

"Someone told me you've been doing your own investigating into Georgia Howards death." He says as he gets comfortable on the chair. I raise an eyebrow, meeting his know-at-all demeanor he's now giving off.

"Who told you that?" I ask and I'm met with a grin.

"Q did." He says casually and I feel my face drop as I turn to my mum. "He mentioned your name and that I should come to you if I want the evidence you've collected." He explains and I roll my eyes.

"So, you're a corrupt police officer?" I ask and he laughs.

"God no, Q and I go way back. He saved my life when I was just 18. When he reached out to me about this, granted I was hesitant at first, but I knew he was right and would always have a plan. So, I agreed."

I take in what he's just said and begin to process it slowly.

"So you're the police officer he mentioned."

He nods. "Guilty as charged. Now Q mentioned that you had brought your mum in on this, is that correct?" He asks and I pause. I never told him my mum was working on this with me.

I nod to him, and he smiles. "How about you tell me what you've gathered so far. I want to know everything." He says as he gets comfortable in his chair.

Ignoring my mums stares as I think of how to start explaining what we had worked out. I'm not sure if I can trust this police officer, and I'm starting to think I have trust issues in general.

"How about you tell me what you can about the case and I'll fill in any blanks I've uncovered." I say confidently. It makes sense, I might be able to keep some things to myself that I can hand over at later date.

He smiles at me and looks at my mum. "You've raised quite a little detective there Mrs Sanders. I'm impressed Juliette." He says as he leans forward and rests his arms on his knees, cupping his hands together.

"As you know, Georgia's body was found by her parents after they came home from work. She was found on the floor, unconscious. I will spare you the gruesome details as it wouldn't be appropriate."

He explains. "We gathered the evidence around the house and moved her body for a autopsy, there we found that she had a seriously lethal dosage of MDMA in her system." I sit back in my chair waiting to hear the rest. "Upon further investigation the medical examiner found that Georgia's body had been cleaned." He says and I frown, disgusted.

"Cleaned? After she had...?" My mum begins to ask but stops herself. "Oh Jesus Christ." My mother prays as her head falls into her hands.

"Did the medical examiner not clean the body?" I ask and Officer Bradley shakes his head.

"Not only had she been cleaned but so had the house." He explains and I get up from my chair, pacing as I'm processing this information.

"You trying to tell me you're going to be treating this as a murder?" I ask and nods his head gently. I begin to feel faint, why would Robert have me investigate something like this? My heart is pounding, and I find myself lowering myself to the floor against the wall. "I can't deal with this." I say placing my head in my hands. It's all too much and I'm trying to keep it together.

I feel someone place their hand on my leg which causes me to move my arms. I'm met with a worrying look from Officer Bradley who gently rubs my leg.

"I know this is a lot to understand Jules. It's a lot to take in. That's why from this moment on, you will not be investigating this any longer. It will be in the hands of the London Police Department." He reassures me and I manage a nod. That does bring me some sort of relief, but also begs the question as to why?

"Jules, we believe that you and your mum have uncovered all the missing answers that we need to this case. You investigated the drug ring, we investigated the murder. We need to join forces on this." He tells me.

"The reason Q sent you on this mission was because if anyone was going to be able to find out what was going on inside the school it was going to be you." He softly says. His tone of voice is comforting, and I feel my heart slowly begin to go back to normal.

"You can trust me." He says confidently and I meet his eyes.

"I'm finding it hard to trust people these days." I express, he's taken back by my answer but nods.

"Well let me prove to you that you can trust me. How about that?" He asks with a small smile. I look to my mum who looks just as distressed as me at this point.

"Okay." I say as I get up from the floor and he stands with me.

"How about you tell me everything you've uncovered."

CHAPTER TWENTY EIGHT

Damian Williams

I move through the crowds of people to get through to the lunch hall. If I want to earn Juliette's trust, I have to do this and not land myself in the shit. Again.

I grab myself a sandwich and begin to look around for Harrison and his little group of criminals. I discreetly pull my phone out of my pocket and click the voice notes section and start recording. She's going to need evidence, and I'm hoping that I can get her some.

I spot them in the far corner of the hall and make my way over. I'm still very unsure as to why Harrison has asked me to sit with them.

I make my way over to them, greeting them with a smile as I approach and gaining a warm welcome from Maura and a look from Holly.

"Here he is." Harrison exclaims as I approach.

"Hi." I say, my smile getting bigger as I grab a seat at their table. Harrison sticks his hand out for a bro-ish high five and gives me a nod.

"What's going on?" He asks with a smile. I shake my head in response.

"Nothing much, what's going on with you?" I ask and he very slowly shakes his head.

"Not a lot my friend." He responds and gives me a smile. "How you finding London is it different from where you're from in America?" He asks.

"Well, the UK is a lot different than the US." I explain. "Like you have different ways of saying things, that's weird." I say and they all laugh.

"We can say the same for you, you just simplify things." He laughs and I can't help but join in. It is very true.

"You aren't wrong." I agree.

"We have a proposition for you." He speaks. I'm briefly taken back by his sudden change in the subject. "Do you currently have a job?" He asks and I frown, slightly confused on where this is going.

"Not currently." I say looking around the group who are now listening in. Curious as to my answer. I have a gut feeling as to what he is going to ask, but surely, I'm thinking this isn't too easy.

"We have a little business on the side that is doing really well, and we need some extra hands." I almost want to laugh. Surely not, surely, he isn't asking me to be a part of the little drug den.

"What kind of business?" I ask. He looks to Maura and Holly who give him a nod.

"Can we trust you?" He asks quietly almost as a whisper. "How do we know you won't blab to someone?" He questions and I look to the girls who give me a very hard death stare.

"Well, I guess you're just going to have to trust me then." I say confidently. I'm hoping I've not ruined it. He gives a look to Maura and Holly one last time before getting super close, leaning over the table.

"We have a little underground business that we would like for you to be a part of. We each earn a cut and the money is good." He explains and I listen carefully and closely. But also get close enough hoping that my phone picks up the conversation.

"What kind of underground business?" I ask and he shakes his head.

"We make some of the best quality molly in London." He begins to explain. I feel my stomach do a dance. I've got him and the girls and they did it to themselves.

"You have a lot of balls asking me to join when there is a cop going round investigating that girl's death." I point out and Harrison doesn't blink. He knows I'm right.

"Oh, I wouldn't worry, we've pointed all fingers to Juliette Sanders. She's currently having a interview with that officer." Maura says, a sour look on her face. I feel my blood begin to boil. With how cold and casual Maura said that I'm guessing this has been planned.

"Wait, don't you tutor her?" Holly asks and I nod knowing that if I say anything my only tone with be sheer annoyance and I don't want them to know that.

"Everyone seems to get tutored these days. Georgia had to be tutored for almost everything. That Trevor Thompson guy. He's so weird." Holly says a disgusted look on her face.

"He's a loner too. But he does what we need him too."

"Jules Sanders will get what's coming to her. We have faked so much evidence against her that there is no way that they won't arrest her."

"She's so weird. Some guy in a hoodie came and saved her the other day it was so stupid. All we were going to do was scare her. But some American dude came to save the day." Maura rolls her eyes; the annoyed tone only frustrates me more. How can they think they could scare her and just get away with it?

"Is he related to you?" Harrison asks and I laugh.

"Just cause he's American he is related to me?" I laugh and he smiles, clearly not impressed by my answer. "No. He's not related."

"Good. So, what do you say?" Harrison asks and I sit forward meeting his gaze.

"I want to see it first before I can decide. I won't say anything to anyone, make me sign a contract I don't care. But I want to see what I might be signing up for."

Harrison hesitates, not sure how to respond or react to my dealbreaker. If it's where I think it is, I want him to either show me so I have evidence or admit where it is so I have that on the footage.

"Fine, we will get you to sign a contract later." Harrison agrees while getting up and putting his bag over his shoulder. The school bell goes off meaning that it's time to get to our 4th lesson of the day.

"We have an exam. Meet us at the library after school." He says before they all walk off leaving me there, shocked to my core that they actually just admitted about the drug den and that they are a part of it. I turn my back to the teachers after I watch Harrison and the twins walk towards the gym to do their exam and pull out my phone to stop the recording. I quickly move it to a section hoping you can hear. I feel my heart skip a beat as I hear the words. "We have a little underground business."

I have to physically stop myself from screaming *yes*! I put the phone is my pocket and quickly exit the hall and try to find a member of staff that doesn't look like they are involved in the drug den.

I go to the reception desk and smile sweetly at the

receptionist.

"Hello."

"Hi love, you alright?" She asks back and I smile bigger.

"I'm great, I was just wondering if you could tell me where the police officer is conducting interviews. One of his co workers dropped some paperwork off for him. They asked me to give it to him." I smile at her and she quickly checks her system.

"Well aren't you sweet. He's doing the interviews in the language block. Go right out of here, up the stairs through the double doors and it's the first door on your left." She says with a grin. I nod to her.

"Thank you so much." I say before taking a right and walking quickly up to the language block.

CHAPTER TWENTY NINE

Jules Sanders

My mum and I place all the evidence in front of Officer Bradley who listens carefully to any theories or speculations that I may have. He doesn't interrupt, which I'm grateful for. I'm nervous as I'm having to present my case to him, everything me, my family and the boys have gathered over the past few days.

I have to admit, if I didn't have Robert, the criminal, on the other end of the MacBook, I don't think I would be able to solve it.

"I agree with you on the basis that someone else is involved." Officer Bradley says after looking the evidence. "Someone is getting them the ingredients and it's not the school."

He looks over what I'm assuming is a report of some kind once more. "So how does Georgia fit in to all of this? What is everyone's theories?" He asks.

"Maybe she found out about the drug den? She could have said she was going to expose them?" My mum says and I nod as that was my theory too, my only thought is that the photos and the distress on their faces when they found out about Georgia's death.

"Harrison, Holly and Maura were all at the school when Georgia was killed." Officer Bradley says.

"You're sure on that?" I ask, and he gives me a very confident nod.

"Harrison was at football practice, and the twins were at the prom committee meeting." He says as he shows us what they wrote in their interview. I exhale, so that is them out of the spin.

"So, what do you know about Georgia's last movements before she died?"

"Georgia left school the same time as everyone else, got in a car and arrived home at 3:50pm. Her security gates confirm that." He explains pulling up the footage on his computer.

I stand up from my chair and begin pacing thinking of all the theories. Now Georgia wasn't one to do drugs, everyone knew that. Yes, people change, but not Georgia. She was known as a princess, extremely high maintenance, cared about what went into her body. The one thing she didn't care for was her studies. She wanted to be a model and school wasn't a strong point for her. Mikki and Katy had mentioned they had overheard Georgia say that the school said if she didn't pick up her studies before the exams, they were going to make her retake year 11.

Suddenly it dawns on me, she must have picked up in her classes otherwise she wasn't allowed to go to prom. Except she was on the committee. So why hadn't she gone to the meeting the night she had died?

"Officer Bradley? Did Georgia's mum mention about a tutor?" I ask curiously. There is no way Georgia, who was in the bottom of every class managed to change her grades herself.

"She did but no one knows his name." He says as he looks over the notes he has. "They said he was quiet, quite scrawny. He looked like he could be in their year or the year above."

I begin to think hard, I doubt that someone in year 11 is helping her, they were probably in the year above they have their own exams to be worrying about.

"I don't know anyone from year 12." I say to him, and he smiles and begins working away on the computer before pulling up the year 12 school photos.

"You might." He says with a hopeful smile.

"I'll try." I say as I sit in his chair and begin scrolling through the sea of year 12 boys. The school isn't even that big and the more I scroll through the photos, I realise that this is possibly useless. I know no boys in year 12. And why would I? Year 9 means you are still fresh meat. You will know nothing unless it's mentioned via gossip.

I keep scrolling and then a name seems to catch my attention and I stop. *Trevor...* why does that name ring a bell?

"Jules?"

"That name rings a bell, and I can't remember why." I say pointing at Trevor Thompsons photo. "It's more than likely nothing."

There is a sudden knock at the door and Officer Bradley looks at us, confusion on his face.

"Maybe it's Mrs. Hadley?" I say quietly and he shakes his head. He gets up from his chair and makes his way to the door. He opens it gently and I hear an American voice and I turn to my mum who looks just as intrigued as me.

The door then shuts, and Officer Bradley looks to the both of us as he holds a phone.

"Apparently you need to listen to this." He says as he sits down getting comfortable and pressing play.

"Georgia was getting tutored in almost every subject. That Trevor Thompson guy. He's so weird."

"Oh my god." I say out loud. Suddenly it dawns on me why the name rings a bell. I click pause on the phone and begin to pace around the room. "Trevor had asked Georgia on a date, and she very publicly told him no. It really embarrassed him."

Officer Bradley's eyebrows raise in suspicion. "When was this?"

"Oh, last year. It was in the food hall. She was so mean about it." I tell him. I know this because of my two little gossips that I can best friends. I have never wanted to hug them more in my life.

"Reckon he's the kind of guy to hold a grudge?" Officer Bradley asks, and I shrug my shoulders.

"Don't know." I speak. "Do you know anything else about him?"

He shakes his head. "Nothing on the database. He has contacts for both parents on his school file. If I was to do a background check it would take a lot longer than you both being here till the end of the day."

I feel myself exhale loudly; I want to be able to solve this as quickly as possible. It seems like we have all the missing pieces for each other's case, we just can't seem to prove that Trevor was the one in Georgia's house, or that he had anything to do with the drug den.

"Wait." He says causing mine and my mums head to turn in his direction. "The email address for his dad is a work one." He says pulling up his phone and typing something in. I watch the realisation hit his face as he turns the phone to us.

"S. Thompson Pharmaceuticals."

"What do they do?"

"They make pills Jules." My mum says and I can't help but feel like everything is coming together. "What's his dad's name?"

"Samuel Thompson." Officer Bradley says looking up from the computer. *Samuel Thompson.*

I frown when I hear the name leave his mouth. "Jules?" My mum asks softly. "What is it?"

"That name…" I begin to say while looking through the piles of paper that we've gathered. "I've seen it before." I say while looking through the piles of paper and realizing it's not there. "Mum where's the list for the black-market buyers?"

She begins to look around the room same as me, rummaging through the blueprints and the pile of papers next to her.

"Here." Officer Bradley says handing me the piece of paper. I go through the names one by one, crossing off any that don't match to what I'm looking for.

Then I feel my heart almost leap out of my chest when I see it.

"There." I say placing the paper down and pointing to the list.

Samuel. J Thompson.

"Jesus…" Officer Bradley mutters underneath his breath. He pauses for a moment trying to gather his thoughts. "But if he has a pharmaceutical company, why would he need to buy it on the black market?"

"Avoid suspicion just like the school, they wouldn't want to be flagged for high amounts of it." Mum explains.

I nod. "If they are going to be ordering a large amount it would mean that they would need quicker shipments and less paperwork. That's why they went to the black market." I speak.

"I could ask Q if there was any way he could send over the shipping address. But I think we've helped you solve this case. You just have to finish off the bits we can't do." I say with a smile.

He laughs at me and nods as he takes a seat. "I think both of you should consider joining the police academy."

Little does he know that's the route I want to take.

"Officer, I think this proves that either Trevor is using his dads name to buy it, or his father is in on it." My mum pipes up. I turn to her who meets my gaze. She has worry in her eyes, and all of this has caused it. Finding out I'm adopted, my father working as God knows what, and getting a case to solve.

I turn to Officer Bradley who rises from his chair. He takes a deep breath before turning to smile at both of us.

"I had this case 2 years. We thought it was open and closed when we arrested Tyler Dunston last year. But then that same pill popped up in a house raid in South London and I realised this was far from over." He says wandering around the room. "I never thought a fourteen-year-old and her mum would solve a case that's kept me up at night for the past 7 months, in 8 days. I'm impressed." He says with a smile. I feel a hand grab mine and squeeze it gently. I turn to my mum who looks as though she's about to cry.

"I can officially say that you have helped solve the case. But you are right Juliette. I need to start doing my job in working out who killed Georgia." He says as he exhales loudly.

"I have a theory." I say to him, and he smiles once more.

"We do love your theories."

I laugh. "What if he didn't mean to kill her? If that's what happened." I say softly. He raises his eyebrows as he looks to my mum.

"You're thinking it was an accident?" He says surprise in his voice. I smile at him.

"That's for you to find out officer. I can't do all the work for you."

Laughter fills the room. "Very true." He agrees.

◆ ◆ ◆

After we sign all of the evidence over to the London Police, we get ready to say our goodbyes. I can't help but feel relief that we've finally been able to help close their case, or should I say almost close it. Gathered it may take them a while to gather the rest of the evidence. But I'm hopeful that it will be soon and that they all get what's coming to them.

"Mrs. Sanders, I would recommend that you take Jules out of school early. Unless you want to go to your last lesson?" He asks and I scoff.

"Absolutely not." I say as I head towards the door.

"Juliette before you go." He says stopping me in my tracks. "The person who gave me the phone, he mentioned that after they had spoken about Trevor there were some quite upsetting things mentioned about you." He says while handing me the phone.

My mum turns to look at me and then back at Officer Bradley. "What could they possibly be saying about her!" My mum exclaims and I place my hand gently on her arm.

"I don't want to know." I say softly. "Whatever it is. I don't need to know. It won't change my life for the better. It would only hurt my feelings. And they are already hurt, battered and bruised." I say softly with a small smile. I do not need to know. It would only cause me to have more negativity in my life. It wouldn't change anything.

"You sure?" He asks once more as I open the door to leave.

"Very sure." I nod.

We head to reception and my mum signs me out, telling the receptionist I have an appointment. The receptionist complains and says are you aware it will ruin Jules' perfect attendance, but I don't care. I don't want to be here for a second longer incase Mrs. Hadley comes out of the office.

My mum signs the forms and we leave the building walking down the walkway towards the car park, the air is fresh, and I've never felt more free. The weight of this case is finally off my shoulders, and I feel like I'm free, in one way or another.

"Jules do you wanna go and do something? Just us?" Mum asks sweetly making me smile.

"Is this because you want to talk about everything?" I ask as we reach the car. When I turn to her, I see the distress in her face, I know she wants to talk I just know I don't have a lot to say.

"I feel like I owe you an explanation, and I haven't really checked in on how you're feeling." She says almost in tears.

I go to her, grabbing onto her arms and holding them gently. "Mum I don't hate you. I understand why you didn't tell me." I say to her, and she removes one of her arms from my grip to wipe her tears that are now flowing down her face. "I get it, you were asked by Robert not to. How could I hate you for protecting me? For giving me an amazing life? For giving me a sister, and a loving family and roof over my head." I say as I go into my bag and grab a packet of tissues. When you have friends that are hopeless romantics, tissues are a necessity.

I hand her one. "I'm mad at the way I found

out and at a certain person, but I could never be mad at you." I say softly to her. Somehow this only makes her cry harder, and in order to stop the tears I throw my arms around her and hug her. She weeps softly into my shoulder for a few minutes, and I let her. It's been a hard few days for us both. I know I'm a Sanders whether or not that is by blood. But unfortunately, by blood I am Robert Quinten's daughter. And whatever comes with the Quinten name, I'm going to assume is only heartbreak and bloodshed and I'm not sure if I want to be a part of that just yet. It's still a lot to grasp.

My mum breaks our embrace and gathers herself, so she doesn't look less puffy. "Your dad would be so proud at how you're handling this. He was so worried." She says in light whimpers.

"Well, I am my father's daughter, and if I didn't deal with hard situations by making a joke, I wouldn't be a Sanders." I say as I open the car door, hinting for her to do the same. "Mum get in the car and stop crying, I'm not going to become a rebellious teenager." I reassure her.

She chuckles as she puts her bag into the backseat. "I think you're getting there if you keep hanging out with Damian and Spencer." She laughs as she climbs into the car.

"Well, I would say you know I'm safe with those two, but Damian I'm not sure I can trust, and Spencer is just enjoying his last days on earth till Robert finds out that I know who he is." I say putting my seatbelt on and then realising I'm missing a brother. "On the other hand, I would probably be dead if I was stuck with Rodger, so I'd count your blessings that it's under your roof and it's with *Tweedledumb* and *Tweedledumber*." I laugh.

She doesn't say anything, she just looks at me and takes my hand in hers and squeezes gently. "I know you haven't forgiven Rodger for what he did, and I know you probably wont. But you should forgive Damian, Jules. He really just wanted to keep you safe." She says softly and squeezes my hand once more. I know she's right; Spencer and Damian didn't do anything wrong. It just hurts a little from Damian, because he was meant to be my friend.

"I'll talk to him eventually." Quickly wanting to move on from the subject. Pulling my hand slowly from hers I place it on my knee and begin to look around.

"Where are we going?" I ask. It takes her a few seconds to respond, clearly, I'm not hiding the fact that I'm still upset with Damian.

"How about we drop the car somewhere and go to have a look in *Waterstones*." Mum says, a smile slowly growing on her face and on mine.

"That is a wonderful idea." I say with a grin.

"Thought you'd like it."

CHAPTER THIRTY

Damian Williams

The freezing cold breeze hits my face and I shiver. I miss America, I miss the heat. Why is the UK so cold?

I check my watch once more and notice it's now 10 minutes after the original meet up time with Harrison. Either he has forgot, or he is playing me like a fool.

I'm debating ditching in a few minutes if he doesn't turn up. The more I stand here, the more I feel as though it's a test. If Harrison and his little gang of criminals wanted me to prove my loyalty surely I've proved it by turning up?

My thoughts are suddenly eased when I see Harrison and Holly come round the corner quickly, looking over their shoulders.

"Didn't think you would show." Harrison states as he walks towards me.

"I'm full of surprises." I say with a smile, which he meets before looking at Holly who rolls her eyes.

"You two done? It's freezing out here." Holly says, her tone annoyed as I tilt my head at her attitude.

"Considering your friend died, you seem in quite a hurry to continue the operation of the drug that potentially killed her?" I state. Her eyes go wide as she looks to Harrison. He smirks, almost as if he is impressed by my truthful statement.

"You know nothing." She states, annoyance in her voice.

"Don't I?" I taunt. She doesn't know what to say, but she looks to Harrison as a way of saying deal with me.

"I like him. Come on, lets go." He instructs as he pushes past me and towards the school. I follow behind like a puppy, impressed that after that comment he didn't just tell me to go home. To be fair it was a awful comment to make, but it was the truth.

"In our defence Damian, we didn't know Georgia was going to die. And although her death is tragic, like the saying goes; the show must go on." He says as we walk into the school. I'm trying to stay close so I don't miss anything that's said, or miss anything that might happen.

"So where you taking me?" I ask as we make our way towards the library. *Bingo.* All of us were right, they moved it underneath the library.

"You'll see." He says with a smirk before turning back around and inputting a code. 7 8 4 1. I'll have to remember that just incase. We walk down a set of steep stairs, and come to a wooden door. He stands in front of it and crosses his arms, almost like he's waiting for me to give him the password.

"Once you go past this door there is no way out. You do as we tell you, when to do it and you don't tell anyone this exists. Understand?" He says harshly. His tone a warning.

"Got it." I say seriously. He looks to Holly who I notice gives him a nod, hopefully hinting to open the door. After a few moments, he does and reveals the gold mine. *The drug den.* In the flesh. Wow.

"This is where we make the best quality molly in London. We have some of the wealthiest clients, from celebrities, to business owners and lastly trust fund kids with way too much money." He begins to explain as we walk through.

On the tables are boxes full of packets of pills, no doubt being ready to go to their buyer very soon. In the corner of the room I notice Mrs Holden, lab coat and goggles on, mixing what seems to be a new batch of molly.

"A year we bring in about £4 million, but that is a good year, it's been quite slow this year since the last site got raided by the police." He explains as we continue to walk through and I take everything in.

"The raid lost you a lot of clients I'm assuming?"

He scoffs at my question and picks up a packet of drugs. "We only lost a few that were made aware, but thankfully it was kept out of the media." He says as he holds the packet of drug up at the light. "This baby goes for £60 a packet." He explains as he hands me the drugs. All of us are very anti-drug considering our guardian is very anti-murder if things don't get done. I don't know much about the drug business, that is something Robert has never invested any money into. But he knows how it works, and I get the sense I'm going to know soon enough from this little band of criminals.

"Expensive." I say as I hand the drug back. He scoffs before turning on his heel and walking towards a door at the end of the hall.

"If you want the best quality, you have to make people believe it." He almost shouts as he is in front of me now, walking quickly towards the door.

"So is this just a trial shift or am I going to get my hands dirty?" I question which causes him to stop in his tracks.

He turns to me, a smile plastered on his face at my bold question. Holly stands quiet, unsure on what Harrison's answer will be.

"Mrs. Hadley would like to see you first, to get you to sign some documents. So it covers our asses." He says as he turns on his heels once more and opens the door at the end.

And to my surprise I see Mrs. Hadley, Trevor and Maura at her computer. They look up at us and I feel slightly nervous as Mrs. Hadley moves from her chair elegantly and makes her way over to where I'm standing.

"Mr. Williams." She greets me as she extends her hand. "I had a feeling that when you were added to my school that you had a sketchy background. So tell me, what have you been in jail for?" She asks with a smirk, which I reciprocate.

"Possession."

"Can you give me a reason as to why I was told you would be starting the school and why you didn't go through the regular process?" She asks while placing her hand that was shaking mine only a moment ago into her blazer trouser pocket.

"My family have money and are close to multiple members of the school board." I state.

She smiles to me before looking to Harrison and giving him a nod.

"Now that you've seen our little operation, you'll know that if anything is ever leaked to the press or to the police, I will know it was you. I maybe inclined to deal with you accordingly." She remarks.

I scoff in her face which earns me a raised eyebrow. "Is that a threat Mrs. Hadley?" I ask with a smirk.

"Consider it a warning. Now, sign the god damn papers and get out of my office. You start tomorrow." She almost growls and walks round to her desk and takes a seat once again.

"Welcome to the H. Operation."

◆ ◆ ◆

I feel a sense of accomplishment as I walk back home. Not only did I get to see the drug den in operation, but I'm now part of it, and I am feeling high off the adreneline.

I make my way through the park looking over my shoulder every few moments to make sure I'm not followed. Its 8pm, and thankfully it's starting to get light outside which is good so I can see where I'm going.

"They buy it?" A voice in front of me shouts and I laugh a little.

"Every word. Did I give a Oscar-Winning performance?" I joke and he chuckles.

"I think so." he laughs.

"Well as long as they don't suspect anything I think we will have enough evidence to put them away for a long time."

"How long do you need me to do this?" I ask as I hand over my mic and the cap with the camera.

"Not long." He says as he gratefully takes the mic and hat from me.

"Officer Bradley?" I ask as he hands the mic and cap to another undercover officer. He looks up at me, hinting for me to continue.

"Don't tell Juliette about this." I say to him and he smiles before walking a little closer towards to me and he places his hand firmly on my shoulder.

"She won't find out until this is all done."

CHAPTER THIRTY ONE

3 Weeks.

Nothing.

Nothing has happened, no one has been arrested, no searches have been done. Just silence.

The day after my interview with Officer Bradley, Mikki and Katy were notorious in demanding what we discussed and why I missed my entire lesson with them. I just said I had signed a form and couldn't say anything. They didn't like that answer, and demanded, quite loudly in front of everyone in the food hall, that I tell them what happened. I repeated it but did earn some looks from the drug den crew.

Marcus is still in London, but is currently doing another task for Robert before flying back to the US tomorrow. But he has popped by the house a few times to check in. I'm grateful for that because on every new visit I always have a new question and he's more than happy to answer.

Damian has been avoiding me in school like the black plague, I know something is going on with him, but every time he and Spencer come for dinner, he denies anything is going on.

Because Damian came too late into the school year, they decided not to have him sit his exams, one because he's too late, and two because he mentioned he has his American SATS. Somehow that qualifies here.

Spencer is trying to live life to the fullest just incase Robert does find out that Rodger went all psychotic. But he seems nicer and that I'll gladly accept that. My grandad described him as a sweet, he's hard on the outside but soft in the middle. You just have to get there. Spencer didn't like being compared to a Werther's Original. But that is now his new nickname. Sweet.

It's the last school week, where teachers give up trying to teach us anything and put movies on. After everything that has happened over the last few weeks, I can't help but feel grateful. I've started to come to terms with the fact that Paul wasn't my dad, and that Amy isn't my mum. But the more I think about it, the more it doesn't matter. Robert will never be my dad; he didn't raise me. I know from multiple people he wanted to, but that doesn't change the fact that instead of raising a baby, he put me up for adoption and adopted older kids. I think that's what is upsetting me the most, I feel as though I wasn't good enough. I feel like I was the burden. No matter how many people tell me that it was to protect me and that Robert has enemies. That doesn't matter. How could you bring a child into this world then not have any responsibility for them, but then adopt 6 other children to make yourself feel better? I find myself starting to resent him and I can't stop myself. I really need to start seeing it from his perspective, but I'm struggling. I'm not jealous, although it may be coming off that way. I do get on with Marcus, we bounce off each other, have the same sort of humor and sarcasm. My mum loves him, she thinks even if I decide to have nothing to do with Robert, that it's good for me to have some sort of connection. That connection being Marcus.

I cannot complain though, my life has been something of a movie the past few weeks. Not even *Jane Rizzoli* from *Tess Gerritsen*'s series could of solved something so quick. I mean she might of, but I want to think I'd be quicker.

My mum and I have been very close these past few weeks. We've been doing more activities as a family, and I think my mum feels as though this has brought us together. I'm so grateful for my mum, who has given me an amazing life, an amazing family. She outdid herself, although she would never admit it.

I walk through to the food hall to meet Katy and Mikki who greet me with warming smile, patting down on the seat next to her. I head towards them, taking a bite out of my apple.

I'm suddenly stopped in my tracks by Harrison, who has an joker-like smile on his face. He begins to get a little too close and I back up. He gives me sad eyes before rubbing his hand slowly across his chiseled jaw.

"Juliette, I hope you know this isn't personal." He says before turning his head towards the window, that shows a swarm of police officers and detectives. I notice Officer Bradley, who when notices me and who I'm standing with, gives his head a nudge telling me to move out of the way. I turn to Harrison who still has that smug look on his face and I'm trying so hard not to roll my eyes.

"Karma is a bitch, Harrison." I say as I walk away not stopping the smile that is growing on my face. I take a seat next to Mikki whos brows are frowning, confused by my encounter.

"What the heck is going on?" She exclaims pointing to the officers outside who begin to make their way into the school. I suddenly feel someone stand beside me and I turn to see Damian. He slowly turns to me, giving me a wink before turning back and watching all of the Officers separate and walk down different halls.

We watch in shock, as I one by one Harrison, Holly and Maura are arrested and their charges listed in front of the entire hall. As they are about to be escorted out, Mrs Hadley comes running through the other doors, shouting some sort of nonsense.

"Excuse me! You can't be arresting my students!" She exclaims getting closer to Officer Bradley.

"I can, and I will. But I wouldn't worry about it, you're going with them." He says while turning Mrs Hadley around and placing handcuffs on her. She's shouting mountains of verbal abuse at Officer Bradley, who looks at me and only rolls his eyes which causes me to smile a little bit.

Mrs. Hadley turns around, and makes direct contact with Damian, "You should be arresting him too." She shouts flustered.

Officer Bradley looks to Damian and extends his hand. "Thank you for going undercover man." He smiles while Damian meets his hand and shakes it.

I feel my mouth drop open as I turn to Damian who is smiling, avoiding my eye contact. "I'm pleased you didn't listen to the rest of that voice recording." He says briefly glancing then back up at Mrs Hadley who has steam coming out of her ears. She turns her eyes to me, filled with rage and anger and mine meet hers with absolute joy.

"Everything was going right. Why didn't you go

down for it." Maura shouts through her anger. I look to Officer Bradley who gives me a nod.

"You should really do your research and check who's a police informant." I say with a grin. I hear gasps around me, no doubt from Mikki and Katy. I watch their faces drop as realisation sinks deep into their souls. I turn to Mrs. Hadley who at this point, is crying in anger.

"Enjoy prison."

Mrs. Hadley makes a questionable angry noise as they are all dragged away. I watch as in order, The ringleader, the dealer and the packagers are all lead away from the school in slow motion for everyone to see. "Oh my god more people have been arrested!" A student shouts and surely enough, Mrs. Holden, Mr. Green and an engineering teacher Mr. Banks, are lead away one by one.

"Oh my god Trevor the freak too!" Someone exclaims and we watch as two police offers have him arm by arm making him walk out of the school. Sooner or later we will find out if Trevor killed Georgia, I would like to hope he didn't. But we can't be so sure.

While everyone watches the window. I turn to Damian, who meets my gaze with a smile.

"Thank you." I say as I get up and throw my arms around him, hugging him tight. We needed this hug, I needed this. I was having so much anger towards him when in reality he did what he said he was going to do. He protected me.

We exit out of the embrace and look at each other for a brief moment. "Friends?" He asks with a smile.

I laugh, not expecting that to be the first thing out of his mouth.

"Yeah, we are friends again." I say as I pull him back in for a hug which he accepts.

"Jesus, took you long enough." He mutters at my shoulder. I lightly smack him on the back which causes him to laugh.

"Don't ruin it." I say in the hug.

"Sorry." He murmurs as I pull away. Officer Bradley walks over to us, a smile on his face which is nice to see.

"I want to thank you both." He says extending his hand to Damian once more who gladly accepts it.

"It was no problem." He says as he looks to me. "This is the person you need to thank." He says pointing at me.

Officer Bradley extends his hand to me, and I accept it. "You get called a snitch you come to me. I'll have them all arrested." He says with a smile. I laugh, more than likely I'll be called a snitch, but when you look at it from my perspective, justice will hopefully be served.

"Any news on if..." I begin to say and he stops me.

"Not yet, but I will tell you if you would like to know." He says with a small smile.

"Yeah, I would, I'd like to know whether or not I

was right." I say with a laugh which both of them join in.

"I want to say you're not, but secretly I'm hoping you are. Either way, they are all looking at a lengthy jail sentence." He says before looking down the corridor. "The school will be closing; I'd call your parents. This is now an active crime scene." He says before being called over by one of the officers and saying goodbye.

I turn to Damian who gives me a nod and I pull out my phone to call my mum and give her the news.

"Jules!" Mikki exclaims punching me in the arm. "Why didn't you tell us!" She shouts.

"OW!" I exclaim rubbing my arm. I am going to recommend that this girl take up boxing classes. She throws a mean punch. "Because I couldn't, and I still can't tell you anything. So don't even think about trying to beat it out of me."

"Damn." She whines while I call my mum. "Also why weren't you two friends?" Mikki asks and I look to Damian while the phone rings. I watch him stutter and I will not lie, it brings me a little joy.

"Er- Because er-." He says looking to me to help him and I just smile hinting he is getting no help from me. "I shouted at her while teaching her fractions." He says eventually. I raise my eyebrows, I guess it's a good cover story. Except those two won't believe it.

"Okay... if you say so." Katy says. My mum finally

picks up and I explain the situation to her.

After I get off the phone with my mum, we are all moved to the new gym in order for the police to keep kids away from the crime scene underneath the library and so parents can pick up their kids.

Mum is with us within the hour, and we are all told by someone who is from the school board, that the school will be closed until further notice. Understandably, parents are absolutely livid that this happened while their kids were at school and in the care of Mrs. Hadley, Mrs. Holden and the rest of the teachers that have been arrested.

My mum is refusing for me to go back to the school, indicating that she will be finding me a new school for September, and I can't say I'm mad about that considering what's happened. Katy and Mikki's parents are the same. All the parents had a quick conversation about it and all agreed that they will be sending us to a new school. Making sure it's one that we end up together and for that I'm grateful. I'm not great at making new friends and I certainly don't want to lose the ones I have.

"Jules what are you doing over the summer?" Mikki's mum asks me as we walk towards the car. The parents have had their good moan about the school, including my mum who has known about the whole situation for weeks but acts like she's as clueless as the rest of them.

"Not sure yet." I say sweetly as we reach our

cars. "I think I might go and see some family who live away." I say and my mum's head whips round, and she looks at me stunned. Granted I should have told her that I'm thinking of maybe going to meet Robert. But I'm still on the fence about it. Robert and I haven't spoken since he gave me that list 3 weeks ago.

"That sounds lovely." Mikki's mum says with a smile.

We say our goodbyes and me and the girls start to plan some things to do during the summer like sleepovers, movie nights and days out.

Mum and I climb in the car while waiting for Ava to finish school. We haven't got more than 30 minutes since the parents spoke for so long. I don't mind the wait as it means I can speak to my mum about how I'm feeling about potentially meeting Robert.

"You upset with me?" I ask her as we sit in silence in the car. The silence was deafening, and it was becoming painful to sit in it.

"Oh Jules, no. I didn't realise you were considering it." She says softly, her voice also quiet and I can hear the hurt in it. My heart sinks, I really should have told her.

"I'm still not sure if I want to do it. It was just a possibility. I know he isn't a good man; the family isn't a good family. But maybe I can get some closure as to why I'm feeling so uncertain on where I stand." I say quietly, my voice very slowly breaking. Over the past few weeks, I've had a lot of time to reflect on everything. On the way I found out, to me now being, by blood a Quinten.

Now for anyone my age, it's earth shattering. And I'm stuck in the middle. "I feel like I'm having a identity crisis." I cry to her. My mum turns to me, tears falling down her cheeks. It's been hard on both of us, no matter how much we say everything is okay, and we are okay. It comes down to it's life changing for both of us, not to mention Ava, who still doesn't know I'm not her sister. By blood anyway.

"Juliette Amanda Sanders." My mum cries pulling me in for a hug. "I understand how your feeling, you want to know where you came from, you want to know what he's like." She says in the hug as I gently cry on her shoulder. "You are old enough to make your own decisions and when it comes to meeting your birth father, if that gives you closure darling, please do it. I'll come with you. We can do it on your terms." She says as she pulls me from the hug and wipes me tears that have fell to my cheeks. "Granted it's more going to be on his terms. He is a criminal after all." She jokes and it causes me to laugh.

She's very right, I probably won't have any say in how, or when I meet Robert. And who says he wants to meet me? He wanted to talk to me, doesn't mean he wants a relationship with me.

"You're right. It will probably be on his terms." I agree as I wipe my eyes. "I have a lot of questions." I say as I continue to wipe my tears.

"Honestly darling, I don't blame you and I do feel like as his daughter you do have a right to know." My mum says softly tucking my hair behind my ear. "But are you ready for that massive life change? To really know what he's like?" She explains and I nod. I've already thought about all this, whether or not I'm ready. I'm not 100% when I'll meet him, I just know I need to for my own sake. And to understand why to him I wasn't good enough to be part of the family.

"I know. I'm still not sure though. So, I wouldn't worry about it." I say with a smile which she returns.

"Oh sweetie. Well, when you are. You tell me and we can do it together." She says softly placing her hand on my thigh and squeezes it gently. "I love you." She says softly. I look up to meet her very teary eyes which mirror hers.

"I love you more."

CHAPTER THIRTY TWO

Since the school is closed, and both mum and I have handed over our informant statements as well as Damian. Summer holidays have come early, and I find myself trying to keep busy. I haven't opened the MacBook for a few weeks, and I don't want to. I'm worried in case he tells me I didn't do enough or that he found out that I had massive amounts of help.

Damian has popped by a few times, and I still haven't seen Rodger, which I'm grateful for. I needed him to stay away from me. It's the best thing for both of us. I hate him and I hate what he did, and he couldn't care less, or he says he doesn't. I can't be 100% on that. He did after all go undercover and take photos for the case as well as get the blueprints of the school. I should thank him for helping but I'm still not sure I can face him.

Officer Bradley had come round the house to let us know that unfortunately Georgia's death was planned and that Trevor had wanted to get revenge since the situation in the food hall. They found a blog online that incriminated him even further and he had planned every single step of Georgia's death and that breaks my heart.

Georgia from what I saw wasn't the nicest person, cared more about her appearance and who she was seen with than how well she did in school. But with that aside, she shouldn't have died the way she did. No one deserves to die like that.

As I put away my schoolbooks for the year, I keep glancing to the box of doom as I've decided to call it. The box of presents that i've received from Robert and no doubt Robert's siblings. The only time I ever looked in it was to add another present. I suddenly feel a wave of curiosity as I can't remember exactly what's in the box. And now that I know that they are from people that I'm related to. The presents inside, to me have a whole new meaning.

I place my books on my bookshelf and walk over to the box of doom. I can remember certain things from inside of it, but I'm not exactly sure on the full contents. I get on my knees, and slowly open the box lid to reveal the insides. The first thing that gets my attention is the Harrods teddy bear that was sent for my first birthday. I pull it out and realise it is quite cute. The blue little coat it has on is still in perfect condition as is the bear. I decide that should be on display and place it on my bed next to my other toys that have been given to me as gifts over the years.

I slowly one by one pull out toys that were given to me when I was growing up, and clothes that I sort of remember wearing. I think my mum placed these in here, I don't remember seeing them, I would of thought mum and dad would have threw them out since they didn't fit me anymore.

I pick up a black box and slowly open it to reveal a necklace with my first initial on. I can't help but smile, I remember getting this one a few years back and telling myself I'm not going to wear some creepy stalker persons present. How silly to think that now; although he is still a stranger, by going through these presents I do start to feel a little closer to him and try to understand him.

He never forgot my birthday.

Or Christmas. I have all of that money saved in a trust for when I'm older and want to do things. Like possibly get my own car or house or start my career. I don't know how much is in there and it doesn't matter. What matters is that he always made me feel included in some way. Although in saying this I still feel resentment, I mean after all – he gave up one kid and adopted 6 others. I have a right to feel as though I wasn't good enough even though deep down, I know that isn't true.

No matter how many times Marcus tells me the story, or how many times the Williams brothers tell me theirs, it doesn't change how I feel. And I do feel hate towards him. I want to have the option to ask him all the questions that have been buzzing around in my head.

Mum has asked me a few times how I'm feeling and whether I have a answer on if I would like to meet Robert and in all honesty, I'm still unsure. Probably because he doesn't know that I know. I doubt the boys told him; they are trying to stay alive for as long as possible.

A knock at the door startles me and I turn my head to see my Grandad Norman standing there, very gently waving his stick. "Hello Romeo." He greets me as he walks in and sits on the bed. My Grandad hasn't been able to walk our stairs in years and I find myself surprised by his visit.

"How long did it take you to get up the stairs?" I chuckle and he shakes his head. I can see he is slightly out of breath, and I stand up from the floor and take a seat next to him on the bed.

"I had some liquid courage." He jokes with me, and I notice the dicky ticker in his hand, and I laugh with him. That drink smells disgusting.

"What can I help you with?" I ask sweetly. He turns his head and has a nosey on over to the box and it's contents. "You going through the box of doom?" He asks. My eyebrows raise at his choice in name for the box. "You called it a box of doom when you were 5. Kind of stuck in my head." He chuckles and I can't help but join in.

"I thought I'd have a look through, see what was in there." I say as I grab the Harrods teddy and lightly rub my thumb over it's cheek.

"Was waiting for you to eventually look through." He says carefully catching my attention. He laughs. "Juliette, curiosity killed the cat." He explains as he picks up the black box with the initial necklace in.

"You know, I doubt he even knew your name in the beginning. No one would have told him. But the J, it symbolises the life you would have had with him and his family, but also symbolises the life that you have with us. Believe it or not Jules, your birthname isn't far off the one your mum and dad gave you. They wanted something so he could always find you." He explains carefully taking the necklace out of the box. "I think he felt a lot of guilt after giving you up." He says softly while placing the necklace around my neck.

"You crawl up those stairs to tell me something?" I ask sarcastically and he can sense that.

"Your mum mentioned that you wanted to meet him, or that you were thinking of meeting him. I think it's a good idea." He says as he moves the J so it sits perfectly in the middle of my chest.

"You think?" I ask softly. He nods to me; he's trying to help me make a decision and I'm feeling grateful. My Grandad chooses to see the good in everyone and I know he's trying to ease the question that's been running in my mind the past few weeks.

"Juliette, he was young when he had you, he is going to make many mistakes." He says in Robert's defense. "But I choose to believe that the decision he made was to keep you safe, whether you think that is up to you. But he loves you." He says softly placing a little kiss on my forehead before getting up slowly from the bed with his stick and giving me a wink.

"Now I need another dicky ticker made and you need to introduce yourself properly to someone." He says nodding his head to the MacBook on the desk. "Your mum is in agreement with me, although it does hurt her that you might be wanting some sort of relationship with him. But she knows that this will help you." He says as he gently rubs his thumb across my cheek. "Your decision kiddo." He says softly with a smile.

He leaves the room and I sit in silence for a moment unsure on what I should do. I know he's right, and for him to come and tell me his opinion on Robert and the situation, it does help me make some sort of decision.

"Well here goes nothing." I say out loud to myself getting up and heading towards the desk and picking up the MacBook. I hesitate for a moment. Will I have a message from him? Will he know that I know? Did the boys cave in and tell him? All these questions are running through my mind even before I lift the lid of the laptop to see if there is anything.

I take a deep breath and lift the lid carefully, seeing the computer come to life, showing my last message with him, which was the list. I close the application and let the computer start up and see if there is any messages from him.

◆ ◆ ◆

25 minutes go by.

Nothing.

I'm sat staring at this computer secretly hoping that he says something but also that he doesn't. The waiting is killing me, and I'm worried that he decided to use me to get what he wanted, which was helping his friend close the case. I get up from the bed. I'm now frustrated. 25 minutes and nothing. Deep down I am telling myself that if he wanted to contact me he would. And if he didn't, he wouldn't. I exhale loudly as I pace at the bottom of my bed thinking of how I should go about this. Do I want a relationship with him? Is this something I want? He should know that I know. But will he care?

I wouldn't ever class myself as an overthinker. But right now? I am. I feel sick to my stomach about this, and all because some man hasn't messaged me first.

Is this what life is like for woman? The constant waiting for a man to finally message you. A message that no doubt will change your life, but will it be for the better or for the worst? Jesus that sounds terrible, I sound whiney in my own thoughts, and I immediately cringe at myself.

"If you want something done Jules, do it yourself." I murmur to myself while opening the application and I begin typing.

The case is solved.

I click send and sit back. I feel the sudden realisation of my actions hit me like a truck and I start to pull my legs up and hug myself. This is some scary stuff. After all, to a lot of other people, I'm messaging a stranger. When to me and my family, he's, my blood.

I feel like I wait forever till I hear the notification sound go off on the computer and I feel my heart fall 1000 ft.

Officer Bradley was just filling me in. I apologise for not getting back to you Jules and congratulating you on the success of your first case. I had some situations to deal with of my own.

I dread to think what those situations probably were. I feel myself hesitate to ask a question in case he tells me I have none left, although my brain is telling me I do. I think for a moment before typing.

That's okay. I understand thank you.

Polite, short and sweet. I don't wait long till I get my own reply.

Juliette, I had some of my boys come to me honestly and tell me that in the middle of this case you were made aware of my relationship to you. Now they admitted the way you found out was severely traumatic and that isn't what I wanted. If you were ever to find out, I wanted it to be your family tell you. Not my psychopath.

I can't help but laugh at the ending of that paragraph. Rodger is a psychopath and I love that he is admitting it. But also, I respect the boys for going to him honestly, before Officer Bradley told him at least, he would have to. Damian went undercover.

I applaud your professionalism and how your family included them, including Marcus. It means a lot to me that you didn't let your feelings get in the way of justice and I see you in the future becoming a great detective.

For some reason, I feel my heart do leaps of joy as I read the rest of that paragraph. I'm pleased I'm not the one to approach the subject first, and I am pleased he knows.

It was no problem, granted I found out in a way that was upsetting. I don't regret it and I have a lot of love for the boys. Apart from the psychopath.

I send it and laugh at my own response. I do hope he reads that and knows not to hurt the boys when they head back to America. I decide then and there that I'm just going to ask.

So, I can ask a question?

I click send and eagerly wait his response. It might be a no. It might be a yes. But I don't have to wait to find out.

Ask away Juliette.

I feel my heart go into knots so quick. He will probably say no. Say something like it's not safe for me right now, or that he doesn't want to meet me he just wanted me to know who he is. All of this is me overthinking, so I just decide to type the message and click send and get it over with.

I'd like to meet you in person. Would that be okay with you?

I feel my heart sink so hard. This is it. There is no turning back now... I suddenly gasp as I read the response that is so sudden on my screen.

Juliette, I'd love nothing more.

CHAPTER THIRTY THREE

Two Weeks Later

I double check that I have everything on my list, although the boys have repeatedly told me that I don't need much and more than likely I'll be shopping while I'm there. Robert and I have been talking almost every day trying to plan this trip, but he assured me since the boys are also coming back to the US, that he will leave responsibility to Spencer, and everything will be fine, and I won't need to worry. But I do.

I've never been to the States before and I'm going with two people I like and one person I hate. Rodger. Unfortunately, he has to come too, and it happens to be on the same flight. *Great.* Marcus headed back to the US to deal with somethings before I arrived.

I close my suitcase and pull it out from the bedroom and towards the top of the stairs. Spencer greets me and takes my suitcase. "What you got in here woman?" He asks as he places it to the ground. "You are going for 3 weeks, not moving over there." He jokes but only Damian and I laugh. My mother stays silent and the paleness on her face indicates to me that she isn't happy with this decision.

I did ask Robert if she could come, but he said just for her safety he would prefer it if she didn't but called her and assured her that I'm in safe hands. My mother made quite a few sarcastic jokes that by the sounds of it he didn't understand, but he managed to convince her despite how much she said no.

"Mum, he's joking, I'm coming back." I say as I pull her in for a hug. She accepts it quickly and I feel my heart hurt a little bit. This is the first time I've gone away without her.

I applaud the fact that she's allowing me to travel to the States with a man my sister says looks like a criminal, a psychopath (that one she isn't happy about) and the "kid" as she calls him. I think at any moment she is about to change her mind, so I exit out of the embrace and give her a kiss on the cheek. "I love you. I'll let you know once we are at the airport." I say as I hug her one more time.

"You better." She murmurs in the hug and I can't help but smile, she really is an amazing woman for letting me do this.

"I'll see you in a couple of weeks." I say as I go and grab my suitcase. I'm quickly shooed away from it by Spencer who gives me a death glare. I take that as he will take it to the car that they hired. No, it's not a taxi, it's a car service. *Rich people.*

I give my mum one last hug before heading down towards the car and Damian opens the door for me, giving me a nod to get in. I tilt my eyes up and see Rodger and I feel myself hesitate while getting into the car. I narrow my eyes at him which causes him to smile. "You going to call me a pedophile today?" He jokes and I scoff before getting into the car.

"Depends on how much of a creep you are today. I have new nicknames I've been crafting too." I say as I put my seatbelt on. I hear Spencer growl from the boot of the car before slamming it shut.

"I swear if you two so much as do my head in for any part of this flight, when we get to the States, I will shoot you both." He says as he puts his seatbelt on, and the driver begins to drive away from the house.

"Now, what's our plan?" Rodger asks Spencer who puts his shades down and pretends he is ignoring him. "Are we putting her on a different plane than us?" He asks sarcastically and I roll my eyes. He really is a child.

"If anyone is getting put on another plane, it will be you. If you weren't such a dickhead you wouldn't have to deal with her. You know what, if you actually talked to her like a decent human being, you would know she's cool." Spencer comes to my defense, and we all look at him in unison, surprised by his response. Spencer looks at our surprised faces and proceeds to look out of the window ignoring us.

"She's not cool. She's a Quinten." Rodger jokes which I do in fact laugh at.

"So is Clarissa?" I point out and I watch the smug look drop from his face. Now that is a look, I want to get every single time he opens his annoying mouth. "One rule for her another for me, eh?" I ask with a smile which he clearly doesn't like. His face stares blankly at me and I know I've won, and it feels amazing.

"You know you claim I ruined your life, yet here you are about to hop on a plane to go and see the very man who abandoned you when you were a baby. How you going to cope when he takes one look at you and realizes you are nothing but a burden?" He says coldly and I feel I chill run through my spine. He really is a narcissist. I smile sweetly at him as I had a feeling something like this would come up.

"Rodger, I have a great support system around me. You did in fact attempt to ruin my life and for a few weeks I had to question myself and my identity but you wanna know something? I'm the kind of person that will see the positives in a negative situation." I say and he quickly shuts up. "Now if we were to talk about your bad behavior, your narcissism and your hatred towards me I think we should look at deep down and your serious issues with woman and why you are drawn to the more unhinged ones because they won't give you the hard truths like I will." I say coldly.

Not taking my eyes off Rodger, I lean closer to him, and I can smell his expensive aftershave. "If you think for one second, I'm going to let you ruin this trip for me, think again." I watch as his face becomes pale and he becomes slightly angry, his nostrils are flaring and the only emotion that is coming through in his eyes is anger and I don't care. "If you aren't going to contribute something positive to this trip. Shut your mouth. You can do that can't you?" I mock with a smile.

I turn to Damian whose mouth is wide open, unsure on where that came from and if I'm honest so am I. I think deep down I was holding it in until I seen Rodger again. "I have never in my life seen you look more like your dad than you did in that moment." Damian says eventually in the silence. I don't say anything back to him I just turn my head and look out of the window. Because I'm not sure whether that is a good thing.

◆ ◆ ◆

We arrive at the airport, and I watch as two men in suits take our suitcases and we are met with a very smiley, blonde haired lady.

"Hello again Mr. Williams." She says to Spencer

who smiles at her with a grin like he's just won the lottery. All of us notice it, although Rodger rolls his eyes and makes an annoying noise.

"Hello Miss Shields. Nice to see you again." Spencer says that grin still plastered on his face.

"If you would like to follow me, I'll get you through security and to the plane. It's waiting for you." She says with a smile and begins to walk through London Heathrow Airport. I begin to become confused at this point, surely, we would be getting a normal flight with everyone else and going through security with the other passengers?

We are led up a set of stairs and towards security, where I notice a long queue and I feel my heart begin to beat normally again, I was once again over thinking and there was no need for it.

"Come on." Damian says as they open up a separate section of security and the boys walk right through. I want to stand and stare in awe, how much stuff do they get away with and what sort of business is Robert and the rest of them into? The more I think about it, the more I realise that I probably don't want to know the answer as I will determine whether or not I get on the plane.

In a matter of 10 minutes, we are through security and the car is pulling up to a private jet. I feel physically sick. These people have some serious money if they have their own jet, and their own security quick pass.

"Robert didn't want us to take you on a public flight in case someone recognized one of us and it all went downhill. So, he sent the plane." Spencer explains, I laugh, this is all so bizarre to me. "I know you'll have a lot of questions but get on the plane." Spencer says and he gives me a light nudge towards the stairs. I shoot him a look in which he ignores, and proceeds nudge me towards the stairs.

"He's a little paranoid, isn't he?" I ask and Damian chuckles.

"You have no idea."

CHAPTER THIRTY FOUR

I wake up groggy and as I adjust to my surroundings, I remember I'm on a plane with the Williams brothers and I feel my beating heart calm just a little bit.

"You snore." Rodger pipes up from next to me. I turn and give him a glare. He is not what I want to wake up to when I'm on a plane. "Like loudly." He continues and I roll my eyes ignoring him.

"Well I'm not so pleased to see your ugly face either so shut it." I say as I undo my seatbelt and head towards the bathroom.

"A lot of girls seem to like my pretty face." He smugly calls after me, I don't bother turning around to him.

"Are they blind?" I hear scoffs and laughter come from the other two Williams brothers who are down the bottom of the plane. This whole thing is insane. I'm on a flight that probably cost more than my house in London and my mums salary in total. It's strange, that this is now my life, that my birth father runs all these different businesses, illegal and not illegal and this is his life. How the other half live. It's insane to me. I wash my hands and open the door back to the main part of the plane where I am met with Rodger and his creepy smile.

"We are landing in 10 minutes you may want to sit down." He instructs with that smile. I ignore him and walk back to my seat and put my seatbelt on. Within seconds he's back to sitting next to me staring at me like some sort of creepy doll.

"What do you want?" I ask ignoring his stares. He doesn't stop, he just continues.

"I want to know why you forgave the other two but you wont forgive me. Come on Juliette, water under the bridge. I didn't mean no harm." He says sarcastically and I roll my eyes.

"Even if I did forgive you, which I don't, you would care less anyway. Is your ego a little bruised from earlier is that what this is?" I mock, he laughs with me, ignoring what I just said.

"Come on Juliette, I know you like me. Maybe not in the way I'm implying but you do like me even if it is just a little bit. You know you wanna be friends." He says with a small smile on his face. I pout at him.

"Aw Rodger your ego is bruised," I say with a smile. "I would rather let Robert shoot me than ever be friends with you." I say coldly and turn away and look out of the window.

Laughter once again erupts through the plane from both Damian and Spencer, and I feel Rodger move from next to me.

"Rodger if you can't play the game don't play. You know I'll always win." I tell his as he moves to and sit next to his brothers.

◆ ◆ ◆

Once we arrive in Michigan, it's still sunny and it's a lot hotter than London is right now. I put my bag comfortably on my shoulder and begin walking down the stairs of the airplane. We are met by 3 cars and what looks like security. I stop next to the stairs and wait for further instructions from the boys who are making their way down the stairs.

I watch as a man gets out of the car in a suit. He presents himself as confident as he strides towards us, sunglasses up and showing no emotion. "Juliette?" He asks as he approaches. I nod slowly not wanting to say anything else. He is tall, intimidating, and has a jawline that could cut you.

He removes his sunglasses so smoothly; you would think this was a movie. He grins at me with the pearliest white teeth I've ever seen in my life.

"My name is Nathaniel. I'm your older brother." He says as he runs up and pulls me into a gigantic hug. I giggle as he swings me around, which I was not expecting. The man who looks like he could kill me and not even think twice about it is a big teddy bear. He places me down and I begin to sort my hair out. "This has been such a long time coming. When dad told me you had decided to come and visit, I begged for him to let me pick you up from the airport, so you had a friendly face to meet before you meet the rest of them." He says with a smile. I look to the Williams brothers who seem to be smiling, even the psychopath.

"It's nice to meet you, Nathaniel." I say as I put my bag back on my shoulder.

"I thought you might want to see another friendly face before we head home." He says as he turns around and gives a nod to one of the cars. I watch as a door opens and a man in a white shirt and black jeans comes from the other side of the car.

"Missed me, sis?" Marcus says while opening his arms and signaling me to come for a hug.

"Absolutely!" I say as I run into his arms, and he hugs me tight.

"You know funnily enough I've missed you." He jokes against my shoulder while he exits our embrace and puts me down. "I think you might be my favorite sister." He says with a wink, and I watch Nathaniel roll his eyes.

"Wait till Alexis hears that she will be so mad." He says while gently pushing his brother.

"Don't blab. She's already given me a bruise this week." He says while rubbing his arm gently. Nathaniel laughs. "I want to be a fly on the wall when you go into your marine training."

Marcus rolls his eyes causing me to laugh. "Nice flight boys?" Marcus calls after the Williams who join to meet us.

"It was until psycho started to be a psycho," Spencer complains looking at Rodger who shrugs his shoulders.

"Whatever."

Both Nathaniel and Marcus shake their heads.

"Well, you are already in the shit for telling her she's adopted so god knows what he's going to make you do." Marcus says before taking my bag off my should and placing it into the car.

"Come on we don't have all day." Nathaniel instructs and we are all shown to different cars. I get paired with my brothers while the Williams brothers go into the car behind.

We drive for what seems like forever and but at the same time, it goes too quickly. Marcus, Nathaniel, and I have been getting to know each other and it turns out we have a lot in common. Nathaniel is the head of the security for the family and provides everyone with a security detail. Marcus starts his training in October, and he is super excited but also nervous. It's all he wants to do, and he is worried that if it doesn't go well, he will be seen as a failure.

I watch as we pull up to a set of gates and the security in front wait for them to open. After a few seconds they open, and we speed through the gates and up a long winding road.

"You guys live in a palace, don't you?" I joke to them, and they don't seem to laugh, only exchange a look.

"Well…" They begin to say, and I watch as the size of the house comes into my view and my jaw drops. It's on a par with a palace and it is the most beautiful most modern house I have ever seen. I do have to give them credit, for people who use guns a lot, they do seem to have a lot of trust in their clients. There are so many open planned windows, it reminds me of the Cullen House from *Twilight*, yet bigger and in less trees.

I climb out of the car, my jaw still wide as I try to grasp the beauty of this place. So, this is how the other half live.

"Juliette if you keep your mouth open like that you will attract flies." Spencer shouts from behind me and I give him a glare.

"This is all new to me. Leave me be!" I shout as I look around. The front of the house is gorgeous but so is the garden. "Wow." I say once more as I take it all in. These people have some serious money.

"Come on, let's get you inside, it's hotter here than London and I feel like you'll burn." Marcus says as we all begin to walk inside. I feel like as we reach the door, my face is in a permanent state of shock and awe at the same time. We enter the front door and I can't even stop myself from gasping. Marble flooring with gold interior everywhere. The outside doesn't match the inside and I can't help but love it. The staircase is gold and huge as it in the main center piece for when you walk into the foyer.

"Stay here. I'm going to get someone who's been dying to meet you." Nathaniel says before leaving me with Marcus and the Williams brothers.

"Well, I don't want to be here for a soppy meeting, see you." Rodger says before running up those stairs, no doubt to go to his room and avoid us all. I turn to my left and watch someone come out of a room at the bottom of the corridor. He begins to walk with Nathaniel, a smile plastered to his face as he confidently approaches me. He's wearing a suit, and it clearly looks expensive. Once he is in a good eyeline I realise that this man might not be my father as he looks a lot older. He greets me with a smile as he approaches me.

"Juliette." He grins. He extends his hand hesitantly unsure on whether or not I will take it. "I'm Peter. I'm your uncle." He says with a smile. I meet his hand and shake it gently, not wanting to be too over eager, but also my gut instinct was right.

"How was your flight." He asks as he places his hands in his trouser pockets.

"It was fine, thank you. I slept the whole way." I laugh, as does he.

"Good, those seats are comfy, yes?" He asks and I nod.

"Very." I agree.

"Boys, leave us please. I'd like to show Juliette around." Peter instructs but never takes his eyes off me. Damian pinches my arm but gives me an encouraging nod before heading up the stairs with both Nathaniel and Spencer.

"After you Juliette." He says extending his hand out to the room on the left as you walk in, which again looks like something out of a palace. I begin to walk in and take in the scenery.

"You have a beautiful home." I say as I move my eyes to admire the room.

"Thank you. Each of us put our own artistic spins within each room." Peter explains. I can only bring myself to nod as I look around the room. I suddenly jump out of my skin when I notice behind the door there is a giant, sculpture of a lion. "Don't worry. Marcel doesn't bite." He jokes with a wink, and I lightly laugh while placing my hand on my heart.

"Why do you have a large lion, that I'm going to assume was once alive in your living room?" I ask. He laughs at me for a moment before pouring himself a glass of water. "Juliette, this is the parlor and waiting area for any guests. And Marcel was a gift from a Prince to your Aunt Felicity." He walks towards me and hands me the glass of water gently.

"I'm going to assume that they are still together if he is gifting her dead animals?" I question, not being able to stop the discomfort on my face. He laughs as he takes a sip of his water, unsure on how to answer the question.

"Felicity doesn't bat for the other team if you understand what I mean." He says. I stare at him blank as I try to understand what exactly he means. But then it hits me.

"Oh! Right!" I say shocked not expecting that.

"She's gay." He clarifies and I nod my head.

"Yep, I got it." I nod, not knowing what else to say.

"Trust me, it was a shock to us all when she came out as gay." Peter says taking a sip of his water.

"Well as long as she's happy that's the main thing, right?" I question and he nods quickly.

"Oh! Absolutely Juliette, we love her no matter what." He says with a smile which I join in on.

"Good." I say as I take another nervous sip of my water. It then dawns on me. "Why Marcel?" I ask as I look back at the lion. "I mean why the name?" I ask curiously.

"Your sister named him." Peter explains and I nod.

"Which one? I've been told I have two." I ask and he smiles while placing the glass on the table in front of him.

"Alexis named him, she's older than you." He explains and I manage a nod. "Can I get you a drink?" He asks sweetly and I shake my head.

"No thank you. I'm fine for now." I say with a smile.

Silence falls between us and although on the way here I had so many questions, I honestly can not think of one that I would like to start with. I think he starts to sense my nervousness and hands me a glass of water from what looks like a drinks trolly and I take it gratefully with a smile.

"Juliette, I'm sure you have questions. But I have a few of my own if you're okay answering them?" He asks softly.

"Of course." I say as I get comfortable on the sofa.

"So, how are you feeling about all this? That is my first question. I mean I'm sure this is all new for you and I heard it was quite traumatic when you found out." He says sweetly and I can't help but feel grateful for his approach.

"I'm starting to come to terms with everything now I think. This is all so new to me." I say quietly and his expression never changes. I find myself fiddling with my fingers which I have never done and I think it's because I'm nervous.

"Juliette, I can assure you - you have nothing to be nervous about." He says almost as a whisper. I look up to him, unsure on how he knew my exact emotion. But I can't help but smile. "You are safe here. And although we haven't got to see you grow up, we did in our own little way." He says with a smile.

"What do you mean?" I ask as he takes a sip of his water before looking towards Marcel the lion.

"Let's just say that is a conversation you may want to have with Robert."

CHAPTER THIRTY FIVE

I sit in silence waiting for Peter to come back. He's been gone almost 30 minutes as he had to take an important phone call and encouraged me to start looking around. I'm hesitant to do that, it's not my place to start looking around someone else house, doesn't matter whether we are related.

I decide that if he said I could look round, i might as well look at the photos around the room.

I get up from my chair and look on every coffee table as well as above the fireplace. Cute photos of Marcus, the Williams brothers, as well as Nathaniel and a young girl who I am assuming is one of my sisters.

I take in each bit of art and I also look over Marcel the Lion to see if there was anything on him but he seems to be for decoration only.

I make my way over to a cabinet that has quite a few photos in. I don't feel upset that I'm not in them I'm only family by blood. I don't know anything about these people or who I'm spending time with. I wouldn't call them family. More acquaintances.

I look inside the cabinet and notice a photo of what I'm assuming is the whole family. They are all smiling in front of the house, even Spencer who I have only seen smile a handful of times in the past few weeks.

I start to feel slightly jealous and I think it's because I was the one that was sent away, when all he did was create a family and not include me in it.

By the way everything is going in my head I sound so bitter and jealous when in reality I should be grateful. I had an amazing upbringing with my Mum, Dad and sister. I had a roof over my head, food in my stomach and a loving home. That I count my lucky stars for.

"Who are you?" A voice from behind startles me causing me to grab my chest.

"Oh! Hi. Er, I'm Jules." I say with a smile, which she doesn't reciprocate.

"Jules what?" She snaps back harshly causing the smile to drop from my face.

"Jules Sanders." I state and she rolls her eyes.

"So, you're one of Rodger's new girlfriends I see." She says while heading to the drinks trolly and pouring herself a drink of something, I'm assuming it's alcohol.

"Rodger's? What? No! God no." I stutter and she roles her eyes annoyed before necking the drink in one and slamming the glass on the trolly.

"So who are you and what are you doing in my dads house?" She questions with her eyebrows raised. I get the sense this girl likes to cause problems, which could only point to one person.

"You must be Clarissa." I say with a slight smirk. Her reputation proceeds her, she is so rude, and incredibly careless.

"So?" She snaps.

"Well Clarissa, I have every right to be in this house considering we both have the same dad." I state. Her expression is emotionless, like she couldn't give a damn who I am. But now she knows I stand here with as much merit as her, I get the sense she's starting to spiral, not being in control anymore. "You speak to all of your siblings with that level of attitude?" I ask sarcastically. I earn myself a scoff this time as she storms out of the room not bothering to know who I am.

"I honestly don't know why you are here. You don't mean anything to any of us, especially dad. So how about you go home back to England with your tea and crumpets and stop trying to ruin my life with my dad. Okay?" She asks harshly to tone in her voice is cruel and also her words hit me like a truck with how hurtful she is, I can't stop but see the jealously pour out of her.

"Clarissa, my mum always said jealousy is a ugly emotion and right now your face is showing it." I state clearly annoying her more. She begins to say something, but I cut her off quickly. "I'm not here to make enemies Clarissa, I'm here to get to know my family and have a relationship with everyone. But I'll be sure to make the least bit of effort with you seeing as the only thing you can give me is a cold shoulder and a bitter speech." I say as I stand my ground.

Her mouth is wide open, shocked by my response to her attitude, and quite frankly so am I. *Where did that come from?*

Instead of arguing with me more, she storms out of the room, shoving past Peter who looks at me with worried eyes as he notices my annoyed expression.

"So, I see you met crazy pants?" He asks with humor in his voice which I have to laugh at.

"That obvious?" I ask as i walk over and take a seat on the sofa once again and take a sip of my water.

"I apologise for her harsh words. Clarissa doesn't like people in general." He says softly which causes me to laugh.

"You don't say. I had been told about her behaviour, I didn't realise her people skills were that bad." I say as a chuckle which he joins in with. "Is that not down to where she came from before

Robert adopted her?" I ask and he shakes his head.
"No. She's just a bitch."

CHAPTER THIRTY SIX

Peter begins to give me a tour of the house and it's a gigantic one. We have been exploring for a few hours at least and he has given me a full house tour, including the William's brothers rooms. Apart from Rodger, who ignored Peter's knocks and has locked his door. Safe to say he really didn't want to see a reunion.

As we walk through the rest of the house and he explains every bit of detail of every room. I'm fascinated but also insanely jealous. I wonder how much these people are worth, or more so how much they make?

Peter begins to show me the back garden, pointing out favourite moments of his as we walk around. It makes me smile a little, this man must be so busy yet he is showing his niece around the grounds of his house.

We reach a small out house where he turns to me with a grin. " I hope you're ready to meet the rest of them?" He asks and I frown at his question.

He opens the door to reveal it completely decorated. Banners and balloons saying 'Welcome home!', cakes and pastries on each table with white and gold napkins that I see have my name engraved on the corner. My breath gets caught my throat and I feel myself begin to tear up.

"Surprise!" People shout as they jump out from behind tables and corners of the room. I get a fright and clutch to my chest trying to calm my beating heart.

"Welcome home Juliette." Marcus says as he pulls me in for a tight hug. I welcome it gladly as I feel my emotions are all over the place right now.

"Let go Marcus! I need a sister hug!" A girl beside me exclaims. Marcus exits out of the embrace and turns me towards the most beautiful girl I have ever seen in my life. Her smile is contagious as she has her arms out, welcoming me into a hug.

"Hi! I'm Alexis, your older sister." She says as she pulls me in for a hug. I can't help but smile as she squeezes me tightly. "I promised myself I wouldn't cry." She says as her voice begins to break. "This has been a long time coming Juliette, we are so pleased you're here." She says as a whisper in my ear.

After a few moments I pull myself away only to be welcomed into another hug by Nathaniel. "Since everyone else is getting one, I have to have another." He says as he spins me round causing me to giggle.

"Nathaniel!" I shout as he spins me once more before putting me down. "Sorry sis, thought I'd get one more in." He says with a cheesy grin.

I turn my attention slightly to meet who I want to say is Ezekiel. "Welcome home Juliette, it's so nice to finally meet you. I'm Ezekiel." He says while extending his hand. He mustn't be a hugger, which is absolutely fine. Everyones different.

"It's nice to meet you Ezekiel." I say while shaking his hand. He smiles to me, which I reciprocate.

"Think that might be the most Ezekiel has spoken all week!" Nathaniel jokes earning a glare from Ezekiel.

"At least I know when to shut up." Ezekiel fires back earning a uproar of gasps and laughter from the rest of us.

"He's got attitude. Okay!" Nathaniel laugh's while extending his hand to Ezekiel and they do a brotherly handshake.

"Okay, lets get this party started. Damian and Spencer will be joining us soon." Marcus says as he puts his arm around my shoulder. "Peter told us you ran into Clarissa." He asks as a whisper in my ear. I nod, not sure if everyone is wanting to talk about her as I'm assuming the mention of her ruins the mood. "She's a bitch, don't let her get to you." He says sweetly as he pulls me in for a hug once again.

"I hope you're ready to answer a ton of questions because we have had these drafted for a year!" He exclaims as he leads me to a seat hinting he wants me to sit there.

"Bring it on."

◆ ◆ ◆

After a few hours of questions, party games and heartfelt conversations, it was time to head towards the house. I can't stop the smile on my face. It's been like a mask ever since I came into the house. Apart from my encounter with Clarissa, this whole day has been something to remember. I feel so welcomed, so wanted and funnily enough so loved.

Each of my siblings head up to their seperate rooms, saying goodnight giving me a hug.

"Juliette, would you like to wait in the parlour for a few moments. I've just been told by security that they are back." Peter explains. I feel myself starting to get slightly panicked as for the first time ever, I will be meeting Robert Quinten, my biological father.

"Come on, I'll go with you." Spencer says sweetly before lightly shoving me towards the front room.

It's empty when we get in there and I watch as Spencer walks towards the drinks trolly and pours himself a drink before pouring me a glass of water.

"To calm your nerves." He says as he hands me the water. I look at him, my eyebrows raised as I look between the glass and his face.

"What's the alcohol for?" I ask confused.

"My nerves." He says bluntly as he drinks it in one before making a sour face. I can't help but laugh.

All of a sudden, I hear the door open and a commotion begin to unfold in the hallway. Spencer looks at me with a warning to stay still as he heads towards the shouting.

"What happened!" I hear Peter shout and a bunch of people shout on top of each other. "One at a time! Come on, the kids are better than you lot." Peter exclaims and I can't help but laugh. Also, curiosity fills me, and I begin to walk around towards the door to get a better look.

"Ask crazy here. Shot up the entire operation. Ruined my brand-new *Louis Vuitton* skirt and I have blood in my hair." One-woman whines. "Not to mention this one is drunk!" She shouts once more. I slowly walk towards the door trying to get a better view as to who is shouting.

"The whole operation was a fucking disaster thanks to Oliver here." One man who stands on the stairs says as he takes off his shirt that is covered in blood. I turn my attention to the boys who stand at the top of the stairs. "Damian, get me another shirt." He says and I feel my heart stop and I freeze.

Oh my god.

"Wait!" He shouts and Damian comes back into viewpoint. "Damian where's…" He begins to say before turning slowly to Peter and then looks up and meets my terrified eyes. I watch him sink into the stairs once he realises I'm there. I'm frozen, I can't breathe, I can't move. All I can see is blood all over everyone and I'm frightened. He rips off his shirt and undershirt while Peter hands him his blazer which he puts on as he almost falls down the stairs.

"Juliette?" He says softly as he approaches me. I hear gasps come from behind him as I'm going to assume Felicity and whoever the other woman realises who I am. "Jules?" The man cries as he reaches down with his blood-stained hands and gently wipes the tears that are no doubt falling down my cheeks. "Oh baby, I'm sorry. I'm so sorry." He cries as he holds my face tightly. "Juliette, breathe please." He begs softly to me, but I can't, I'm so frightened I feel like I might die.

"Robert." I hear a familiar voice speak and my heart begins to beat again as I'm no longer faced with Robert, I'm now faced with Damian. "Jules, come on. You're okay." He says as he lifts my arms and pulls me in for a hug. I instantly get my breath back and I grab onto Damian so tight and cry into his shoulder. He soothes and calms me down as I watch Robert fall to the floor in shock at to what's just happened.

"Go get changed and bin the clothes now!" I hear Nathaniel instruct them and I hear them one by one all scatter, even Robert. "Damian, she alright?" Spencer asks as I feel someone rub my back gently. I feel Damian nod before pulling away to look at me.

"You good?" He asks and I nod lightly. Before pulling away and wiping my tears. "The blood." I cry and Damian places his hand on my shoulder. "I know. *I know.*" He says softly as he let's Marcus hand me a glass of water. I gratefully take it, my hands still shaking and the fear still rushing through my veins.

"He knew she was coming today!" Spencer shouts to Peter who only nods. "He was laughing as she had a panic attack!" He shouts once more, and I realise they aren't talking about Robert; I think they are talking about Oliver.

"I'll talk to him." Peter says softly to try a calm Spencer's anger which when I look up, doesn't seem to budge.

"You told me I had to protect her in London, I didn't realize I had to protect her from her own Uncle here." He says to Peter. Who looks at Spencer with a look I can only assume is, I will talk to him.

I walk over and take a seat and hold my glass in my hands. I have never felt more frightened in my life. I've been here under an hour, and I've already had one experience with this new crazy family.

"Juliette, do you need anything?" Damian asks placing his hand on my shoulder. I shake my head, not feeling like talking. One by one I hear them all leave leaving me in the parlor to try and digest what happened.

CHAPTER THIRTY SEVEN

Damian keeps me in his room the rest of the night and if I'm honest I'm grateful. Robert hasn't made a effort to talk to me yet, and truthfully, I needed some time to process what I had seen yesterday. It wasn't exactly how I wanted to meet my biological dad, but I can't change what happened. And by the conversation I overheard between Spencer and Marcus, Oliver had planned the entire thing. He had found out in the car that I was on the plane and only hours away. He wanted to prove that I wasn't good enough to be in this family.

I decide while they are all in some meeting I would go exploring once again. This place is huge, and I will no doubt get lost, but I guess that's the fun of it. I start by walking down long corridors and down any side ones that looked interesting.

As I reach one of the doors at the bottom of the corridor and try it. It's open. I gently turn the handle and open it and I feel my mouth drop open as I walk into possibly the most beautiful library I have ever seen.

There are books on every single wall that go all the way to the ceiling. I feel as though I'm in love and would happily get lost in here.

I head over to one section of the bookshelves and find myself looking at first editions of books that are 100s of years old. "It's beautiful, isn't it?" Someone says in the silence, and I almost jump out of my skin. I look to see Robert standing in the doorway, less bloody than yesterday and in more comfortable clothes. "Juliette we never got properly introduced." He says as he enters the library. I don't feel as frightened today, although every time I look at him; I am reminded of the man who had blood all over his hands and the thought makes me sick to my stomach.

"Juliette, I'm Robert." He says while extending his hand to me.

I hesitate for a moment as I'm reminded of the blood for only a second and then it goes back to normal. I meet his hand confidently as I shake it. "It's nice to finally meet you," I say with a warm smile.

I'm the first to pull my hand away but he doesn't

seem to mind. "Do you like to read?" He asks and I nod. "I like a lot of crime novels and teenage books. But these first editions are very cool." I tell him and he nods in silence. "I'm sorry for freaking out yesterday. I've just never seen that much blood on so many people, I just got a bit spooked." I apologise. He's taken back by my apology as a look of confusion fills his face.

"Jules, if anyone should be a apologising it's me, not you." He reassures me. I don't know how to respond so I just decide nod is better than nothing and I don't want to come over as rude.

"How about you tell me about yourself while we go for a walk in the garden?" He suggests. I look at him for a moment and I realise we have very similar eyes and eye colour to each other and the thought makes me smile.

"I'd like that." I say confidently. I'm not lying either; I do think that having some fresh air might do me some good today.

"Perfect, let's go." He instructs and leads the way to the garden. The whole house is like a maze, and although I feel as though he would never admit it, he did get lost once or twice on our way to find the garden.

We walk through the freshly cut grass smell and the flowers and it smells different than it does in America, or at least I think it does.

"Juliette, you can ask me anything, I'm an open

book." He says with a smile as we walk through. I think for a moment on my first ever question. Now he's mentioned it, I can't seem to think of one.

"How about I go first, you will probably have so many you can't choose from, right?" He asks and I nod, nervously.

"How is your mum?" He asks and I feel relief for a moment, talking about anyone but myself is easy and I'm grateful for his choice in question and I think he can see the relief on my face when I look up.

"She's good. She's been doing really well." I tell him and he smiles for a moment.

"She was so lovely to me on the day your parents came to collect you. I never used to like being hugged or touched by anyone. But your mum, when we first met was so grateful, she was the first person I had hugged in a very long time." He explains and I feel my heart about to burst. My mum has always been a hugger, always. That's one of the many reasons why I love her.

"That's mum for you." I say in a laugh which he joins in. It's silent for a moment as we let the good feeling between us fade.

"I'm sorry about your dad." He says with sorrow in his voice and I meet his eyes. He means it. I don't think he ever thought I would lose my dad as young as I did. But it has shaped me into the person I am today. I would like to think he would be proud.

"Who were those people also covered in blood

yesterday? Are they your siblings?" I ask changing the subject and he nods very quickly.

"They are. You met Peter when you arrived, then there is Felicity, Serena and Oliver." He says as we continue to walk through the garden.

"Oliver, has a bad reputation, doesn't he?" I ask and once again, he's quick to answering with a nod.

"Unfortunately, yes, that is the downside to Oliver. I can't even tell you there is a upside to him. The man is constantly miserable." he jokes. I don't laugh, seeing how he was laughing after a panic attack I overheard he caused, I'm going to try and avoid him for as long as possible.

"I think it was Felicity said that Serena was drunk. Is she always drunk?" I ask. He hesitates for a moment before looking at me with sad eyes. I guess that is my answer, everyone struggles with their own demons, and everyone has a way of fighting them off.

"She's a lovely girl, she just makes bad decisions." He says quietly as we continue to walk. We reach a field of apple trees and the sweet scent in the air makes me happy.

"I have to ask otherwise I will go crazy." I say as we walk through the field. "Why did you tell my mum she couldn't ever tell me?" I ask.

He pauses in the field unsure on what to say. I stop in my tracks also, hoping to not hear some lie. "Juliette, you want to know a secret?" He says to me as he walks closer to me. I'm not massively in front of him on this field but I am a little bit. "The lies we tell are to protect the ones we love and adore from harm." He says softly as he reaches my face and gently rubs his thumb across my cheek. "But the secrets we keep, are the reasons we fight off our demons in our nightmares." He says while slowly removing his thumb from my cheek. "What I'm saying is, we told you a lie to protect you. But we suffered with the secret in silence out of love." He says softly.

"That is a very touching speech." I say with a smirk and he laughs before moves his hand away and it goes into his pocket.

"You have my humor." He states with a smile before walking onwards.

"When I sent you on that case, I thought it was an open and shut one, you got some evidence for the London police, and I got to know you. What I didn't realize was how difficult it was to stop you from putting yourself in danger." He explains as we begin to walk over to a bench in the corner of the field. "You are very like me when I was young." He says with a smile no doubt remembering the good times. "When I first got handed the business after my father died." He continues.

"What exactly is the business?" I ask and he chuckles trying to find the words to say.

"We own many legitimate businesses that are worth millions but also some smaller ones." He says with a grin. I nod, but also pout a little as I digest the information.

"So basically, you're a criminal?" I ask and he laughs out loud. He can't deny it and he can see on my face that I can see through his crap.

"Basically yes."

"Oh, how fun, I'll be the police detective with a mafia father. How exciting!" I joke, but he laughs.

"I promise you it's not a bad thing to be related to a Quinten." He says with a smile.

"So, you just kill people for a living?" I ask and he is taken back by my question for a moment. "Even people that didn't deserve it?"

He pauses for a moment before looking me in the eyes. "You're more like me than you think Jules. I maybe a monster in your eyes but I am your father whether you like it or not." He speaks clearly and I feel a shiver go down my spine. The air is now thick with tension, and I have found myself becoming quite sheepish in his presence. I am not like him; I know I'm not. But he is right, he is my birth dad and that I can not change.

"Speaking of being related." I say as I decide to slightly change the topic. "How come I was put up for adoption, yet you adopted 6 kids after me?"

I watch as he is taken back by my answer and for a few moments he doesn't have anything to say. "You've thought about this long and hard, haven't you?" He asks and I nod. I feel like this, and another question I have are two staples in a way that I can properly start to come to terms with who I am now I found out I'm adopted.

"As Marcus had mentioned to you, not that long ago. I was in a really dark place after I had to give you up. I didn't want to. I wanted to keep you, raise you and be a good, great father even. But I couldn't leave the family business to Peter, it wasn't fair on him. He didn't want it, and I had been groomed as such to take over the family business once my father died." He explains. He takes a deep breath before continuing.

"There was a hit on us for 2 years at the time when you were born. Everything had to be done under the radar, we had to stay quiet, and we had to stay out of sight. About a year after you had been born and your mother had taken off, we had dealt with the hit, and we were back to running our empire. But I felt lost, because I couldn't have you. But I couldn't be the man to rip a child away from parents who love them. You were better off with your parents, they could keep you safe. I couldn't." He begins to get emotional. "I then decided that if I wanted to be a father, I wanted children that would be able to take over the family business if anything was to happen. Then I adopted Nathaniel. Then Marcus, Alexis and Ezekiel and lastly Tommy and Clarissa." He explains. "I know how it must make you feel, I completely understand, and you have every right to be angry at me. I did what I had to do to protect you. You deserved a life away from this." He says as he takes my hand in his.

Although it is hard to hear, I do understand a little about the situation he was in. If it made him happy then I'm happy.

"What about my mother what happened to her?" I ask and Robert shrugs not knowing what else to say.

"After you were born she took off. She left a note saying 'I'm sorry.' and that was the end of it. I tried searching for her for years. Just after a while, I decided that maybe she never wanted to be found or she changed her name." He says as he begins to get emotional once again. "Believe it or not Juliette, I loved your Mom. I still do, even after all this time." He chokes up. I can't help but get upset myself. Marcus said that he never dated or loved anyone after her. Maybe he really did fall for her.

"Was I a mistake?" I ask in the sadness. He looks up at me, his eyes slightly bloodshot from the tears as he takes my hand and holds it tight.

"Never." He says almost as a whisper. "The only person who made a mistake was me." He states. "I didn't fight harder to keep you. I wish I had." He says as he slowly pulls me in for a hug which a glady accept.

We stay like this for a short while and I'm grateful. There is so much emotion in this hug. We are both so emotional and it has been fourteen years in the making. I'm hugging my dad. My biological dad. And although he terrifies me slightly deep

TORRIE JONES

down, I'm willing to dance with the devil.

CHAPTER THIRTY EIGHT

5 Days Later

My time here in America is flying by. I've been spending as much time as possible with my siblings and the Williams brothers, minus Rodger and Clarissa of course. Those two are up to no good somewhere else and as long as they stay away from me, I'll be happy as can be.

I've spoken to my mum every day since I got here, she's constantly wanting updates and asking what I've been doing. I think she's worried that Robert will be including me in his illegal activity when in reality that is so far away from the truth.

My siblings as well as the brothers have been

showing me what it's like to live in America. Taking me to all the best food spots, we've been watching movies, shopping. It has been the best few days so far and the week has only just started.

As we sit watching another episode of *The Big Bang Theory* and laugh at Sheldon's shenanigans suddenly the TV is turned off and whines and groans fill the room from my brothers. I turn around to find Peter, Felicity and Serena standing in the doorway of the room. Peter is holding a file and just seeing one of them makes me incredibly nervous.

"What is so important that couldn't wait a hour? I was on the phone with Steven Holliday about securing the Switzerland deal." Robert complains as he comes in the room glaring at his siblings.

I look to their faces but I can not place the emotion which makes me sick.

"What is going on?" Marcus asks breaking the silence.

"Jules will you stay for a moment? The rest of you, scoot." Peter instructs. We all exchange a confused look with each other and without a fuss, one by one, I am left on the sofa on my own, now feeling physically sick.

Peter makes his way over to the corner of the room to the desk with a laptop.

"Peter, what's going on?" Robert asks curiously as he stands closer towards the sofa, never breaking eye contact with his older brother. I can see the pain in Peter's eyes as he begins typing on the laptop.

"Remember 13 years ago when we hatched Operation Red Head?" Peter asks Robert who can only nod slowly with his brows frowned. "Well today that comes to a end." Peter says as he turns the computer around.

"What's operation Red Head?" I ask while makeing my way over to the computer. Robert turns to me, his eyes wide as he clearly is caught off guard by this whole thing.

"Operation find your mother." He says quietly causing my eyes to widen at his response. *They found her?*

"Juliette, so you have a bit of a back story. Your Mom and Dad both met when they were young, your Mom's name was Arielle, although she gave us many different names that night." Peter begins to explain.

"You were born 9 months later and Robert had left Arielle to rest and went and got a coffee. When he got back, she was gone and there was a note saying I'm sorry." Peter continues. I feel my heart sink, why would she abandon her own baby?

"Now we have spent the last 13 years tracking her down. We couldn't find anything or anyone who matched Arielle's description at the time we were all in London. It was like she never existed."

"So, she was just invisible to everyone but all of you?" I ask and Peter shakes his head.

"Juliette at the time we were hiding from

something, but she wanted some sort of normal life." He explains. I look at him and I shake my head.

"I don't follow." I say to him.

"Neither do I." Robert pipes up.

Peter groans in annoyance as he stands over the desk. "Arielle was young when she had Jules wasn't she, we reckoned about 16." Peter asks Robert who nods. I turn to him, a disgusted look on my face which he ignores but it does cause Felicity to giggle.

"What I'm saying is, I found her." Peter says in annoyance when he realises he isn't going to get the reaction he wants. I watch as Robert's eyes pop out of his head as he tries to process it.

"Is she alive?"

"Yes, and trust me. None of us seen this coming." He says with a slight smile on his face. You can tell he is so excited to tell everyone about what he's found but by the silence in the room from Felicity and Serena, I'm going to assume this isn't anything good.

"What is it?" Robert asks impatiently after a few moments, and we watch together as Peter turns the laptop around to show a group photo, or more so a family photo. I look at it carefully trying to work out which one is my Mum, but I can't work it out, there are quite a few young people in this photograph.

"Who should I be looking at?" I ask as I turn to Robert who has gone as white as a ghost.

"The red head Juliette." Peter tells me and I look closer to the screen. She's dressed in a wedding dress, her bright red hair is curled and her veil is beautifully laced with diamonds and on the top of her head is the prettiest tiara I've ever seen.

Robert falls into the chair next to me, disbelief plastered all over his face. I turn my attention back to the photo and focus on the text underneath.

"King Edward of Haroux and Queen..." I begin to say but am completely cut off as my mouth falls wide open at the name. *Queen Arielle... surely not.*

"Did you photoshop this?" I ask as I look up to my uncle. He frowns at my response.

"What's photoshop?" He asks, clueless. I roll my eyes.

"This is clearly a joke. Please tell me this is a joke." I plead, humor but also annoyance in my voice. I turn my head to Robert, who sits in his chair, still as can be.

"August, 2000. She always told us that the 1st of August she had to make one of the biggest decisions of her life. The same date she got married." He says from his seat, no emotion in his tone of voice as he is completely baffled by the image in front of us.

"Juliette, your birth mother's a Queen."

The Secrets We Keep
10th October 2022

ACKNOWLEDGMENTS

To my wonderful family who have supported me throughout all of this, thank you. To my girls, my dames. Caitlin, Megan, Andrea (who helped me with the series name), Olivia, Madison and Kilee. Thank you for pushing me to write the book, I wouldn't of done it without you. To Kellie, Laura, Char, Lewis, Fallon, Elise and Demi for believing in me when I didn't think I had it in me. To my fabulous cover artist Amie, who amazes me with her talent every single day.

To my lovely troublemakers who I adore more than life who have stuck by me through thick and thin. Who knew trouble would end up being an author?

I also thank you reader for taking your time to read a story that floated around in my head for years, who, until I got forced into it, was going to stay in my mind or on scraps of paper forever. I hope you love these characters as much as I do.

ABOUT THE AUTHOR

Torrie Jones

Torrie Jones is a author born and raised in Newcastle-upon-Tyne in the UK. She grew up reading and watching crime shows because of her Grandad and eventually incorporated that into her Hidden Jules series. She is a content creator, makeup artist and podcast host. She has a dog called Penny and a cat named Sheldon.

You can join her on her socials:

TikTok & Instagram: @torriemaryjones & @torriejonesauthor

Join her Facebook group: Trouble's book club. Check out her website: www.torriemaryjones.com

Printed in Great Britain
by Amazon